Storm

MEN OF HIDDEN CREEK

HJ WELCH

Cover design by AngstyG.

Createspace Edition.

ISBN-13: 978-1986788779

STORM

For my nana xxx

Hunter had no idea what he was doing. He just knew he couldn't abandon Chase now.

They were sitting on the sofa in Chase's cramped living room. Hunter had willed himself to take hold of Chase's hands, to assure him that this was what he wanted. Even if he wasn't totally sure himself. His heart was pounding in his chest, but he had to be brave.

What did they really have to lose? They had already kissed. All that had told Hunter was, despite his inexperience with men, he wanted more. It was clear Chase did too.

Hunter licked his lips, stalling for time. Part of him was as scared as he'd always been to admit this was how he really felt. The other part of him couldn't tear his gaze away from Chase's mouth, and how soft it looked.

Chase had his eyes closed and was breathing fast and shallow. '*I can't believe a guy like you would be interested in me,*' were the words he'd just used. Could he not see how wonderful he was? He was a brilliant father and a caring person and cute as fuck to boot. Hunter wanted to prove his doubts wrong once and for all.

Hunter needed to let go. So what if he'd always thought of himself as straight? He wasn't and that was all there was to it. Hunter had gay buddies and had always considered himself an ally. Discovering his own feelings for another man shouldn't be a big deal.

Chase was so easy to fall for as well. Adorable but still sexy. Shy but also fierce. Hunter didn't question the delicious ideas that were running through his mind. He knew he wanted Chase, to claim him as his own. Chase was aware he hadn't done this before, so he wouldn't judge if they fumbled the first few steps. Besides, fumbling under the covers sounded like an excellent plan to Hunter right about then.

He leaned forward, inching his lips closer to Chase's slightly parted mouth. "Can I kiss you again?" Hunter murmured.

"Oh god, yes," Chase replied, his eyes still closed.

He was trembling but Hunter sensed it wasn't all from nerves. The way he was panting was pure lust. He wanted Hunter desperately, and that was one hell of a turn on.

There would be no turning back from this. But Hunter had known that for some time now. The chemistry between them had been building to the point of no return. In a way, it was inevitable that they would eventually end up here.

Where their hands touched it felt like crackling electricity. The brewing of an oncoming storm. Hunter brought their lips together, feeling that powerful connection even more.

The kiss was gentle to begin with. Hunter delicately probed with his mouth and tongue, feeling his way against Chase's lips. Chase moaned and slid his fingers through

Hunter's hair, urging him to get closer. Hunter couldn't think of anything he wanted more.

He shifted his position, wrapping his hands around Chase's hip and the back of his neck. His slim frame fit perfectly under Hunter's large one. Like they were designed to go together.

It broke Hunter's heart that Chase thought so little of himself. To his mind, the whole town hated him and he wasn't worth taking a chance on. It must have been so hard for him, thinking he had to face the world all alone.

He wasn't alone anymore. He was a father, and if Hunter got his way, they could be something together too. He wasn't sure exactly what yet, but it was okay to take things one step at a time. They didn't have to use labels, but he wanted to make his feelings clear.

"I want you to be mine," he said between increasingly heated kisses.

Chase gasped and shuddered against him. The sensation made Hunter quiver as well. Chase wriggled and dropped down on the couch, dragging Hunter with him so he was laying on top of him.

"Yes," Chase whispered. "Fuck, yes. All yours."

Hunter's chest felt like it exploded with warmth. He may have been unsure how to have a relationship with a guy, but that had to be a good start. Chase was his.

He rolled his body along Chase's as they passionately made out. Kisses fervent, hands wandering and hard cocks jutting against each other's bodies. Hunter had been worried he would reach a point at which he'd be freaked out by the strangeness and have to stop and think before he could continue. As there didn't seem to be any danger of that happening, he decided to just keep going.

Chase's stubble rubbed against his chin, the friction causing tingles to run over Hunter's skin. Chase felt like a man, and smelled like one too. The faint scent of his soap and shampoo and natural musk was wholly male. Hunter loved it.

He wasn't afraid. He knew Chase had faced a lot of hardship, and by accepting his sexuality, Hunter was opening the door for prejudice himself. But all he cared about was having Chase by his side. He could deal with anything else life threw at him if he got to keep Chase.

He blinked his beautiful green eyes and looked up at Hunter. It was clear from the noticeable bob of his Adam's apple he was nervous. But the way he clung to Hunter's shirt also conveyed his desperation.

"Take me to bed," he rasped.

Hunter was more than happy to do as he was asked.

CHAPTER ONE

CHASE

Chase Williamson had no idea how he was supposed to be feeling.

To begin with, he had been totally numb, and some of that sensation still remained. But now he was also confused, panicked, terrified. Nothing good.

And yet, he was the adult in this situation. He blinked and looked at the small girl fiercely hugging her stuffed dragon on the seat beside him. If he was feeling like this, she had to be suffering a hundred times worse.

Lyla Hart. His daughter. He could count the number of weekends they had spent together on his fingers. To call himself her father would be quite a stretch of the imagination. But in what felt like the blink of an eye, he was now all she had.

He could feel the eyes of Mr. Preston from social services on him like a hawk. But Chase needed a minute to absorb what was happening.

Amanda couldn't really be gone. They had managed to

stay friends since their school days, but it didn't take a genius to work out that she and Lyla were better off without a loser like Chase in their lives. He could barely help her with child support. He didn't know anything about being a parent.

She had done just fine on her own. Except now they were throwing words around like 'brain aneurysm' and 'sole custody' and Chase felt maybe he was going to pass out.

Dr. Felix looked at him with what felt like genuine sympathy. She was a stout Asian-American woman with short, graying hair and bifocal glasses. Her hands gripped the file on her lap tightly as she waited for Chase to say something, anything, to the news that his high school girlfriend was dead and he was now responsible for five-year-old Lyla.

The staff at the hospital assured him that it had been instantaneous, that Amanda hadn't suffered when she had blacked out and lost control of the car. Luckily, Lyla had been at school. But she was old enough to understand something real bad had happened and her momma wasn't coming back.

She was so tiny, even for her age. Just a little doll of a girl lost under a mountain of red curls. She was sucking her thumb and wrapping a lock of hair tightly around one of her fingers. Her gaze was vacant.

Chase wanted to cry. Amanda had been nice to him as well as funny with her head screwed on right. She had a good office job – or at least she *had.* She couldn't really be gone, could she?

"Mr. Williamson," Mr. Preston said, somewhat gruffly. They were in a small admin room away from the ER where Amanda had been brought. "Do you understand what we're telling you?"

Chase nodded. "Lyla is going to come live with me now."

"As her biological father, Amanda Hart named you as Lyla's next-of-kin." Mr. Preston peered at his notes. His mustache was so large, Chase wasn't sure how he could see over it to read the paper in his hands. "We – social services – will be in regular contact through your first few months together to ensure everything is suitable for Lyla's care. You hardly have an outstanding record, Mr. Williamson."

Chase winced. He didn't need anyone reminding him of that. In twenty-three years he hadn't managed to achieve anything of note in his life. Except for Lyla. Now, he had to prove he was worthy of being her father.

"I know," Chase stammered. "I'll do my best. I have to. Nothing is more important to me than my little girl."

Mr. Preston glanced at his notes again as if he found that very hard to believe.

Chase risked looking at Lyla again. She was determinedly staring at the floor, her face blotchy and her eyes brimming with tears. Apparently, one of the ER nurses had sat with her for some time, explaining as best they could that Momma had gone to heaven.

Chase didn't have many friends. Or any, really. He'd kept his distance from Amanda out of respect, but right then he really could have done with her no-nonsense, ballsy attitude. She would take charge and know what to do.

But she was gone. Chase had to step up to the plate now.

"It's late, Chase," said Dr. Felix sympathetically. "You should probably think about taking Lyla home for some rest. We can finish up the rest of the paperwork tomorrow or later in the week."

Chase nodded, rubbing his face. "Um, yes, of course."

At least Lyla had a sort of room at his place. She hardly

ever slept over, so it wasn't decorated in the way a kid might like. But there was a bed and he would get everything from her mom's apartment to make her feel as comfortable as possible. Luckily, he had a key to their place at least.

He didn't have a booster seat for his car though. He didn't have any food in the fridge. He didn't have a hair brush or bands. Lyla always brought any toys she wanted to play with over herself. For crying out loud, he didn't even have a TV.

"Mr. Williamson?" Dr. Felix said again. She looked like she understood his pain and fear, but they didn't have any other choice.

Not unless they wanted Lyla to go into the system.

For a terrible fleeting moment, Chase wondered if that might be better. He pictured Lyla with a loving foster family, able to give her everything she needed.

But she was *his* little girl. He couldn't abandon her like that. He had to fight for her. He was the parent now. He wasn't allowed to freak out. He had to take charge, look after his little girl.

"Sorry, we'll, um, get out of your hair now," he said. He brushed his jeans and rose to his feet, trying to ignore how queasy he felt. "Lyla. Do you want to come home with Daddy?"

Lyla's lip trembled. "I want *Momma,*" she cried, breaking into pitiful sobs.

Chase could feel his heart breaking all over again. She didn't deserve him. She deserved Amanda.

He swallowed, forcing himself to grieve later. "I know, sweetheart. I'm so sorry. But Daddy's gonna take real good care of you, I promise."

He crouched down in front of her and opened his arms.

She hiccuped twice before finally giving in and throwing herself at him, crying her eyes out.

Chase wasn't strong enough. He couldn't do this. But somehow, he managed to stand and nod at Dr. Felix and Mr. Preston. "Thank you. Y'all have been very kind."

He snuggled Lyla and her stuffed dragon to his chest, as if somehow he could protect her from the world. Together, they made their way through the busy ER and out into the evening twilight.

"So, um, you feel like McDonald's?" he asked.

The few times they had been out before, he had taken her for a burger and fries. She was a sucker for a strawberry milkshake, that much he did know. He tried to remember how much cash he had on him. Even if it meant him not eating tonight, he'd get her whatever dinner she wanted. He would get paid in a couple of days, so things would just have to stretch until then. He wasn't going to make Lyla feel like she was unwanted or a nuisance.

But she didn't respond in any way. She simply continued to cling to him for dear life as they walked to his banged-up car.

He had enough gas to get them home and maybe run a few errands tomorrow. He figured there would be a hell of a lot to do to even begin untangling this mess. He was thankful at least his place wasn't far from the hospital.

In a flash of inspiration, he realized he had some towels in the trunk from when he'd used them to protect the seats from the blazing sunshine. He folded a couple up and improvised a booster seat. Lyla allowed him to place her in the back and buckle her up.

"What do you say, kiddo?" he asked. He brushed her wild

red hair away from her face where it had stuck to her damp cheeks. For now, she was just sniffling. But he was under no illusion that she was done crying. "You want a shake and fries?"

Lyla shook her head, then looked out the window. Dusk was falling over the parking lot and Chase could hear the crickets starting up their chorus.

"Um, how about fried chicken? Or pizza?" He figured she was too young for anything spicy like tacos.

Startled, he realized he wasn't completely clueless after all. He'd worked that out by himself. Maybe there was other stuff he could up with on his own too.

"I wanna go home," she said, rubbing her freckled, button nose. She still wouldn't look at him.

Chase sighed. Amanda's apartment was rented, so the landlord would want to find new tenants as soon as all the legal issues were straightened out. He toyed with the idea of letting her sleep one more night in her regular bed. But that seemed cruel. Like he was just delaying the inevitable.

"We have to go back to Daddy's house now," he said, hoping he was doing the right thing. "Then tomorrow we can go and get all your toys and clothes. But...you're going to be living at Daddy's house now."

Lyla continued to stare out over his shoulder where he was crouched by her seat. "Okay," she mumbled.

Chase made one last check that she was buckled in okay. He was terrified he had gotten it wrong. Whatever else he did, he needed to get a booster seat as soon as he got paid. Would the cops pull him over if he didn't have her set up right?

He decided to hurry home as soon as he could. McDonalds

was on the way, so he would just grab a couple of meals to go and just hope she nibbled on some fries.

Then...

Then he had to be a parent. For the rest of his life. He sat in the car gripping the wheel as his panic threatened to overwhelm him. He was breathing fast and shallow, but he couldn't seem to get any air into his lungs.

He was never going to be able to manage this. Amanda was supposed to be the parent, not him. They both knew he didn't have what it took.

But if he didn't, social services could take her away and put her into the system. Then she really wouldn't stand a chance. He wouldn't do that to her.

So, he started the engine and pulled the car from the lot. "Just one thing at a time," he whispered to himself. "Just get food. Then put her to bed. Then you can face tomorrow."

He wasn't sure tomorrow would be any better. But he was going to give everything he damn well had to do his best for Lyla.

CHAPTER TWO

HUNTER

When he woke drenched in sweat and tangled in the bed sheets, Hunter Duke had no idea where he was. For several, long, tortuous seconds, he gasped for air, hand clutching at his chest as he stared into the darkness of the room.

Gradually, his heart began to slow down, and his memories kicked in. He was home. His new home. He was safe. Everything was fine.

He closed his eyes, even though there was very little light in the room. It helped center him in the here and now. The ringing in his ears slowly faded and he felt able to breathe again.

He smoothed down the sheets under the illusion it would be more comfortable. But he'd been struggling to sleep in a bed since he'd come home from his last tour. Something about knowing he wouldn't be going back was causing his body to rebel. The mattress was too soft, the comforter too heavy, the room too quiet without twenty other guys snuffling around him.

Hunter rubbed his forehead and stared at what little he could make out of the ceiling. The bulb had a cheap paper lampshade on it. He'd need to think about a replacement.

There were a thousand little chores he had to consider now that he owned his own home. But the idea of being anywhere permanently still seemed like such a foreign concept to him. He couldn't really commit to it.

Had he made a mistake, coming to Hidden Creek? His buddy Connor said it would be a good place for a new start. Maybe Hunter just needed to give himself some time to settle in. It had only been a week, after all.

It wasn't even oh five hundred hours, so he turned on his side and tried to get some more sleep. He only had a couple more days off to enjoy before he started his new job on Monday. He didn't want to waste one of them being tired and grumpy. But even though he couldn't remember what he'd been dreaming about, the adrenaline from the nightmare was still thrumming in his veins.

He wondered if there would ever come a time where he wouldn't be haunted by some of the things he had seen out in Afghanistan. Sometimes, when he closed his eyes, it was impossible to escape the images that danced in his mind. He had hoped that moving to a new town would help put his time in the Marines behind him. Now he wasn't so sure it would be that easy.

Eventually, he gave up on sleep and found his running shoes in a box with the rest of his workout gear. After all the moving of furniture and other boxes, he hadn't felt the need to exercise until now. But an early-morning jog might be just what he needed to shake off the uneasiness lingering from his dreams. Plus, it would give him a chance to explore the town further.

He used his phone to map out a route that would take him a couple of miles. Nothing too strenuous. Since coming back to the States he had updated his music collection, so he enjoyed running along the sidewalk with a new playlist as dawn broke.

Hidden Creek was a cute town in Texas, not far from Houston. The houses in his neighborhood were large with neatly trimmed front yards. All the cars parked outside were no more than a couple of years old. Apart from the occasional basketball hoop outside, they were difficult to distinguish between one another. It was quiet but still welcoming, or so Hunter hoped.

It had been ten years since he'd left home and joined the Navy as a hospital corpsman. When he'd been between tours, he'd stayed with his folks back in Oklahoma. But changing his career had made him want to change his scenery too, so Hidden Creek had seemed as good a place as any to settle down.

The prospect of staying here for years was almost too difficult to imagine after a life of constant movement. If he hadn't been at sea, he'd been on base, or, in the case of his last tour, serving with the Marines rather than the Navy out in Afghanistan.

Hunter slowed his pace as he neared his street, rubbing the perspiration from his forehead. It wasn't that he regretted transferring from the Navy to the Marines. He knew he had done a hell of a lot of good during his time there. Besides, he'd grown restless at sea, writing out prescriptions and giving flu shots. He had wanted a change of pace.

Ten months had been more than enough for him to appreciate that, actually, there was nothing wrong with slightly boring days. There was a lot to be said for routine and the simple pleasure that came from treating people for non-life-threatening maladies.

He never wanted to watch anyone die again so long as he lived, let alone another buddy.

With a sigh, he jogged toward his home. He'd made a promise to himself to keep looking forward now his days of service were over. No sense dwelling on the past when he couldn't do anything to change it. The future was open to him, full of unknown possibilities he was determined to seize.

It would be nice to meet a lady. Other guys he'd known over the years had wives and girlfriends waiting for them back home. But Hunter had never seemed to find the time for more than a few dates with anyone. Now, with such a big house, he could see himself with someone special, maybe even a couple of kids.

He smiled. Wouldn't that be something?

"Morning!"

He pulled his earbuds out and stopped the music on his phone. Looking over he could see his neighbor at her front door, collecting the paper. She was a plump woman with curly brown hair that looked to be going gray. She waved to Hunter and gave him a warm smile.

"Hello," he called back, slowing to a halt in front of her yard.

"You're the new guy, aren't you?" his neighbor asked, walking down the pathway. She shielded her eyes from the increasingly strong morning sunshine. "You just moved in."

"Yes, ma'am," he said. He offered his hand to her, hoping it wasn't too sweaty. "Hunter Duke."

"Shelly Duvall," she said, impressing him with a firm handshake. "What brings you to our little town, then?"

"Work," he said simply. He wasn't used to chatting with strangers, but the way she rose her eyebrows suggested she expected more of him. "I start at the doctors' office on Monday. I'm the new physician assistant."

"Oh well, isn't that great," she said, clapping her hands together. "And your wife, what does she do?"

Hunter smiled awkwardly. "No wife, ma'am. It's just me."

He could have been mistaken, but he swore he saw a glint in her eye. "A handsome young fellow like you won't stay single for long, I'm sure," she said with a wink. "Now, you look parched. Can I tempt you with some homemade lemonade?" She half-turned and pointed back toward her house.

Hunter's initial reaction was to decline. He didn't know Shelly and he always struggled for conversation with strangers. But the fact that she had invited him in at all gave him pause. Seeing as he was a big guy and his tattoos were visible, he would have expected her to be wary of him. Most people were, especially as he knew he struggled to be friendly more often than not. But she appeared to have no hesitation in inviting him inside her home. It would be rude to refuse.

"That would be lovely, ma'am," he said.

She waved her hand and led him back up the path to her front door. "Aren't you all manners and politeness. Please, call me Shelly."

She pulled her keys out from her sweatpants and unlocked the door. It was a little strange that she'd closed it when she had hardly even left the house. But Hunter soon realized why she had as soon as they stepped into her hallway.

He couldn't help but laugh as several balls of fur catapulted into their legs. Over half a dozen Golden Retriever puppies all clamored for their attention. Their tails bashed into Hunter's naked calves as they wagged furiously.

"I do hope you're not allergic to dogs," said Shelly proudly. "Our latest litter is waiting to go to their forever homes, so the house is a little full right now."

Hunter bent down to stroke some of their ears. "Not that I know of," he admitted. He didn't have much experience with dogs apart from the trained ones he had occasionally served with. But these were absolutely adorable. "You're a breeder?"

"For nearly fifteen years now," she told him as they walked toward her kitchen. The pack of puppies scampered around their feet as they were joined by a couple of older dogs as well. "Ever since my daughter left home. She'd be about your age, I guess."

As hints went, it wasn't all that subtle. Hunter tried to muster some enthusiasm for the idea that maybe Shelly's daughter might be lovely. Someone he might even connect with. But all he could do was smile politely and continue to pet the many dogs.

The dogs' interest in the newcomer waned slightly. As they spread out over the kitchen, one pup in particular caught Hunter's eye. He blinked, making sure he was seeing correctly.

"And who's this little guy?" he asked as the dog in question hopped over to him to get his head scratched. And he did literally hop.

He only had three legs.

The little fellow didn't seem to care as he bound over to Hunter, wagging his tail and nipping playfully at Hunter's fingers. But where his front, right leg should have been, there was simply a furry round stump, just past his shoulder.

"Oh," said Shelly. There was a touch of sadness to her voice as she placed a glass of lemonade on the kitchen table where he was sitting. "He's our special guy. The runt of the litter, he was just born like that. Perfectly healthy otherwise, but sometimes things like this happen."

Hunter used one hand to pick up his drink and take a sip. It was indeed very good. The other hand was preoccupied petting the special puppy's soft fur.

"Of course," he said. The dog didn't seem to know he was different to his brothers and sisters after all. "Has he got a home to go to like the others?"

Shelly smiled and sat in the chair next to Hunter. "No," she said. "Not yet, anyway. People tend to overlook a pup like that when there are so many pretty ones to choose from. But, maybe when the rest are gone, someone might want to take him. Otherwise, I guess we'll keep him." She shrugged. "We haven't really got the room for another big dog, but I wouldn't take him to a shelter or anything."

Her voice became a little gruff and she stood suddenly. She busied herself by putting clean dishes away from the dishwasher.

Hunter looked down at the pup. He deserved a home like any of the others, surely? A trooper like him would be just as good as a four-legged dog.

Without really considering what he was asking, he looked up and caught Shelly's gaze when she moved between the cupboard and the dishwasher. "How much do you usually sell the puppies for?"

She paused, blinking and glancing down at the mass of golden fur happily wandering around her kitchen. "Well, usually, I charge seven fifty for one, or seven hundred each if people take more than one. But I would be willing to sell him for less, if it meant he got a home where he'd be loved."

Hunter bit his lip. What was he thinking? He knew nothing about dogs. This was crazy.

And yet...all he could picture was having someone else in his big house. How much less lonely it would be with another little body helping fill all those rooms with a bit more life. Anything he didn't know, he could look up on the internet. Hell, Shelly was right next door if he got especially stuck.

She was right. This little buddy needed a home where he'd be loved *because* he was different. Not in spite of it.

"No," he said slowly. "I'll pay full price. He's just as good as any of the others. That is-" he looked up and smiled "-if you'd want me to have him?"

Shelly's mouth dropped open before she quickly snapped it closed again. "Really?"

Hunter picked up the pup, who squirmed happily in his arms, trying to lick his face. "I might need a bit of help," he admitted with a laugh. "But...yes. I'd love to take him home."

CHAPTER THREE

CHASE

Chase wished the doctors' waiting room wasn't so busy. As was usual when he went out and about in town, he could feel the odd stare coming his way. He hunched his shoulders and dropped his head, willing people to leave him alone.

There wasn't much remarkable about his appearance to cause such interest. He had always been desperate to try and blend in, to not stand out. Brown hair, green eyes, medium height and slim build. Since he'd been old enough, he'd worn a short bit of scruff on his face to try and appear older than he was, manlier. But aside from that, he didn't feel he stood out from the crowd all that much.

Except people still occasionally talked about the Williamson boy. How he'd knocked up Amanda Hart, even though they all thought...well...*you know*. Didn't he swing for the other team?

Chase watched Lyla and tried not to feel sad. He would hate for her to ever think that the only reason she had come to exist was because her dad was trying to convince himself that he really did like girls, not boys. Convince himself and everyone who had ever kicked the crap out of him.

It was irrelevant now. None of the small-town gossip or disapproving looks mattered in the slightest. The only thing that was important was doing the best he possibly could for his little girl.

Unfortunately, he wasn't sure he knew the first thing about being a parent. As proved by the tantrum Lyla had suddenly, inexplicably, started throwing.

One second she had been absolutely fine, sitting playing on the floor with her stuffed dragon and some battered trains from the toy basket at the doctors' office. The next, she was wailing at another little boy who had approached her, batting him away with the dragon.

Chase leaped to his feet as the boy's mother equally lurched forward, pulling her son to safety. "Can't you control her?" she cried, hugging the boy to her chest.

"Sorry, sorry," Chase said breathlessly, hugging Lyla close to him as well. "Sweetheart, it's okay. What's wrong?"

She sobbed into his work shirt. Hopefully it would dry before he had to go on shift.

"Bo-Bo is *mine*," she cried pitifully. "I don't want to give him away!"

Bo-Bo was the dragon she hadn't let go of since Chase had brought her home three days ago. Since her mom had died. Right now she had her hand wrapped so tightly around his neck her little knuckles were turning white.

Chase guessed maybe the poor boy she'd bashed had unknowingly asked to play with Bo-Bo. As much as he didn't want to excuse her aggressive behavior toward another child, he thought he understood at least. Bo-Bo was her main source of comfort since her whole life had been turned upside down.

"You don't have to give him away," Chase murmured through her red hair. It was already in a tangle, despite his best efforts to tame it this morning. Maybe he should start carrying a brush around for when the curls rebelled? "Bo-Bo isn't going anywhere."

Thankfully, Lyla managed to calm down before the display board showed her name. He didn't want the physician assistant to think he wasn't capable on their very first visit to the doctors' office.

Chase hardly ever came in for appointments, but he figured he needed to bring Lyla for a check-up with his doctors' office as soon as possible. From the time they had spent together in the past, he knew she was a very active child and often spent most of her playtime outdoors. If she fell out of a tree and broke her arm, he needed to know she had the right insurance for a trip to the ER.

He kept her on his hip as he walked them around to the right room. Hopefully the appointment wouldn't take long as he needed to get Lyla to school and himself to work. He'd been lucky enough to get an early morning slot, so neither of them would need to take any time off.

He had wanted to ask Bernie, his manager at JJ's Fresh Goods, for compassionate leave. But that didn't pay so well, and he was on thin ice as it was at the store. A couple of late days here and there, an unfair complaint from a customer and his lack of qualifications meant he was lucky to still have a job at all. Lyla was now relying on him to earn a decent enough income to support them both.

The school had been extremely helpful in taking their

circumstances into consideration. They already had a counselor set up in-house, and Lyla was set to meet with her this afternoon. Mr. Preston from social services was apparently going to work with the counselor too, which made Chase a little nervous.

One thing at a time, he told himself sternly as he knocked on the door with a large number five painted on. The plaque read 'Hunter Duke.' Chase wasn't sure he had seen him before.

"Come in," a deep voice rumbled through the wood, so Chase turned the handle and walked both himself and Lyla inside.

He almost tripped as he laid eyes on their physician assistant. He definitely hadn't had an appointment with this guy before. "G-good morning," he stammered, closing the door behind them. "Uh, this is Lyla. We're just here for a check-up."

The guy, Hunter, smiled and indicated the vacant seat opposite him. "Of course," he said.

He had thick, dark hair, brown eyes, and strong cheekbones that complemented his sturdy jawline. Even sitting down, Chase could tell he was several inches taller than himself and built like a linebacker. Muscles were straining under the forest green shirt he wore.

Ordinarily, Chase did very well hiding his reactions to meeting a gorgeous guy like that. But Mr. Duke had caught him totally off guard.

This wasn't the time or the place. Chase felt even more ashamed than he usually would at succumbing to his desires. This wasn't about him, it was about Lyla. So he could feel guilty and angry at himself later.

"Hi, Lyla," said the PA. "I'm Hunter. Am I okay to give you a quick look over today?"

Lyla said nothing from where she was sitting on Chase's lap. She just swallowed and looked down at Bo-Bo. "Sorry, Mr. Duke," Chase said. "She's feeling a bit shy."

"Hunter, please," Hunter said warmly. "And don't worry, Lyla, I'm a bit shy too. It's my first day, and you're my first patient. So you'd be helping me out big-time if I could just listen to your heartbeat with my stethoscope." He wiggled the circular end of the stethoscope at her. Miraculously, Lyla gave him a twitch of a smile.

"How about I hold Bo-Bo so Hunter can listen?" Chase suggested.

Her lip wobbled and Chase knew he'd fucked up, but Hunter came to his rescue. "Oh, no. I think we should listen to Bo-Bo's heartbeat too. Don't you agree, Lyla?"

Dubiously, she frowned at the end of the stethoscope he was now holding up to the stuffed dragon. Then she tentatively held Bo-Bo out for inspection.

Hunter made a show of pressing the stethoscope to Bo-Bo's belly, nodding to himself and humming as he pretended to listen. "Well, that's excellent. What do you say? Your turn now?"

Lyla bit her lip, then nodded. Hunter moved swiftly, lifting up her T-shirt enough to press the metal circle plate against her heart. He was quiet as he really did listen this time, then nodded.

"Very good, honey. Okay, next we can check yours and Bo-Bo's ears, then a few other things to make sure you're all nice and healthy. Sound good?"

Chase's chest filled with gratitude for how nice Hunter

was being. Lyla still wasn't smiling exactly, but she was relaxing a fraction as the examination went on. He took her pulse and felt the glands under her jaw. He checked her ears for any sign of infection then used a thermometer there as well to get her temperature. Everything came out just fine.

Until Hunter found the bruises.

Chase hadn't really even thought about it. But Lyla had a scrape on her knee, a bluish mark on her arm and one on her hip, then several yellowing spots along her arms and legs. She had probably gotten them last week, roughhousing in her backyard, but Chase didn't miss the flicker of concern in Hunter's eyes.

"Lyla's an outdoorsy kid," Chase blurted. "She plays horses and goes on quests with Bo-Bo, and she loves Little League."

Hunter smiled at him, but it didn't reach his eyes. "Lyla, your mommy usually brings you in to see the doctor, right?"

Chase felt all the blood in his veins turn to ice. Lyla froze, going still as a board in his lap. Tears burned at the back of Chase's eyes.

"Uh," he said, unable to stop the tremble in his voice. "Lyla lives with me now," he said. He tried to give Hunter an imploring look over Lyla's head, begging him to understand and not ask any more questions. "If you like, I can give you Mr. Preston's number at social services? He can maybe explain a bit more."

Hunter watched him for a moment. "Okay, sure, that would be great."

He pushed a pad of paper over to Chase along with a pen. Chase managed to get his phone out with one hand and thumb through his contacts to find the right number. He didn't want to let go of Lyla, and she was certainly clinging to him and Bo-Bo for dear life.

They finished the rest of the examination in strained quiet, silent aside from Hunter's occasional question or instruction. Lyla was sniffling again, but at least she wasn't howling the place down. Chase wondered what kind of day she would have at school now. Whether or not he would be called in because she was fighting later.

He wished he could keep her at home, but that wasn't possible. At least he'd had the chance to put gas in his car and give it a bit of a tune-up, so they had been able to drive over to Amanda's place yesterday and get most of Lyla's things. It was going to devastate her when the landlord rented it to someone new and they couldn't go back again. But at least for now, she was getting used to staying in her room at Chase's place with her creature comforts around her.

Chase couldn't wait to get out of the office. For a second, he'd allowed himself to be grateful that someone in this god forsaken town wasn't looking at him like he was a total failure. But now Hunter thought he was neglecting his daughter. Or worse, *hurting* her. He felt sick to his stomach as the check-up finally came to an end, and he rose to his feet.

"Mr. Duke," he said softly, his voice wavering with emotion. He paused on their way to the door with Lyla back on his hip. He looked directly at the PA. "I appreciate your concern. But there isn't a single thing on this Earth I love more than my baby girl. Now that she's living with me, I hope I'll get the chance to prove that."

Whatever else anybody around here thought of him, he wouldn't stand for any kind of accusations that he was a danger to his child.

Hunter held his gaze, then nodded. "Thank you, Mr. Williamson."

Chase kept his head down as he walked with Lyla through the waiting room and back out into the sunshine. "Are you okay, pumpkin?" he asked.

She shrugged and leaned her head on his shoulder.

Humiliation burned through him the more he hashed over the appointment in his head. Damn Hunter for bringing up Amanda and upsetting Lyla. Didn't they have up-to-date records from the hospital? He had explained the situation to reception when he'd made the booking, for crying out loud. Had no one told Hunter what had happened?

As much as he was cross about that, the accusation that he might be hurting his own daughter pained him more. No one in this whole town thought he was good for anything. A high school dropout who got a good girl pregnant, ruined her life, then refused to marry her.

No one was interested in listening to Amanda when she said she didn't want to get married either. Or the fact that she finished high school just fine and graduated proudly with her baby bump. People had already made up their minds that the Williamsons were poor, trouble, and generally best avoided.

Chase ground his teeth as he clipped Lyla into her new car seat. "What's wrong, Daddy?" she asked, her green eyes wide. She was wrapping a curl of her hair around her finger again.

"Nothing, sweetie," he lied. He rubbed his face, then did his best to smile at her. "Let's get you into school, huh?"

She didn't say anything as he closed her door and got himself into the driver's seat. She just started sucking her thumb. He inhaled slowly, then turned the key in the ignition.

The engine spluttered and rolled over. Chase gasped in

horror as he looked in the rearview mirror and saw a white plume of smoke drift up from the exhaust pipe. The ignition gave up and stuttered into silence. Dead.

He looked down at the steering wheel, unwilling to believe this was really happening.

If he didn't have a car, he was fucked.

CHAPTER FOUR

HUNTER

HUNTER COULDN'T BELIEVE he'd fucked up so badly on his very first appointment. He'd been slightly terrified to see a child patient for the first time, but it had been going so well. Her dad had appeared nice too. A little nervous, perhaps, but sweet.

Then Hunter had jumped to conclusions when he'd seen all the bruises, and worse still, mentioned Lyla's mother.

Mr. Preston from social services had been almost delighted to confirm that, yes, Amanda Hart had just suffered a brain aneurysm while driving. He seized upon the idea that Chase Williamson might be anything less than a perfect parent. But Hunter had hung up the phone before he could do any further damage.

Because it was his first day, the office had given him a light schedule and he didn't have his next patient for another fifteen minutes. So, just on the off chance he'd get lucky and Chase was still somewhere around, Hunter dashed out into the waiting room. A quick scan of the area told him he was too late. But then he glanced out into the parking lot.

Chase was standing by an ancient-looking Ford Focus with the hood propped up and his hands in his hair.

Hunter blew out a sigh of relief. "I'll be back in a moment," he told one of the receptionists. "I just need to have a quick word with my patient."

She nodded, her attention already on the ringing phone on the desk.

Hunter jogged out into the warm spring sunshine. Chase was completely absorbed in fretting over the inside of his car and didn't see him approach. He wasn't a big guy, but in that moment, he seemed especially fragile.

"Mr. Williamson?"

Chase all but leaped out of his skin. "Shit – I mean..." He looked at Lyla inside the car, but Hunter doubted she would have heard the profanity. She was still hugging her dragon toy and staring out over the parking lot with her thumb in her mouth.

"Is everything okay?" Hunter asked.

Chase hugged himself. "Yeah, fine," he mumbled.

Hunter was almost certain that wasn't the case. But then he remembered why he had come out here in the first place. "Mr. Williamson," he said again. He felt horribly awkward, but he just had to get over that. The mistake was his, so he needed to fix it as best he could. "I'm so glad I caught you. I can't apologize enough for what I said in our appointment. I was completely ignorant of the facts. I didn't mean to cause you and your daughter distress."

He watched as Chase took a shaky breath in and out.

Then he offered Hunter a weak smile. "That's okay. It's obvious you didn't know. It's...well, it is what it is. I'm just worried about Lyla. This is hardest on her."

That didn't sound like a man who had just lost his wife, leaving Hunter to conclude that their relationship must have been more complicated than he first assumed. "Of course," he said, unable to think of anything else. "Look, are you sure you're okay? Your car doesn't smell too great." There was definitely a chemical odor in the air.

Chase grimaced. "I don't know," he bemoaned. He jammed his hands in his brown hair again, making it stick up at odd angles. It was kind of cute. "It won't start and there's smoke coming out the back end."

Hunter was grateful to focus on a problem he might be able to fix. Chase didn't seem too mad that he had put his foot in it about Lyla's mother, but Hunter still felt crappy. He had probably been overly-cautious about the bruises he'd seen, too. But Lyla was the first child he had examined and he hadn't wanted to take any chances.

Looking at Chase now though, he didn't appear like the kind of guy who'd hurt a small child. And Lyla was indeed tiny for her age. Social services would look into it either way, but Chase was clearly upset about his car and yet wasn't losing his temper.

"I don't suppose you know anything about cars?" Chase asked meekly. "I have to get Lyla to school. Then my shift starts in an hour and a half. I don't really have time to call a tow truck."

Hunter rolled up his sleeves. "Have you noticed anything off with it lately?" he asked, peering under the hood. It was filthy. At least ten years old and never been cleaned, if Hunter had to guess.

Chase rubbed the back of his neck. "Not really. I did a few things yesterday evening after I put gas in it. Checked the tire pressure, topped up the oil-"

"How much oil did you put in?" Hunter asked. He quickly located the top of the dipstick and unscrewed it to remove it from the engine.

Chase pointed at one of the caps. "That's where the manual said to top it up. But it never reached the marker, so I just stopped pouring after a while."

Hunter sighed sympathetically, the dipstick held in front of him. "The marker isn't by the cap. It's here." He turned the thin metal rod in the sunlight so the oil glistened. "Can you see the two dots? The level should be between them."

It was about two inches above the top marker. Chase had massively overfilled the oil.

"Fuck," Chase whispered. The color dropped from his face. "Oh fuck, have I destroyed my car?"

"How much have you driven since you topped it up?" Hunter asked.

Chase shook his head. "Just to here. So, about ten minutes."

Hunter smiled. "Don't worry. We can fix this. I've done it before."

Chase pointed toward the hood. "You put too much oil in your car as well?" he said, not sounding convinced.

"No," Hunter said with a chuckle. "But a private did on one of the Jeeps on my last tour. You're lucky, I know how to undo it. No need to call out Triple A."

Chase covered his face with his hand. "Thank you," he muttered. "Fuck, I can't do anything right."

"Hey," said Hunter. He touched Chase's elbow, making him drop his hand and look at Hunter again. "Easy mistake to make. The important thing is your car will be okay."

Chase nibbled his lower lip between his teeth. "Lyla really needs to get to school," he said. His voice sounded as fragile as he had looked despairing over the car's engine. "It's my first morning taking her. I can't..." He scrunched up his face and shook his head. "I can't screw this up."

Hunter checked his watch. "What time is she due there? Is it close?"

Chase shrugged, his gaze on Lyla in the backseat of the car. "If we start walking now, she'd probably only be twenty minutes late. Better than not showing up at all."

"And driving?"

Chase looked back at him. "Five minutes, if the traffic isn't too bad."

With a grin, Hunter fished his keys out from his pocket. "I've got ten minutes until my next patient. I'll drive you guys as close as I can. You hop out and walk her to class, then make your way back here. Then we can get the oil out from your car after I get through my next appointment."

Chase stared at him like he'd lost his mind. "You'd do that? For me? *Us,*" he quickly amended.

Hunter nodded. It was the least he could do after the mess he'd made of their appointment. "But we gotta be quick."

Chase didn't need telling again. He dashed around and scooped Lyla up from her seat. "Hey, sweetie," he said as she wrapped her little legs around his waist. "Nice Mr. Duke is going to give us a ride. Pretty cool, huh?"

Her eyebrows climbed almost all the way up into that mane of red hair. "I won't miss school?"

"Not if we hurry," Chase said. He snatched up her small backpack covered in dinosaurs and shut the door. Hunter dropped the hood then Chase locked the car. "You ready?"

Lyla eyed up Hunter, then gave a cautious nod.

Hunter grinned. "Let's do this."

CHAPTER FIVE

Hunter had a nice car. Chase thought it was maybe a Toyota from when he'd glanced at the outside as they were getting in. It was clean and spacious and Lyla's booster seat fit nicely in the back. This was the kind of car she should be riding in.

"So, um, you were in the Army?" Chase asked to fill the silence. He was anxiously watching the clock, but they had a few minutes still to get Lyla to school. Traffic wasn't too bad, thank goodness.

Hunter glanced at him. "Navy, then Marines," he said. "I was a corpsman, so easy enough to transfer to a physician assistant."

"Wow," said Chase. Then he felt dumb. Someone that all-round impressive didn't need a loser like him confirming he was awesome. He should just shut up.

But Hunter seemed determined to make it worse. "How about you? You ever serve?"

"Oh, uh, no," he replied. "A bit too physical for a runt like me."

Hunter arched an eyebrow. "Plenty of different types of guys that serve."

Chase felt his face heat up. How did he explain that he'd had enough trouble with people tormenting him at high school? The armed forces weren't the place for a sissy like him.

But now Hunter probably thought he was judging him. Like Chase thought he was too good for the military or something? What could he say to assure Hunter he was more than good enough without sounding pathetic? Or worse, like it was a come on?

Fuck. The sooner they got out of the car, the better. Hopefully, it wouldn't take too long to fix the mess Chase had made of his oil and then he could bury this embarrassing encounter forever.

"Were you a soldier?"

Chase saw Hunter look in his rearview mirror at Lyla. He smiled. "No sweetie. I was a medic. Kind of like a nurse. I helped make the soldiers better when they got hurt or sick."

Chase glanced over his shoulder at her. She was frowning, deep in thought.

"So...now you're a doctor?"

"I'm a physician assistant," Hunter said. Chase had noticed that he wasn't afraid to address Lyla directly, and his voice was patient when he spoke to her. "It's kind of between a nurse and a doctor."

"Why?" Lyla asked.

Hunter glanced at Chase as he merged lanes. "Why what, hon?"

"Why are you a...uh, nurse here and not a soldier nurse?"

Chase felt his eyes go wide. "Oh, Mr. Duke might not want to talk about that, sweetie."

Lyla chewed her lip. "Oh," she said. "Sorry, Mr. Duke."

But Hunter shook his head and smiled at them both. "No, it's okay. I don't mind." He was quiet for a moment as he drove through town. They weren't far from the school now. "I guess, it's really tough to be in the Marines. So I thought I'd come home and start a new job where I could make some new friends."

"Oh!" She sat up in her seat and pushed her wild hair back. "Did you grow up here, too?"

Hunter gave her an apologetic look. "No, sorry, I meant home to America. Hidden Creek is my new home now, so I can make some new friends here."

"Like my daddy?"

Chase spluttered. "Oh, look," he cried a little too loudly. "There's the school. That's fine, Mr. Duke, you can drop us here."

Hunter smiled at him though. "It's fine. I can get you a little closer."

"Sorry," Chase mouthed at him, mortified. He'd hate for Hunter to think this was some sort of ploy on Chase's part to befriend him.

Hunter shook his head, though. "No problem. I only just met you guys, Lyla, but maybe we could be friends. Hey – do you like dogs?"

Lyla's head snapped around. "Dogs are the best. I saw a dog once, and it had a bowtie, and then it ate my pizza, and then I saw it chase a bicycle and my friend Milly's dog barfs in the backyard then eats that too, but he doesn't bite, even though you should ask nicely before petting him...and...did you know dogs are so smart they can find bombs and cookies and dogs are the *best*."

Chase blinked. He'd never heard her talk so much in one breath.

Hunter laughed. "Wow, sounds like you know a lot about dogs, huh?"

Lyla nodded. "Momma said we could get a dog soon, but..."

Chase knew it would be like this. It had only been a few days. But damn, it was so hard. He scrambled to think of something to say to take Lyla's mind off of her mom just before going into class. He couldn't exactly promise that *they* could get a dog. Chase could hardly afford to look after himself, let alone Lyla *and* a dog.

As was becoming habit, though, Hunter came to the rescue.

"Well, how would you like meet my puppy?" he asked. "You and your daddy could come over for dinner one night this week."

"A puppy!" Lyla squealed, balling up her tiny fists in excitement. "Oh, can we Daddy? Can we? *Please*."

Chase felt beyond awkward. He tried to keep his heart rate down but he was freaking out. Hunter wouldn't want to hang out with him. He'd make buddies down the gym or with other people from the doctors' office. But his daughter's face was filled with hope and delight.

"Um," he began, glancing at the clock on the dash of the parked car. They really needed to go. "I don't know. We don't want to be an imposition, Mr. Duke."

Lyla's eyes got wider, if that was possible. "He asked us, Daddy. *Please*."

Hunter gave Chase's knee a pat. Chase did his best not to quiver at the contact, but it was like the skin tingled with electricity where Hunter's hand touched his leg. He smiled at Chase.

"Honestly," he said. "I'd love to. It's the least I can do. And you can call me Hunter. I insist."

Chase swallowed, unable to see how he could get them out of this. "Okay," he said reluctantly.

Lyla cheered and hopped out of the car with her bag. Chase hadn't even realized she had unbuckled herself. "Thank you, Mr. Hunter!"

"Sweetie, wait!" Chase cried, fumbling with his own belt.

Hunter placed that strong hand on his knee again. "It's cool, you've got this," he said firmly. "We'll talk more back at your car."

"Oh, all right..."

Chase scrambled out of the Toyota in a daze. What the hell just happened?

He shook his head and rushed after Lyla as she skipped up to the front gates of Hidden Creek Elementary. "Are you okay, hon?" he asked. "Do you know where you're going?"

"Yes," she said, looking up at him as if he was a dummy. But she then slipped her tiny hand into his and his heart melted just a little. He was desperate for her to feel comfortable with him. To trust him. He couldn't let her down.

Therefore, when she asked her next question, there was no way he could say no.

"So, we can have dinner with Mr. Hunter and his puppy?"

Chase looked down at her as they walked along with the other kindergartners and their parents. He would do anything to make her happy and he had never seen her face light up like it had when she'd talked about the dogs.

He was convinced Hunter Duke wouldn't want to be associated with someone like him when he got to know more people in the town. But for now, maybe if Chase just thought of it as a playdate for Lyla and the puppy, it wouldn't be too awkward between him and Hunter.

"Sure, sweetie," he said. He was rewarded with another squeal that made some of the other kids look.

"Really? You promise?"

"As long as Mr. Duke says it's okay," he said. "We'll organize a day when I see him back at the doctors'."

"Can we go tonight?" she asked eagerly.

Chase couldn't help but laugh. "I don't know. But if we're lucky, maybe sometime this week?"

Eventually, he was able to coax her into going into her classroom. He watched fondly as she was enveloped by the throng of other kids. She remained easy to spot, though. Her hair was a crazy red cloud that bobbed around her head with every step she took. Tomorrow, he would absolutely come prepared with a brush.

He turned to walk back out of the school. As he did, he caught a couple of the moms nearby whispering together. They were staring his way.

Immediately, he dropped his head, shoved his hands in his pockets and walked with purpose toward the exit. He didn't want to know what they might be saying about him. The thought that other kids might be unkind to Lyla because their folks didn't like her dad broke his heart.

It felt like a long walk back to the doctors'. Chase hoped Hunter had made it back in time to see his next patient. He was ashamed that he'd been such a moron and now required Hunter's help to fix his car. He had patients to see. He shouldn't have to be running around after Chase's stupid ass. Guilt and humiliation warred with each other all the way back to the parking lot.

What kind of man didn't know how to top up the oil on his car? He was useless. While he waited for Hunter to come back out, he searched online for advice on how to get the oil back out again. But his data was low, so he stopped after a couple of minutes. Hunter sounded like he knew what he was doing. Chase had just hoped to look slightly less clueless when the other man returned.

Chase only had to wait a couple more minutes before Hunter's large form emerged from the doctors' office. He wasn't overweight or scarily muscly, from what Chase could tell. It was simply that his frame was bigger than average and he was toned on top of that.

Scowling, Chase turned his head away. He never allowed himself thoughts like that, not unless he went to a bar specifically looking for a bit of company. Even then, Chase treated those encounters as a requirement to be completed as soon as possible. A necessary release. He wasn't about to start allowing himself to daydream about a guy he knew, particularly when he had been so kind.

It was already hot, so Chase had been sitting with the doors open to let a breeze through the car. As Hunter neared, he stepped out onto the pavement and waved. Then felt like an idiot, so shoved his hands back into his pockets again.

"Hi," he said as soon as Hunter was close enough to hear. "Thanks so much for this. I can't believe I was so stupid."

Hunter was carrying a bucket which he placed on the

ground by the car. Inside was a wide gauge syringe and a coil of tubing as well as a roll of paper towels and a packet of disposable rubber gloves.

He frowned at Chase over the sunglasses he had put on. "Hey, it's no trouble, I swear. Stop beating yourself up."

Naturally, that only made Chase feel more incompetent. Not only was he burdening Hunter with this task, but he was also pissing him off.

Although...Hunter didn't seem pissed off. He smiled and touched Chase's elbow again. "Everybody makes mistakes. It's good you caught it before you did any real damage to your car. Now, let me show you what to do."

"Oh, okay," Chase said. He'd hoped Hunter would stick around. But of course he had patients to see, a job to do.

Hunter winked at him, his glasses adorably on the tip of his nose. "Don't worry, it's easy."

Together, they attached the tubing to the nozzle of the syringe. Then they fed the tube down where the dipstick went. After that, they pulled back the top of the syringe to withdraw a measure of the oil, which they pushed back out from the tubing into the bucket. Chase wore the gloves and did the first few sucks with Hunter looking on.

"That's it, you got it," Hunter told him, clapping Chase on the back.

Chase couldn't help but smile, feeling the tips of his ears warm up. He couldn't remember the last time anyone but Amanda gave him any genuine praise.

"Thanks," he mumbled.

Hunter nodded at the engine. "I'd say do about twenty of those, then check the dipstick again. You'll be good to go in no time."

Chase looked down at the slightly dirty oil they had already extracted. "What should I do with all this once I'm done?"

Hunter pointed toward the back of the surgery. "Leave it by the dumpsters back there, and I'll take care of it."

He nodded and made to walk away.

Chase's heart was in his throat. He'd *promised* Lyla they would go visit Hunter's dog and go for dinner. But he couldn't find the words to bring up the offer without sounding needy.

Luckily, Hunter clicked his fingers and turned back around. "Almost forgot about dinner," he said brightly. He fished a pen and small pack of sticky notes from his pants pocket. "I mean-" he expression fell "-if you want to? I don't want to be an imposition."

Chase couldn't help but splutter. "It's *me* that's the imposition," he said. "I've got you out here fixing my car and driving us to school on your first day of work."

But Hunter shook his head. "I just have the one buddy here in town," he said. He sounded a little sad. "Connor. He's going through some stuff of his own. I'd be honored to have you and your little girl come over."

Chase thought maybe he was just being polite and honoring his invite to Lyla. But Chase was so keen to please his girl he decided that was okay and accepted the offer anyway.

"Well, that would be swell," he said. "Thank you."

Hunter scribbled on the small square of paper. "Here's my cell. Drop me a text and we can work out a day and time, then I can try and text you directions." He chuckled and rubbed the back of his neck, flexing his bicep as he did so. Chase determinedly ignored the sight. "I don't even really know where I live yet."

Chase couldn't help but laugh. It was probably the relaxed atmosphere between them that gave him the confidence to ask. "Lyla was kind of hoping we might come over tonight. But I understand if that's not enough notice for you."

Inexplicably, Hunter's face lit up like a Christmas tree. "That would be wonderful," he said, apparently sincere. "If you come over about seven, would that be too late for her?"

"Not if we ate soon after that," Chase answered, proud he knew what time his little girl needed to be heading to bed. He was already sounding slightly more responsible.

Hunter checked his watch, then smiled warmly at Chase. "Give me a text, and we'll work out the details. Let me know if she has any favorites or allergies, and I'll see y'all at seven?"

"On the dot," Chase confirmed.

He watched Hunter go back into the doctors' office with his heart hammering in his chest. There was no reason why it should be, he told himself sternly as he turned and got to work again on the car. This was *not* a date. This was so Lyla could meet the puppy.

Chase didn't do dates, anyway. So there was nothing to worry about. He just needed to get this damn oil out and get to work at JJ's. Then he could figure out how he was going to make it through the evening without making a fool of himself.

Again.

CHAPTER SIX

HUNTER

Hunter had no idea why he was so nervous. Well, other than he had managed to somehow burn the pasta and forgot to get juice and didn't know if the mini brownies he had bought would be suitable for dessert. What if Lyla was allergic to nuts? They didn't specifically have nuts in, but they might have been made in a place with nuts. Chase hadn't said she was allergic, but...

"Enough," he said out loud to Trooper as he scampered around at Hunter's feet. "This is ridiculous."

Trooper barked in agreement.

Hunter was getting himself all wound up, worrying what he and a five-year-old would be able to talk about. But Chase would be with them, too. A perfectly capable adult, who could presumably hold a conversation with no problem.

Hunter stirred the pasta and wondered not for the first time what had caused him to be so rash. The old him, before Hidden Creek, wouldn't have invited a stranger over for dinner, even if his kid was as cute as a button. Was he really feeling that guilty over his faux-pas at their appointment?

Or was he really hoping he and Chase could become buddies? They didn't seem to have all that much in common. But for whatever reason, Hunter felt drawn to him all the same. He had learned during his active duty that it was important to trust his instincts. So, if his gut was telling him they could be friends, why not listen?

He hadn't had long after he finished work to go to the store (after he had found it) and pick up groceries. So he'd fallen back on one of his old favorite recipes his mom had taught him before he left home. A simple pot of spaghetti with a cheesy ham, leek and mushroom sauce. It was one of the only things he knew how to actually put together, so he hoped Lyla and Chase liked it.

When the doorbell rang, he made himself take a deep breath in and out. "Nothing to worry about, Marine," he told himself. "Who knows? You might even have fun."

Trooper was already having a ball. He bounced around Hunter's feet as they walked from the kitchen to the front door, wagging his tail and yapping.

Hunter whistled sharply, like he'd seen on the videos online. He needed to be firm and show the dog he was the alpha of the pack. Sure enough, Trooper quieted down.

Pleased, Hunter opened the front door with a smile. Chase was standing on the front step looking even more anxious than Hunter felt. Lyla was in front of him, and Chase had both his hands resting lightly on her small shoulders in what looked like an attempt to stop her jumping up and down. It appeared that Chase had tried his best to tame her unruly red hair, which made Hunter smile even more.

"Hello there," he said to them both.

Then Trooper used his nose to push past Hunter's legs and launch himself into the arms of the five-year-old.

Hunter jerked forward to pull them apart, worried how the puppy would behave that close to an excited child. But the two of them were immediately squealing and barking as she hugged him close and he did his best to lick the freckles off her nose.

"Oh my god!" she shrieked. "I love him, oh my god, Mr. Hunter!"

Hunter laughed. Chase visibly relaxed and managed to laugh a bit, too. "Would you like to come inside?" Hunter asked.

"Yes please," said Lyla.

Hunter tried whistling, but Trooper was too hyper. So he gently pulled the pup back indoors by his collar. Lyla was only too happy to follow him, pulling her sparkly pumps off as she went.

"Hi," said Chase, then cleared his throat. "Um, this is for you."

He thrust a cheap-looking bottle of red wine Hunter's way. Confusingly, he seemed to be blushing. Maybe he was as rusty at hanging out with other guys as Hunter was?

Luckily, Hunter hadn't met a red wine he didn't like. Most of the guys he had hung out with over the years preferred to drink beer, which was fine. But a glass of red was Hunter's go-to and would do the trick nicely with the pasta he was cooking.

"Thank you," he said graciously. Or at least, he hoped it was gracious. He held his hand out toward the hallway. "Come on in. Did you find the place okay?"

Chase nodded and stepped inside. He brushed his hands

down his jeans. The light green shirt he was wearing was a button down, which suited him better than the grey polo he'd been wearing earlier. Hunter thought it might actually have been the same uniform he'd seen the clerks wearing at the JJ's grocery store.

"It was only a ten-minute walk. Lyla showed me some of the cool, big houses on the way."

As if on cue, the little girl came bounding back up to Hunter from where she and Trooper had already raced in to the kitchen. She tugged on Hunter's pants at the knee.

"Excuse me, Mr. Hunter," she said in all seriousness.

"Yes, Lyla," he replied, equally grave. He guessed she was going to ask about Trooper's missing leg.

But instead she smiled up at him and curled a lock of hair around her finger, pulling it taut against her head. "What's the puppy's name?"

"Oh," said Hunter, pleasantly surprised. "It's Trooper."

"I like that," she said brightly, then skipped away to chase him around the kitchen again.

Chase came and stood beside him, watching the two play. "He looks like a little trooper," he said.

Hunter nodded, even more pleased. "That's what I thought."

He fetched two wine glasses down, then remembered he hadn't bought juice.

"Um, I've got milk Lyla can have," he said guiltily. "Or water. I'm sorry, I totally forgot to buy juice or soda."

But Chase shook his head as he leaned against one of the kitchen counters. "She's not allowed soda yet. Water will be great. Thank you."

Hunter was able to waste a few minutes pouring their

drinks while he struggled for something to say. It was easy when he was talking to patients, most of the time at least. He could just discuss whatever was wrong with them and only had to throw in a bit of chit-chat here and there.

"Oh," he said as a thought occurred to him as he was handing over Chase's wine. "You're not driving, are you?" He'd said he'd walked, but Chase wanted to make sure. "Is the car okay?"

Chase shook his head, accepting the glass. "No, the car is fine, but we wanted to walk. For the fresh air."

Hunter recalled the budget bottle of wine and the comments about the large houses, so he thought maybe Chase was saving money on gas. Hunter approved of him being sensible, but it also made him determined to spoil his guests a little bit. He got out salad and bread rolls to go with their pasta as well.

"Can I help with anything?" Chase asked.

He was cradling his wine glass like it was a shield. Hunter was sort of relieved he wasn't the only nervous one, but he was hoping they'd all have a fun time tonight. Keeping busy always made him feel less agitated too.

"You could set the table," he suggested. "The cutlery's in this drawer here-" he banged it with his hip "-and the dining room is through there."

Chase gave him a grateful smile. He placed the glass down on the side, then occupied himself putting all the necessary bits and bobs in the right place while Hunter dished up their food.

He almost gave Lyla the same portion size as the two of them. But he looked at the size of her then decided to give her a third of what they were having. When Chase came back to take their plates, he nodded approvingly.

"Thank you, sorry, I should have said."

Hunter had noticed that Chase apologized a lot. It didn't annoy him, but he did wonder why that was.

"It's fine," he assured him. "Lyla can eat whatever she wants. I won't be offended if she just has the bread."

Hunter was impressed though. When they called her to come sit down, she didn't need to be told twice. That might have had something to do with the fact that Trooper was just as eager to come to the other room as well, and sat by her chair when they all settled down.

"No feeding the dog scraps from the table," Chase warned. It was endearing to see him be the firm parental figure.

Hunter knew he wanted kids someday. It wasn't a question for him. But without even a girlfriend on the horizon, he doubted that day would come any time soon for him.

For a while, they ate their food in slightly strained silence. Lyla picked out all her leeks and mushrooms which made Hunter feel bad. But she ate the cheesy pasta and ham well enough. When she got halfway through her meal, she began to tear little bits off her roll and nibble them from her fingers. Chase had barely touched his wine, but Hunter was drinking his a little too fast to compensate for the increasing awkwardness. He placed the glass back down, resolving not to sip from it again until he'd finished his dinner.

"So, Chase," he said. The words came out stilted, but he pushed on regardless. "What do you do? When you're not getting stranded in parking lots, I mean."

He meant it as a joke, but Chase bit his lip. Hunter cursed himself.

"I work at the grocery store in town," he said, fiddling with the salt shaker. Hunter had guessed correctly about his uniform. "JJ's Fresh Goods. Nothing special." His smile didn't meet his eyes. "Not like you. I bet your folks are real proud of you."

Hunter swallowed his mouthful of food. He didn't like the idea that Chase's parents might be looking down on him for working in retail. At least he was supporting his daughter, even if things hadn't worked out with her mom. And now, he was her sole provider. It had to be tough.

"Yeah," he said. "They're happier now I'm back in the States, I guess." He nodded at Lyla and Trooper. "They can't wait to meet Trooper. He's a great dog, isn't he?"

Lyla came back to life. "Oh, yes," she said. She nodded so hard her hair shook in a ginger cloud around her. "I like him so much. Can I please come see him again?"

"Mr. Duke is very busy, honey," Chase said quickly. "I'm sure he has other friends too that will want to see him."

Hunter was hurt that Chase wasn't all that interested in getting to know each other. But he still smiled at Lyla. "I'm not that busy," he said, looking back and forth between father and daughter. "And Trooper seems to really like you. You'd be welcome over any time I'm home to come say hi."

Lyla gave a little clap. "I really like him, too. May I be excused to the bathroom?"

The jump in conversation threw Hunter slightly. Her mind seemed to race a mile a minute. "Of course. It's upstairs. Do you need me to show you where it is?"

Lyla shook her head and hopped down from her seat. "Can Trooper come with me?"

Hunter laughed as the puppy immediately jumped to her side. "I don't think I could stop him if I wanted."

Happily, the dog and the child skipped off to find the bathroom. Lyla chatted to Trooper until the door shut on them.

"I'm sorry," said Chase. When Hunter looked at him, he was focusing on pushing his pasta around the plate. "That's extremely kind of you, but we've put you out enough today."

"Have I done something to upset you?" Hunter asked. He'd learned to be direct after all his years of service, and he didn't like the idea that Chase seemed so reluctant to keep up the friendship.

But his astonished expression when he looked back at Hunter surprised him. "No," Chase stammered. "No, of course not. I mean...it's just..." He sighed, then grabbed his wine glass to take a large gulp. "You'll probably soon get talking to people and realize you could keep much better company than me. If...if you really don't mind Lyla visiting Trooper, I'll bring her over to say hi. But, yeah, as the new guy I'd advise looking elsewhere for friends."

Hunter glanced upward. There seemed no sign of Lyla coming back down yet. He leaned back in his seat and regarded Chase. "Can't I decide my friends for myself?" he asked.

Chase nibbled on his lip. "Well," he said slowly, also glancing toward the ceiling. "How about I give you the facts? Then we can head off, and you can make up your own mind."

Hunter nodded. "Sure." Was this something to do with Lyla's bruises after all?

Chase took a fortifying breath. "I got Lyla's mom, Amanda, pregnant when we were eighteen. It was just a stupid teenage mistake – I mean not using a condom," he added in horror, his wide eyes snapped back to Hunter. "Not Lyla. She's the best thing that ever happened to me."

His sincerity moved Hunter. He reached forward and placed his hand over Chase's smaller one. "Of course," he said. "I'm a medic, I know these things happen."

Chase looked down at their connected hands. Slowly, Hunter withdrew his, hoping he hadn't crossed a line.

"Well," said Chase, frowning. Like he wasn't used to people being understanding. "She wanted to keep the baby, and I was happy to support her however I could. But we didn't want to get married. We knew it wasn't the right thing to do." The door opened upstairs, and Chase looked up and inhaled sharply. "A lot of people around here saw that as my fault."

He glanced nervously at Hunter, then wiped his hands with a napkin and stood up. Hunter watched him swallow, then plaster a smile on his face.

"Hey, baby," Chase said, his voice strained as Lyla and Trooper came back into the dining room. "Are you ready to head home?"

Lyla's face fell. "Already?" she asked.

"I'm afraid it's nearly your bedtime," Chase said.

"But next time," said Hunter as he also rose to his feet, "y'all can come over earlier and have more playtime with Trooper. I promise."

Chase blinked and frowned at him. But Hunter wasn't an idiot. He could make up his own mind and he knew that he liked both Chase and Lyla. He didn't care their history was unconventional, or what any local gossip might say.

Lyla clapped her hands again. "Okay, promise," she said firmly, nodding her head and shaking her hair about. "Bye-bye, Trooper! I love you!" She managed to hug the puppy clumsily and kiss his head, despite his wriggling. Then she scampered off to get her shoes.

Chase eyed him warily. But Hunter shrugged and walked over to him. "How about we just see if we enjoy hanging out? You'd be doing a lonely vet a favor, and I think spending time with Trooper is doing Lyla some good too."

"Well, yeah," said Chase, turning his head the way Lyla had run. "I agree on that." He looked Hunter up and down. For the first time, Hunter realized how green his eyes were. "Okay, I guess, if you're sure?"

Hunter let out a breath of relief he wasn't aware he'd been holding. "Yeah," he said. "I'm sure."

CHAPTER SEVEN

CHASE

It was amazing how much Chase's house had changed in the past couple weeks.

It wasn't ever a place he had taken pride in before. When his good-for-nothing father had passed three years ago, he had left the property to his only child, Chase. It was the sole decent thing he had ever done for him.

Chase had thought about moving, selling up and relocating somewhere completely new without so many memories to haunt him. But Lyla had kept him here. Although he hadn't been a huge part of her life, he had done what he could for her, and wanted to remain close. Besides, even with a good deal of the mortgage paid, he couldn't afford the excess costs it would take to move elsewhere.

So here he had remained. In this one story, two-bedroom dump that echoed with all the awful things his dad had ever said to him.

But in the few weeks Lyla had been with him, a transformation had started to happen. For one thing, it had forced

Chase to clear out a bunch of junk that had been lying around. Boxes of magazines and his dad's old trophies and rusting pots and pans from the garage. VHS and cassette tapes that he no longer had the means to play. A rickety wardrobe that had just been taking up space in the corner of his bedroom. He'd filled his car and taken load after load to the dump.

For the first time he could remember, Chase felt like his home was opening up. That there was space to breathe. The room where he slept was starting to feel more like his, despite having changed the bed as soon as his dad was buried and gone. He couldn't afford new sheets, but since Lyla had arrived, he had mixed up two of the bedding sets he already owned to create a slightly different color scheme of blues and grays.

Amanda's parents, Lucy and Paul, had been in town for the funeral. They were good people. Paul's health still wasn't great, hence the early retirement in Ocala. But they loved Lyla dearly and were clearly devastated over Amanda's death.

Chase had tried to help them to a certain extent with emptying Amanda's apartment while they'd been around. But they didn't seem sure what to make of him. To be fair, they didn't *know* him. He was just the boy who had knocked up their daughter then refused to marry her. So, he tried not to blame them for their wariness. But it was hard when they were still questioning how fit he was to be a parent and offering to take custody of Lyla themselves, despite Paul's health issues.

However, that did now mean that all of Lyla's possessions had filled up Chase's house, lighting up every room with her artwork, toys and photos. He made sure that Amanda's smiling face was everywhere, staying close to them both.

His small, childhood bedroom had been where Lyla had

slept on the few occasions she'd visited in the past. But since she'd moved in, they had properly redecorated together. The walls were now cream instead of the pale blue they'd been before, and she had brought all her purple knick-knacks from her old room. Comforter and lampshades and rugs, all various shades of purple, bringing life to the room.

Lyla loved spaceships, dinosaurs and fluffy animals almost equally, as was evident by her clothes, toys and furnishings. Chase had hung brightly colored movie posters on the walls with Sticky Tack and plugged her nightlight into the wall. As far as a kid's bedroom went, he felt like it wasn't half bad.

Chase realized the next Saturday morning as he sat drinking coffee that this was the first time he might ever have felt close to happy under this roof. But then he immediately felt guilty because the reason Lyla was with him was that Amanda was gone.

He and Lyla had good days and bad days dealing with their grief. Unfortunately, today was one of the bad days.

Chase tried not to panic as Lyla tore through her room, screaming at him. As it was a Saturday, he had told her she could wear anything she wanted. Anything at all. But she was still flailing around in her underwear. From what he could tell through her tears, her hair hurt (he hadn't brushed it yet) and he was the worst for making her wake up (he hadn't, she'd gotten up all by herself) and why couldn't she go swimming? (He said he'd take her.)

The last straw came when she insisted she wanted to go jump out of the window so she could ride the horse on her sweater that she wouldn't put on and then shouted was too hot to wear before calling him a stupid head.

"Lyla, *stop it!*" Chase roared, feeling like he was going to burst into tears himself.

The doorbell rang, causing them both to stop and look toward the front of the house.

Of course, this was the morning social services was due to call.

Lyla hiccuped, her wide eyes almost as red as her hair. Chase tried not to panic. "Please," he whispered. "Please, baby. I promise we'll go swimming and I'll even get you some ice cream. Just let me get you dressed and fix your hair."

Her lip wobbled and for a moment he was hopeful. But then she dropped her head back and started wailing again.

The doorbell rang for a second time. Chase's heart was like a jackhammer in his chest. He saw no option but to pick up the squirming Lyla and answer the door.

He tried to rehearse what he was going to say in his head. But it was difficult with Lyla crying and wailing under his arm like a wriggling roll of carpet. It was like he pushed through fog to reach the door and pull it open.

"I'm so sorry-" he began. Then stopped, snapping his mouth closed.

Hunter was standing on the front step, the little three-legged Trooper straining against the leash in his hand. "Hi," Hunter said.

He looked wary, probably because Lyla was only in a T-shirt and panties and was lying horizontally across his hip. But at the sight of Trooper, she dialed her sobbing down to sniffles and put her thumb in her mouth. Good. That was a sign that she was finally calming down. He hoisted her up so she could sit upright.

"I thought you were..." Chase trailed off, not wanting to

admit to Hunter that social services were coming over to check on him. "This is a nice surprise, isn't it, Lyla?" he bounced her on his hip. She didn't reply, but she kept her eyes on Trooper and didn't resume her crying, so that was a win.

"Oh no, is this a bad time?" Hunter said. He took a step back and looked uncomfortable. "We were just walking past and Trooper wanted to say hi." He raised his eyebrows at Lyla, as if asking if she wanted to say hi back.

Chase could have wept in relief when she popped her thumb out of her mouth and waved tiredly down at him. Trooper gave her a bark.

"We've got someone coming over," Chase said, conceding that much. "But Lyla wasn't feeling so great. Maybe now we can get you dressed though, sweetie?"

"Oh dear," said Hunter in his talking-to-kids voice. He stepped back up to the door. "What's the matter, Lyla?"

She shook her head and rubbed her eyes.

"Come on," said Chase kindly. He sensed victory was at hand and wanted to pounce while she was calmed down. "Let's go get you dressed properly, huh?"

She didn't answer, but she did drop her head onto his shoulder and grab a fistful of his T-shirt as she hugged him. He kissed her forehead.

"That's it, darling."

He smiled at Hunter, still waiting across the threshold. He couldn't deny it was damned good to see him. After their aborted dinner on Monday, he'd been wondering if Hunter had really meant what he'd said about wanting to be friends. Chase had forgotten that he'd told him where he lived in their texts. Not explicitly, but enough that a smart guy like Hunter could figure it out. After all, no other house had his battered old car parked outside.

"Would you like to come in?" he offered hesitantly. Seeing as Trooper had done so much to calm Lyla down, Chase hoped he might continue to do so. Also, there was something about Hunter that calmed *Chase* down, as silly as that was.

Hunter's face broke into a gorgeous smile. Damn. Even with everything that was going on, Chase had still found a few idle moments to wonder if there was any chance Hunter was into dudes. Then he'd stopped himself each time because Chase would never risk going with anyone from Hidden Creek. Not even the hunky medic.

"We'd love to come in," Hunter said. "If that's all right with Lyla?"

Finally, that got a response from her. She nodded and put her thumb back in her mouth. Chase blew out a sigh of relief.

As quickly as he could, Chase took Lyla back to her room. He slipped on her favorite little green alien T-shirt with black pants and then carefully ran a brush through her hair. She was still sucking her thumb and mercifully didn't put up a fight. Every few seconds, Chase glanced out into the living room to see Hunter watching Trooper carefully as he sniffed around the furniture.

"There's coffee in the pot if you want some," Chase called out, aware that he was being a bad host.

Hunter smiled at him, which did funny things to Chase's insides. "That would be great, thank you."

Chase didn't make fancy coffee often. It was only because Mr. Preston from social services was on his way over that Chase wanted to make a good impression. Plus, JJ's had some Guatemalan beans currently on sale, so with his staff discount they had actually been affordable and he'd splurged just for this. Now he was glad he was able to offer a cup to Hunter as well, though.

When Lyla was finally presentable, Chase sighed in relief from where he was kneeling in front of her. She sniffed the last of her tears away and rubbed her freckled nose. "Sorry, Daddy," she mumbled.

He gave her a hug. "It's okay, pumpkin. Do you want to go say hello to Trooper and Mr. Duke now?"

She nodded. "Yes, please."

He led her by the hand to where Hunter was standing in the kitchen. He'd let Trooper out into the small, shabby backyard where he was happily chasing his tail and snapping at the leaves rustling in the warm spring breeze. The grass was all yellow and dead still from the hurricane damage. Chase didn't know how to fix it.

Hunter turned from where he was watching the dog out the back door.

"Wow," he said to Lyla. "Don't you look great?"

She managed a small smile. "Thank you, Mr. Hunter," she whispered.

He pointed outside. "Do you want to play with Trooper?"

She nodded, already running for the yard. But Chase reached belatedly after her. "Don't mess up your clothes!" he cried.

Lyla waved and nodded, then skipped after Trooper. Hunter was already looking at him inquisitively. Chase busied himself by loading the dishwasher.

"Your folks coming over?" Hunter asked. He was going for casual, but Chase could tell he was curious.

"Uh, no," Chase admitted. He didn't want to lie to Hunter,

and Hunter had already told him he wasn't put off by his past. The fact he was standing in his home went some way to convincing Chase he really meant that. "This was my parents' house. My mom left a long time ago, and my dad passed three years back."

"I'm so sorry," Hunter said.

Chase scoffed. "Don't be," he said automatically. But then he realized how bitter he sounded. He cleared his throat and turned to look directly at Hunter. "Sorry, that's nice of you. But my dad didn't like me any more than I liked him." That was a nice way to say he was quick to lash out with both his tongue and his fists. "I don't remember my mom," he lied.

Hunter looked like he was even sorrier to hear that, but he didn't say anything more on the matter. Chase could tell he was still wanting to know who they were expecting to visit. Familiar shame filled Chase's chest.

"The truth is," he said reluctantly, "social services is coming over. I think they would rather send Lyla down to her grandparents in Florida. But I'm her dad and official next of kin. So, for now, they've agreed not to disrupt her life any further."

"That's good," said Hunter.

Chase shook his head. "I wasted so much time thinking I wasn't good enough to be in her life. Now, I'm terrified they're going to take her away from me."

To his horror, he couldn't stop the tears that blurred his vision or the thickening in his throat. He turned hastily and wiped a cloth over the already clean counter.

"Hey," Hunter said. His voice was much closer than Chase would have expected, and the next thing Chase felt was his big hand on his shoulder. "It's going to be okay. You're doing great."

Chase turned to face the taller man. "I'm barely holding it together," he whispered, his voice cracking. "I can't do this. She deserves better."

Chase wasn't quite sure how it happened. But he suspected Hunter, this man he hardly knew, pulled him into an embrace. Chase melted against his broad chest, allowing Hunter's large arms to envelop him. "It's okay," Hunter said soothingly as Chase tried to dial back his emotions. He needed to be strong for Lyla.

Chase couldn't remember the last time he'd been held by anyone. Not like this, like they were protecting him from the world. "Thank you," he said, his voice raspy.

A knock at the door startled them apart. Chase cleared his throat, feeling embarrassed. He hoped Hunter didn't feel too weird after their moment.

"Oh well," Chase said, resigned. "I guess you'll get to meet Mr. Preston, too."

It probably wasn't ideal that Chase had a strange man around the house. In fact, he became very worried very quickly that it was going to look extremely bad. But Hunter was just here as a friend, and Lyla loved Trooper. Anyone with eyes could see that. And Hunter wasn't gay. Neither was Chase, officially. So he did his best to tell himself he didn't have anything to fret over.

Hunter gave him an encouraging smile as he headed for the door. Chase prayed to whoever might be listening that the universe would be kind to him for once. With one final steadying breath, he reached for the door handle and plastered on his best smile.

CHAPTER EIGHT

HUNTER

Mʀ. Pʀᴇᴄᴛᴏɴ ᴡᴀᴀ as unpleasant as Hunter had imagined him to be from their brief conversation over the phone several days ago: a bulbous walrus of a man. He took his time wandering about Chase's small house. The way he patted his large belly and stroked his bushy mustache set Hunter's nerves on edge. Hunter didn't know Chase very well. But he disliked the idea of him being judged by a man who was obviously comfortable in life, if his round belly and expensive suit were anything to go by.

"Where is Lyla?" Mr. Preston asked, his voice a nasal squeak.

"Outside, playing," Chase stammered. He was wringing his hands. Hunter felt the urge to put himself between him and Mr. Preston.

"I brought my puppy over to see Lyla," he said, addressing Mr. Preston. "Hunter Duke. We spoke on the phone the other day regarding Lyla's circumstances."

"Oh," said Mr. Preston, suddenly a lot more interested in

Hunter. "You're the Marine, aren't you? It's an honor to have you come to stay in our little town. An honor indeed, sir. Thank you for your service."

He pumped Hunter's hand fiercely without waiting to see if Hunter wanted to shake in the first place.

Hunter grimaced and withdrew his hand from Mr. Preston's sweaty palm. He hated when people said things like that, because he had no idea what to say back. 'Thank you?' He appreciated that people supported him giving his time and risking his life to protect their country. But rarely did they know what that truly entailed. He didn't like being put unjustly on a pedestal.

Especially not by someone who raked his eyes over Chase like he was a rabbit trapped in the sights of a fox. "How would you say Lyla is doing, Mr. Williamson?" he asked.

"I, um," said Chase. Then he took a steadying breath and relaxed his shoulders. Hunter was proud of him. "She's been good, sir," he said steadily. "Obviously, this is a very difficult time for her. But she's adjusting well and coping as best she can."

Mr. Preston smiled like a snake and fetched a beige file from his brown suitcase. "Really?" He rubbed his whiskers and flicked through the sheets of paper in his hands. "Because her teachers have said differently. Did you know she has been called to Principal Irwin's office twice this week?"

Hunter glanced outside to where Lyla was scampering about with Trooper, happy as could be.

"Yes," Chase said, nodding. "Yes, and I've spoken to the school about that."

Mr. Preston rose his eyebrows and scanned his file of papers. "And you're happy about this?"

"Well," said Chase. "I'm not *happy,* but-"

"Why do they think she's acting out?" Mr. Preston interrupted.

Hunter thought that was just cruel. "Excuse me for butting in," he said in a friendly tone. "But in my medical opinion, I feel it is entirely natural for a young child to display her grief in a number of ways. Acting out and fighting, although not ideal, is only to be expected." For adults, too, he wanted to add.

But Mr. Preston looked up and narrowed his eyes at Hunter. "As I recall," he squeaked, "you contacted my office with concerns for the child yourself. May I ask what you're doing here today, Mr. Duke?"

Hunter held his head high and met Chase's eyes. "Yes. It was my mistake. My notes hadn't been updated yet and I regrettably put Mr. Williamson and his daughter in an awkward situation. As far as I can tell, Lyla is a content, healthy girl going through a very sad period in her life the best she can. Her father is doing admirably."

Chase gave him the warmest, most grateful look Hunter had received from anyone in some time. It stirred something unfamiliar in his chest, like a balloon expanding.

"And the cuts and bruises you highlighted?" asked Mr. Preston, obviously hoping to stir trouble.

Hunter eyed him squarely. "Lyla is clearly an active child," he said. He jutted his chin toward the kitchen window. They could all clearly see her and Trooper playing tug-of-war with a large stick. If this man was looking to drive a wedge between Hunter and Chase, he would have to try harder than that.

"I see," said Mr. Preston, making a note with his shiny silver pen. "So, if you aren't concerned for the child, may I ask again what you're doing here?" His eyes flicked to Chase who looked away, uncomfortable. Hunter wasn't sure what the exchange signified.

"I'm new in town," Hunter said with ease. It was the truth, after all. "After our appointment, I apologized to Chase. Then we've kept in touch."

From what Hunter knew of the kind of things child protection services were interested in, he thought having a friendship with a physician assistant would go in Chase's favor. As someone educated who cared for the community, Hunter would be seen as a good influence. But Mr. Preston quirked his eyebrow and wrote something else down on one of his sheets of paper.

"I think it would be a good idea to summon the child now," said Mr. Preston. He looked up expectantly at Chase.

"Oh. Sure," he said with a timid smile. He glanced at Hunter, who gave him a reassuring nod, or at least he hoped. Then Chase crossed through the house to lean out of the back door.

"Lyla! Could you come here, please?"

"Can Trooper come, too?" her voice drifted faintly in through the door. Hunter couldn't help the grin that crept on his face. It was a good thing Hunter wanted to be friends with her dad, because Lyla was quickly becoming inseparable from Hunter's dog.

"Of course, sweetie," said Chase.

He glanced warily over at Mr. Preston as they all waited for the duo to come back into the house. Chase took the opportunity to get Mr. Preston a cup of coffee. He looked at it like it was dishwater and grimaced as he took a sip.

Lyla and Trooper clattered back onto the kitchen tiles. Then Lyla looked past the dining table through the open-plan house to where Mr. Preston was standing in the den.

"Oh," he said with a chortle, putting down the coffee right next to a coaster. "It seems like you forgot some of your dog!"

Lyla regarded him in confusion. Hunter was glad he was slightly behind Mr. Preston because he knew he flashed a look of pure anger at him. How dare he make fun of Trooper's missing leg?

"Lyla," said Chase. He placed a hand on her back and gently steered her foreward. Trooper loped along by her side. "Do you remember Mr. Preston from social services? He's here to say hello and check up on you."

"Why?" Lyla asked. She pulled at a lock of her hair and gawped warily up at Mr. Preston.

Mr. Preston laughed heartily, which Hunter didn't think was entirely appropriate given the circumstances. Mr. Preston ran his hand down his waistcoat and leaned over so his whiskery face was closer to Lyla's. "Aren't you a pretty girl?"

Lyla scowled and hid behind Chase's legs. "Who's that, Daddy?"

Chase kept his cool. Hunter resisted the urge to go stand by the two of them and his dog, but he didn't want to be seen as interfering.

"That's Mr. Preston, honey," he told her. "Can you say hello?"

Lyla's scowl deepened.

Mr. Preston laughed, but there was a nasty edge to it as he shot Chase a look. "Her social skills aren't as developed as I would like to see," he said. He pulled a grim-looking handkerchief from his breast pocket.

"I'm sure Lyla is just-"

Mr. Preston cut Chase off once more by honking his red nose into the handkerchief. Chase grit his teeth and looked tearful. Hunter bunched his fists up and didn't know if he should speak up again.

"That's better," said Mr. Preston. He folded up the snotty cloth and slipped it back into his pocket. Hunter's stomach rolled. "Now, Lyla," he said, full of self-importance. He bent down to look her in the eye, speaking to her as if she was an idiot. "Sometimes grownups have to check how other grownups are behaving. That's my job. I need to make sure your daddy is a good daddy."

Lyla's face dropped. It was in moments like that Hunter appreciated how small for her age she was. "I'm sorry, Daddy," she whimpered, pulling at his jeans. Fat tears welled in her eyes. "I'm sorry," she stammered. "I'll be good, I swear."

"Hey, hey," said Chase, dropping to a crouch and pulling her into his arms. "It's okay. You don't need to say sorry."

Lyla was crying in earnest now. Hunter felt a rush of anger toward the social worker for upsetting her so much. He didn't pause as he strode over and dropped down to kneel by her as well.

"What's the matter darling?" he asked, rubbing her back.

Both she and Chase looked at him, but Chase's expression was grateful once again. Lyla was fearful. "I yelled at Daddy."

Understanding crossed Chase's face. "Oh," he said to Hunter, then glanced up at Mr. Preston. "That's okay, hon. We just had a little misunderstanding. We're friends again now, aren't we?"

"Lyla," said Mr. Preston sternly. "Can you tell me why you shouted at your father?"

"Because I'm a bad girl!" Lyla sobbed and threw herself into Chase's neck. Trooper was whimpering and nudging both Lyla and Chase with his wet nose.

Hunter stood up. "She just had a tantrum," he said softly to the social worker. "I was here. Like I explained earlier, it's natural for a grieving child to act out. They can't express themselves in any better way."

Mr. Preston stroked his mustache and glared at Hunter. "I would appreciate it if you didn't speak for the child." Hunter almost got whiplash from his change in tune. He obviously wasn't enough of a war hero for him anymore.

"She's clearly distressed," said Hunter calmly. "She thinks she's in trouble."

Mr. Preston scoffed. "You're not in trouble," he said to the back of Lyla's head with a laugh. "Lyla. Can you look at me please?"

"Sorry," she said again, peeking around her shoulder with watery eyes. Trooper forced his head under her hand, and she petted him absently, calming a little further.

Chase shook his head. "You don't have to say sorry, sweetie. The man is here to see Daddy, not you. He wants to make sure I'm a good daddy."

"Oh," said Lyla earnestly, understanding his meaning better this time. "Yes, mister. My daddy is a very good daddy." She hugged him tighter, her red curls almost enveloping Chase's whole head. He subtly pushed some of them back so he could still see Mr. Preston.

"I apologize, Mr. Preston," he said. "I don't want you to get the wrong impression."

Mr. Preston was scribbling in his file again. "And what impression would that be, Mr. Williamson?"

Chase gently squeezed Lyla's hand, still crouched on the ground. "That because I wasn't as involved in Lyla's life as much as I should have been before this isn't the right place for her now."

Mr. Preston gave him a tight smile, but his eyes were cold. "We shall see, won't we?" Chase opened his mouth, but Mr. Preston continued speaking before he got the chance to say anything. "In the meantime, I shall continue to liaise with Principal Irwin, as well as Dr. Felix from Hidden Creek Memorial. Have you seen her again to do a physical examination of Lyla yet?"

"I already forwarded her my report," said Hunter. He was getting angrier by the minute. Chase and Lyla were going through an extreme transition. Mr. Preston seemed to have no compassion for them, let alone respect.

Mr. Preston gave him a tight smile. "I think we'll let Dr. Felix see for herself, hmm?" He turned back to Chase. "The school will be sending me weekly reports of Lyla's grades and her behavior, as well as any tardiness on your part. I would like you to keep a detailed food diary of the child's nutritional intake." He narrowed his eyes. "We'll know if you aren't being truthful."

Chase gulped. Lyla trembled. Hunter had enough.

"Is all this really necessary?" he asked. "Chase is clearly doing the best he can."

Mr. Preston rubbed his mustache and the underside of his nose with a pudgy finger. "You're new in town," he said to Hunter. His tone was attempting sympathy but it came across as condescending. "So there's probably some things you don't know about Mr. Williamson here. Trust me, a respectable fellow such as yourself probably doesn't want to be seen in a neighborhood like this. You'd best be heading home."

"I'm good, thanks," said Hunter coldly. Wow. Chase wasn't kidding when he said some folks around here weren't fond of him.

Mr. Preston laughed humorously. "Suit yourself. Though, if you ever want to come around for dinner, Mr. Duke," he said, his tone shifting back to simpering. "My family would just love to host a real American hero." Mr. Preston placed his hand on his heart and shook his head. "I dare say my daughters would love to meet you." He smiled, like a shark sensing blood in the water, then narrowed his eyes at Chase. "I shall be in touch, Mr. Williamson." He plastered on a fake smile, then gave Lyla a clumsy wave. "Bye-bye, Lyla," he cooed. "See you soon!"

Lyla sniffed and rubbed her eyes. Trooper barked and hopped about on his three legs. Hunter and Chase watched Mr. Preston pick up his brown briefcase and walk out of the house in furious silence. He didn't bother to close the door behind him, so Hunter marched over and did so for him, slamming it a little harder than was probably necessary.

"Jerk," he grumbled, turning back to face Chase still kneeling on the floor with Lyla. "Are you okay?"

Chase's gaze dropped to the thin carpet. "Told you," he said in a defeated tone that made Hunter even angrier. If Chase thought Mr. Preston's behavior had convinced Hunter that Chase was no good, he'd be surprised. It had done quite the opposite.

"He can go jump off a pier," Hunter growled. He tried to

shake off his anger as he crossed the room again and crouched down the other side of Lyla, who was sucking her thumb.

"Amb I in twouble?" she whispered around it.

"*Oh, no,*" Chase and Hunter said, practically in chorus.

"No, honey, you did fine," Chase insisted.

He looked rattled though. Hunter scooped Trooper up for a hug so Lyla could pet him too.

"He was just a bit grouchy because he had to work on a Saturday," Hunter told her. Lyla managed a weak laugh. "Hey, your daddy said something about ice cream earlier. I don't know about you, but I could really go for a banana split right about now."

Lyla gasped, the sparkle back in her eyes as she dropped her thumb. "With sprinkles?"

"Absolutely," said Hunter. "What do you say? My treat."

"Can we, Daddy?" Lyla asked.

Chase looked like he debated the offer for all of three seconds. Then he nodded. "That would be lovely, Hunter," he murmured. "Thank you."

He stood, lifting Lyla to his hip and looked at Hunter with sincere appreciation.

"I reckon you're right, kiddo," said Hunter, getting Lyla's attention.

"About what?" she asked.

Hunter smiled at her and Chase. "You've got a *great* dad."

CHAPTER NINE

CHASE

Like Chase, Amanda hadn't been a rich kid. He had only gotten to know her during senior year when they'd taken algebra together. But from the conversations they'd had, he understood that money had been tight at her home too, although for slightly different reasons. Her dad had high medical bills and crappy insurance. Chase's dad had been an alcoholic asshole.

But it had left them both knowing what it was like to go without. So it didn't surprise Chase that Amanda had done everything in her power to give her daughter the very best she could.

No one could ever call Lyla spoiled, not by any means. She and Amanda had lived in a modest, rented apartment. Lyla had plenty of nice clothes, but they were from Target and Walmart. They had only ever been on one vacation and even that had just been camping.

The one thing Amanda had really splurged on was extra-curricular activities. Dancing. Swimming. Choir. Little

League. She'd even enrolled Lyla in one of those clubs that taught kids etiquette. How to behave like little ladies and gentlemen. Lyla did everything.

Because Amanda paid for a semester or whole year at a time, Chase wouldn't have to worry about fees for a while. But the money he was spending on gas alone to get her across town was something he hadn't really considered.

His job as a checkout clerk at the JJ's Fresh Goods wasn't exactly demanding. So he was using the down time on his current shift trying to balance his books while he passed item after item over the barcode reader. The little *bleep bleep bleeps* kept him company as he smiled at customers who were often too engrossed in their phones to smile back.

JJ's was an old-timey, quaint sort of place. It almost served as a tourist destination as much as a store with its burlap bags of grain, wooden beams and jars of colorful candy. Of all the establishments in town to work for, it wasn't that bad.

Chase spent the morning devising the most cost-effective meals he could for the rest of the week. Thank god for cheap frozen vegetables, otherwise neither of them would get any nutrients. That wouldn't look good on Mr. Preston's food diary.

There was only so many times Chase could make them chicken nuggets, fries and corn, though. But it was better than going hungry. He'd just have to see what else was on sale if he wanted a bit of variety.

As it was a Tuesday, he'd have to take Lyla to dance class once school was out. Although his boss, Bernie, thought Chase was about as useful as moldy bread, he'd been surprisingly good at rearranging his shifts so Chase could work while Lyla was at school. Chase would finish up here, then drive her to the dance studio. But if he planned efficiently enough now, he could fly around the store before he left and do a quick shop with his employee discount card.

He hated the thought that Lyla would have to stop dance soon. That was one of the activities that charged by the semester, though, and it wasn't cheap. She loved contemporary the most, where they made up little routines to Little Mix songs. So maybe they could just stick with that one and drop ballet and lyrical?

"Excuse me?"

Chase blinked back to the here and now. A middle-aged woman was waving a wad of coupons in his face.

He'd been so busy finishing scanning her shopping he hadn't heard her question. He quickly looked around to check Bernie wasn't in earshot. Luckily, he only saw Jake, the produce manager who was much nicer. He even waved at Chase as he caught his eye.

Relieved Bernie wasn't there, Chase looked guiltily back at the customer. "I'm sorry, ma'am?" he said.

"I *said* are any of these valid," she said scornfully. "Honestly, it's no wonder your generation is so lazy. You're always daydreaming and all fancy yourself reality TV stars."

Chase stared wordlessly as she glowered at him. He wasn't sure he really deserved her ire against every millennial out there. But he managed to muster a smile and take the crumpled bundle of coupons.

"My apologies, ma'am," he said. "Let me check for you now."

She huffed and crossed her arms, not taking her beady eyes off him while he put each one through. He tried not to get flustered like usual.

Then he thought of Hunter.

He would never have gotten through that social services visit on Saturday without him. So, as stupid as it was, Chase took a long breath in and imagined Hunter was standing there by his side right then. This woman could get as huffy as she liked with him. He would just keep smiling and do his crappy job that paid his bills so he could care for his little girl.

This was what being a parent was. Amanda hadn't loved the office where she'd worked. But it had given her a decent enough paycheck and benefits that Chase couldn't dream of. At least Lyla would be eligible for death benefits until she hit eighteen. If social services let him keep her.

He banished that thought and sorted the coupons out into those that were valid and those that weren't. He couldn't do anything about Mr. Preston now. But he could try and stop this woman from lodging a complaint against him.

"There you go, ma'am," he said. Luckily, the pile of coupons he'd been able to validate was larger than those he handed back, so she seemed satisfied enough. With a tut, she took the scraps of paper back and shoved them inside her purse.

Once she had left, Chase was gifted with a string of people on their lunch breaks who just wanted to checkout as fast as possible with no chit-chat. That was fine by him.

His mind was filled once again with Mr. Preston and Hunter.

Chase had numerous feelings about the visit. It was difficult to unravel them, and he was still struggling days later.

For starters, the fact that Hunter had just swung around in the first place. He had no reason to be this kind. Chase tried telling himself it was because he saw the positive impact the puppy Trooper had on Lyla's mental health. That little dog brought her immeasurable joy that kept her buoyant for days.

But it wasn't just that. Hunter talked to Chase like they really were friends. He'd taken them all out for ice cream and chatted about his hometown and how his dad used to take him out for sundaes every weekend after they played catch in the park. Chase had been briefly envious of his relationship with his dad, but it didn't linger. He couldn't be jealous, not when Hunter was going out of his way to spoil Lyla the way Amanda would have wanted. When he'd promised her ice cream, the best Chase could have done was a box of store-brand popsicles. Hunter had gotten them all banana splits with the works.

Chase tried telling himself that he was being nice because they had gotten off on the wrong foot in their appointment. But this went above and beyond mere duty.

Which left Chase to conclude that Hunter genuinely liked them. Liked him. When they'd walked back from the ice cream parlor on Saturday, Lyla and Trooper had run ahead, leaving Chase alone with Hunter. They had plenty of awkward pauses. Neither of them were very gifted at conversation. But by sheer luck, it turned out they were watching the same crime drama on TV and had been able to pass the rest of the walk home enthusiastically theorizing about who had done it.

They had only hung out twice. But Chase was finding it harder and harder to deny that he really liked Hunter. Usually, he didn't have high standards when he hooked up with a guy. If they were just going to get off, Chase only cared that the other dude wasn't repulsive or creepy. He'd never allowed himself to particularly crush on anyone, not since his disastrous high school years. He'd learned right off the bat to keep those thoughts as hidden away as possible.

But Hunter was new and dangerous. He made Chase not want to hide.

Although he'd never come out, the town pretty much knew Chase was gay. He'd been tormented mercilessly at school, enough to force him to drop out just to escape. He thought he'd always stay in the closet. There didn't seem to be a scenario he could imagine where he'd ever make himself so vulnerable as to admit the truth.

But Hunter made him truly wonder for the first time. What would it be like to have a boyfriend?

At this point, his logical brain would kick in and tell him to stop being such a fool. Hunter was a handsome, successful hunk of a man. There was no way he'd be gay or bi, and even if he was, he wouldn't be into a loser like Chase.

Would he?

Chase didn't have enough experience of having friends to fall back on. But totally straight dudes didn't make friends with people they had nothing in common with then go out of their way to help them out and be buddies. Did they?

Could Hunter actually be interested in him?

As much as the possibility excited Chase, it also came with its own set of worries.

He'd only just become a full-time parent. Lyla was his priority above all else. He couldn't be so selfish as to start fantasizing about Hunter and if they might get together. All his effort had to be toward getting Lyla through this transition. If Chase was incredibly lucky, he might even get official full custody of her. He couldn't focus on anything else while that was still in doubt.

Amanda's parents were nice enough people. But they didn't think that much of the boy that had knocked up their little girl. If they felt he was unfit, they would fight for custody themselves, despite their ailing health.

So, even if Hunter was potentially interested in Chase, Chase would have to ignore it. As much as it hurt his heart. Because...*damn*. Hunter was hot as all fuck and had a great job and was kind and all the things Chase found most attractive in a person. But Lyla came before all of that.

Which was a good thing. Because Chase hadn't missed the looks Mr. Preston had given him during his visit on Saturday.

From what Chase could gather, Mr. Preston had jumped to a few conclusions about Hunter being there. Chase could tell he was wondering if the two men were dating, and he clearly disapproved. Whether he thought that was an unstable environment for Lyla to be in, or if he was plain homophobic, it didn't matter. Chase couldn't risk anything jeopardizing his custody of Lyla.

His heart grew heavier as he made it through the rest of his shift. It was becoming more and more obvious to him that he would have to do his best to discourage contact with Hunter. Chase couldn't risk his feelings getting deeper or the slim chance that Hunter might feel the same. Not if Mr. Preston would count a relationship between them against Chase in his case.

Like always, Chase was on his own. He couldn't rely on anyone else for help. It was just him and Lyla against the world.

By the time he left to pick Lyla up from school, he almost believed himself.

CHAPTER TEN

Slowly, Hidden Creek was beginning to feel like home.

At the end of his second week, Hunter had allowed his colleagues to take him out to a bar to celebrate how well he was settling in at work. They were a nice group, fun without being too rowdy. He guessed that was to be expected from a bunch of doctors and nurses. They also didn't ask too many invasive questions about his military past.

It was funny. Since getting Trooper, Hunter found his nightmares weren't as bad as they used to be. Or, more precisely, he still had them. But thanks to Trooper being there whenever he woke up, he was able to calm down and banish them far quicker than he had in the past. Something about the little guy was able to focus Hunter's troubled mind when nothing else had worked.

He made sure to say hello to his neighbor Shelly whenever he saw her. He'd even taken over some lasagna when he'd made too much for himself. She loved seeing Trooper's progress, and Trooper loved seeing her and his doggy parents regularly.

Hunter had so far managed to evade being set up on a date with her daughter. But he suspected it was only a matter of time before he gave in. He wasn't even really sure what was holding him back so much. She sounded like a lovely person.

For now, though, he was just enjoying his new beginning away from the military. The sleepy small-town lifestyle suited him so far. It had been a long while since his time was his own. The strict regulations of the Navy and Marines had been good for him in his teens and twenties. But now he was nearing his thirties, a little more freedom was appreciated.

He was still working out what to do with that free time, admittedly. It had been nice to find himself with whole evenings to just watch a movie or take Trooper out for walks as long as they liked. But he'd always been a busy, social person. So he was eager to make new friends and fill his week with activities. Even if it was only grabbing a coffee or sharing dinners.

Maybe because he was slightly anxious about building up a new social sphere he noticed when Chase became less and less responsive with him. He wasn't rude or anything. But Hunter could tell when he was being fobbed off.

He hadn't forgotten their conversation over dinner at his place. It made him wonder if Chase was being distant because he was still worried about not being a worthy friend, rather than he wasn't interested in getting to know Hunter.

Therefore, Hunter had persisted in keeping in touch. He just sent texts asking how Chase and Lyla were, sometimes accompanied with photos of Trooper. But after the last five went unanswered, Hunter decided he had just cause to feel worried something might be actually wrong. So when he finished work for the day one sunny Thursday evening, he stepped out into the parking lot and gave Chase's cell a call.

Each ring he told himself not to be disappointed if Chase let it go to voicemail. After all, he and Hunter didn't really know each other. But for whatever reason, Hunter really wanted this friendship to thrive over all his others. Chase was a great guy.

Hunter couldn't help the big smile that split across his face when Chase picked up.

"Hello?" he said. He sounded frazzled.

"Hi, it's Hunter," he said. Maybe Chase hadn't checked caller ID.

Sure enough, he let out a little 'oh' noise. "Um, hi. How are you?"

Hunter put his hand in his pocket and kicked absently at a stone on the tarmac. "Good. Is this a bad time?"

"Oh, um, no," said Chase unconvincingly. "I'm fine. Just, uh, busy."

"Oh, sure," said Hunter. That sounded a bit like Chase was dismissing him. But then Hunter remembered that Chase didn't think enough of himself and might need help. "I was just worried because I hadn't heard back from you in a while. Is everything okay?"

There was a pause on the other end of the line. Hunter even took his phone away from his ear to check they were still connected. But then he heard Chase sigh. "I...I guess I'm feeling a bit overwhelmed," he admitted.

Hunter seized on the opportunity. "That's totally normal. Anything I can help with?"

Another sigh. "I don't think so. I have to try to make a

costume for Lyla's parade thing, but...it's just not happening at all."

Hunter chuckled kindly. "I can't say I have a ton of experience with that. But I went out on enough Halloweens as a kid. I might remember something from what my mom used to do for me if you wanted help."

"Yeah?" There was cautious optimism in Chase's voice.

Hunter didn't want to overstep his mark. But it sounded like Chase might genuinely benefit from his assistance.

"Listen. I've just finished work," Hunter told him. "Why don't I give Trooper a quick walk then come over? Have you guys eaten?"

"Um..." said Chase. That wasn't a yes.

"I could pick up some take out, if you like?" Hunter offered, really warming to this plan. "If I walked Trooper a slightly different way, we could pass Victory Boulevard and grab some Chinese?" Hunter had been recommended the place from one of the nurses and had eaten there twice already. Their sesame chicken was something else. "Does Lyla eat that, if I get her something plain?"

"I couldn't ask you to do that," Chase protested weakly.

Hunter smiled. "I'd like to. If you don't mind having us over again? Unfortunately, it seems you've become my best friend by accident, so you have to entertain me when I'm bored," he joked. But he was only half kidding. This was ridiculous. He'd been less nervous asking girls out on dates.

He could practically hear Chase chewing his lip. "We'd love to have you over," he said. "And I can't even remember the last time I had Chinese."

Hunter grinned in silent triumph. "Excellent. We'll see you in about an hour."

Hunter had a crazy amount of food. But in his haste, he had neglected to ask Chase what he actually wanted. So Hunter had bought a dozen or so dishes including rice and noodles. There was bound to be something in there that Chase liked. With any luck, he'd like enough of it that he'd be able to keep the leftovers for tomorrow's dinner as well.

Trooper had enjoyed having a slightly different walk. It was amazing that his missing leg didn't seem to slow him down much at all. Hunter didn't have a lot of previous experience with dogs, but he would have thought being down a limb would make him tire more quickly.

It made Hunter think proudly about the guys he knew who had lost limbs during their service. They were some tough sons of bitches, that was for sure. Troopers, just like his awesome pup.

He managed to hold the bags of takeout with one hand while keeping the leash looped around the other as he knocked on Chase's front door. Hunter noticed the front yard was looking neater than the last time he'd been around. The old car had been washed, too.

Hunter was busy admiring it when the front door opened. Lyla's happy squeal soon caught his attention though.

"Hunter! Trooper!" she said from next to her dad's legs. She jumped and clapped her hands, her wild hair bouncing with her.

Chase rubbed the back of her head. "I don't know if she really believed you'd come," he said softly. He smiled and ushered Hunter inside.

"Of course," said Hunter beaming. "I'm sorry we weren't here sooner, but I had to wait for dinner."

"Momma and I used to get noodles," said Lyla nodding. Hunter froze and he saw Chase do the same. But Lyla just knelt down to unclip Trooper's leash and pat his head as he excitedly licked her face. "Did you get noodles?"

She looked up expectantly at Hunter. Apparently, she was able to talk about her mom without bursting into tears. Hunter thought that was damn impressive.

He gave thanks that he'd bought plain chow mein just for her, as well as rice and plain chicken. It seemed safest for a five-year-old. But the fact it was her favorite made him feel like a hero.

"Of course," he said. "You can't have Chinese without noodles."

Chase went a bit bug-eyed at the number of cartons in the bags but didn't comment. Instead, they put all the boxes on the dining table, then got down three plates and glasses of water.

"You can try whatever you like, sweetie," Hunter said. "As long as Daddy says it's okay. Nothing's spicy."

Lyla crawled up into one of the seats and Chase helped her pick out some food for her to try with her noodles. She loved the sweet and sour pork and the mushroom foo young. Hunter felt proud of her for trying so many new things. She even attempted to use the chopsticks, even though most of the time she just speared one through the bits of chicken then used a fork on the noodles. At least she wasn't afraid to try.

Would it be like this with his own children? Hunter found it hard to picture when Lyla was in front of him. She was one special girl.

Hunter was so glad Chase had relented and invited him

over. Whatever barrier he had put up between them seemed to have gone again as the three of them had dinner. Trooper eagerly waited by their feet for scraps to drop, completing the picture.

Hunter had the foolish thought that this felt like a family. But that was crazy. He was just glad that Chase trusted him enough to be his friend and help out with Lyla. It was in his nature to help people. That was all.

As he'd hoped, there was more than enough left over for Chase and Lyla to enjoy as their dinner the next day. So while Chase put his daughter to bed, Hunter boxed it all back up again and put it in the fridge. It wasn't exactly full.

Hunter sighed. Chase was obviously struggling to make ends meet and that killed him. For now, the best he could probably do was wait for opportunities to help out. That was what friends did, after all.

He didn't have to wait long for Chase to come back out again. "She's exhausted," he said softly as he closed her door and came down the short corridor and into the central space of the house. "She wanted to stay up and play with Trooper, but when I told her he was sleeping too, she nodded right off." He laughed and looked at the conked-out puppy on the rug by the sofa.

Hunter smiled too. "She's a good kid. You're doing great with her."

Chase shook his head. "Ah, it doesn't feel like it," he said glumly. "She's struggling at school and I can't keep up with all her clubs." He rolled his eyes and sighed. "This parade costume, oh my god. Who gets time to make things like that?"

"Does it have to be made?" Hunter asked. "Can't you get something store bought?"

Chase shrugged. "There's a specific theme. Anyway, I think the other kids might tease her." He bit his lip and looked off into the distance. Hunter could imagine that was a nightmare for any parent. Worrying their kid was getting picked on somewhere they couldn't protect them. Chase shook himself and brightened. "Would you like a beer? I've been saving a six pack," he said with a laugh.

"I'd love one," Hunter said, eager to put him at ease.

Chase dug into the bottom drawer of the fridge and cracked two cans. They settled on the couch where he handed one to Hunter then rubbed his eyes. "If I talk to you about dad stuff will you lose your mind?"

Hunter chuckled and shook his head. "Of course not. That's why I'm here."

Chase sipped his beer and narrowed his eyes at Hunter. "You could be in town watching a Rangers game," he said. "Not working out little girls' parade costumes. I warn you, there's probably going to be talk of glitter at some point."

Hunter laughed, softly so as not to disturb Lyla or Trooper. But he was sincere. "Dude, I have other friends to watch baseball with and shit. I like this family stuff. We can sort your costume, then maybe watch some ball if you want?"

Chase shrugged. "Not really into sports. But I could see if there's a decent movie on while we brainstorm?"

"Sounds great," Hunter assured him.

They soon had something with explosions playing quietly on the screen while Chase opened up his ancient laptop. He rubbed his eyes and sighed. "So, Lyla does this thing called Little Ladies' Etiquette. They have a float in the Spring Parade in a few weeks. The theme is 'Princesses.'"

Hunter thought that sounded like a fairly typical theme for

small girls. But Chase's tone suggested it wasn't that simple. "Do they all have to pick a different one?"

"Yes," said Chase with a scowl. "And some other parent already snagged Merida." Hunter gave him a puzzled look, so Chase hastily typed on his laptop. "The Scottish girl from Disney's Brave. I know things like this, now," he added with a laugh.

He showed Hunter the images that had come up of the character. She had wild, red curls, just like Lyla's hair, as well as a large bow and arrow. "Oh, but that's perfect," said Hunter. "Surely another kid would just have to wear a wig?"

Chase scoffed. "Exactly," he said. "I think they picked it just so Lyla couldn't have it."

That didn't seem likely to Hunter. Why be so petty? "I'm sure they'd switch if you asked."

But Chase shook his head and bit her lip. "The other girls..." he said quietly. "Well, it's normally well-off families that send their kids to these classes. Lyla struggles to fit in. I'm not sure she even likes it."

"Then why do it?" Hunter asked.

"Because her mom wanted her to," said Chase. Although he was fighting it, the sadness was clear in his voice. "She paid for the full year. So, now I need to come up with another princess. But Merida's the only one Lyla likes. The feisty ones with weapons are her favorites," he said with a laugh.

"Wasn't there a Chinese princess who went to war?" Hunter asked. Disney wasn't his forte, he had to admit.

"Mulan," said Chase with a nod. "But one of the actual Asian girls has already taken that."

"Fair enough," said Hunter.

"Daddy?"

They looked up to see a rumpled and sleepy Lyla wandering down the corridor, her blanket trailing from her hand behind her. "Sweetie," said Chase, jumping to his feet. "Did we wake you up?"

"I heard you say Merida," she said with a yawn as Chase scooped her up. She snuggled on his lap and sucked her thumb. "I wub her," she said around her hand.

Chase soothed her hair back. "I know you do, hun," he said. "But we need to think of something else Daddy can dress you as for the Ladies parade."

"Does it have to be a character?" said Hunter. "Could she just wear a pretty dress and a crown?"

Chase sighed. "She doesn't really like dresses," he said quietly over her head. "The few she has are denim. I don't think the other girls would understand."

Hunter rubbed his chin. "Well, you know there are other princesses aside from Disney. Lyla, do you like Star Wars?"

Her eyes widened. "You mean Porgs?" she asked.

Hunter blinked in confusion, but Chase came to his rescue. "She hasn't seen any of the films, but she's seen ads for Porg toys on the TV. She likes them and the Ewoks."

"Well," said Hunter carefully. He wasn't sure if this was a dumb idea or not. "Star Wars has a princess called Leia. That's almost like Lyla, isn't it?"

Lyla sat up in Chase's lap and took out her thumb. He took that as a sign of interest. So did Chase, as he typed into the search engine. Sensibly, he looked for 'Princess Leia white dress kids' so no gold bikinis came up.

Lyla gasped and sat forward. "Gary," she said, pointing at one of the pictures of Carrie Fisher that came up.

Hunter and Chase frowned at each other. "That's Princess Leia, honey," said Chase.

Lyla shook her head. "She's the general and she has a dog."

Hunter didn't follow, but Chase's face lit up. "Oh, you're so right. Look." He opened a new tab and brought up a different set of photos. They were all of an older Carrie Fisher holding a black French Bulldog. His tongue was falling out of his mouth in all of them. "The dog's name is Gary."

"Yes, yes!" said Lyla excitedly. "That's the general!"

Chase smiled and kissed her head. "Aren't you clever, pumpkin," he said. "Well, when she was younger, General Organa was Princess Leia, and she wore that white dress with her hair in buns. She even had a blaster gun. Would you like to be her for the parade?"

Lyla turned her whole body to look at Chase. "Can I?" she whispered.

"You can be anything you want," Chase promised. Lyla nodded and turned back to look at the screen filled with images of Princess Leia.

Hunter caught Chase's eye. "Will Little Ladies' Etiquette think that's the right sort of princess?" he asked, playing devil's advocate.

But something wild danced in Chase's green eyes. For the first time, Hunter really saw the family resemblance between him and his daughter.

"She's the right sort of princess for my baby girl," he said. "She's a fighter."

Hunter couldn't argue with that.

CHAPTER ELEVEN

CHASE

WHEN LYLA FELL ASLEEP AGAIN in Chase's arms, Hunter said it was probably time he headed off. He scooped up his sleeping puppy and bade them goodnight.

This was a good thing, as Chase wasn't sure what might have happened if Hunter had stayed. When Lyla was back in bed and they didn't have dad stuff to talk about anymore, Chase didn't trust himself not to do something foolish.

He had promised to distance himself from Hunter. A promise he'd broken when he'd caved and invited him over for dinner. But so few people had been genuinely nice or kind to Chase during his life, it was like a drug he was becoming addicted to. Hunter was his weakness.

It was probably what had made Chase feel reckless after he put Lyla back to bed and he found himself alone again. He not only finished his beer, but Hunter's barely touched one as well. He wasn't used to drinking these days, so the alcohol went to his head a bit harder than he would have expected.

Which was most likely why he took himself off to bed early, stripped naked, and slipped between the sheets.

It had been a long time since he'd felt horny. But with the beer zinging through his system, he didn't fight his body as he lay in the dark and reached down to stroke his cock, bringing it to life.

He tried not to think about Hunter as he shivered and gasped, but he couldn't help it. Hunter was so commanding in his own gentle way. If he insisted on swooping in and saving the day constantly, it was only natural that Chase would fantasize about Hunter taking care of him in other ways.

He pushed the doubts he had over Hunter's sexuality away. In his mind, Hunter was a hot-blooded, tender lover of men. He would know exactly what to do to make Chase feel good, the way Chase's other lovers had never bothered to try.

It was probably very wrong of him to fantasize about his friend in a sexual way, but Chase decided he could feel guilty later. After not jerking off for weeks, his prick was already eager to go, his climax not far off. Chase didn't have any lube or lotion at hand, so he paused to lick his hand instead, and soon he was leaking precum that helped with lubrication as well. He gritted his teeth, throwing himself into it without pause.

As scenarios went, it was probably the tamest one Chase had ever imagined while getting himself off. But all he could picture was Hunter kissing him while he jerked Chase's cock. That was all it took before he was coming all over his hand, his back arching as he gasped for air.

Chase flopped back against the mattress, boneless. "Fuck," he whispered to himself in the dark as his heartbeat calmed down.

The guilt threatened to creep in before he even finished cleaning himself up. But, for once, Chase went easy on himself. It was just a release, and he had imagined someone comforting him. Lately, the only person who had done that was Hunter. Hunter never needed to know about it, and Chase promised himself never to do it again. After all, he was a twenty-three-year-old guy. Just because he was a full-time dad now didn't make him numb below the waist.

Maybe he'd be upset with himself in the morning when he was sober. Possibly even ashamed. But right now, it was the perfect release for all the tension he had been storing up the past few weeks. Sleep enveloped him like a warm blanket, and he didn't stir until his alarm went off several hours later.

THE MORNING FLEW by in its usual whirlwind fashion. Lyla typically found something to dither over while Chase was trying to get her to school. This morning it was putting her shoes on, despite Chase telling her three times she needed to do so.

But they got out the door regardless. Chase's daily prayer that his car would start worked, and he was able to walk her through the school gates with five minutes to spare. Traffic was also on his side.

So that was how he found himself outside JJ's with ten minutes to spare and his phone in his hand. He was scrolling up and down his message history with Hunter.

He wasn't feeling great about his drunken actions last night. But he was able to soothe himself somewhat that nobody else ever needed to find out. So that left him with the unavoidable truth that, yes, he probably was falling for Hunter. But given that he was more than likely straight, Chase could safely and quietly nurture a private crush for a while.

He hadn't gotten close enough to anyone to feel a connection in years. The butterflies in his stomach whenever he thought about Hunter were a rare indulgence. When everything else in his life was an uphill battle, why couldn't he let himself have this bit of fun?

He was perfectly aware that it would most likely all come down in flames. Pining over a guy so out of his league, one who probably wasn't even into dudes, was a recipe for heartbreak. But it was like having chocolate in the fridge. Chase couldn't stop thinking about it and wouldn't be happy until he got it.

As long as he went into this not expecting anything physical, why couldn't he enjoy Hunter's company? The man actually seemed to want to be friends with him, unlike most people in this town. So if Chase was careful not to let anything slip, that could be okay.

Mr. Preston surely couldn't object to them being friends either, could he? Hunter was ex-military and a physician assistant. It was difficult to get more respectable than that.

Hunter would probably be at work by now. But Chase wasn't allowed his phone while at the checkout, so he fired off a quick message now that Hunter could pick up later.

Thank you so much for yesterday evening, he wrote. He almost put 'last night' but that definitely implied something more intimate had taken place. *I managed to find a second-hand Leia costume for ten bucks and a video tutorial on the hair. Lyla's going to love it. You're our hero.*

He wondered if that was a bit much, but he pressed send anyway. No sense overanalyzing every single thing. If he did that, he wouldn't have even sent the text. He'd probably get an hour into his shift and regret it horribly. But for now, he was feeling a little giddy at his daring.

He leaned back in the car seat and turned up the radio, hoping to center himself before having to start his shift. But a ding on his phone distracted him.

It was Hunter.

Chase was a little ashamed of how quickly he unlocked his phone. He eagerly opened the text, gobbling up Hunter's words.

That's great news! She's going to be the best princess on that float ;) I hope y'all enjoy the leftover Chinese tonight. Trooper and I are jealous!

Something wild and crazy took over Chase.

You could join us again, if you like?

As soon as he tapped send, he really did regret that one. What the hell was he thinking? That was incredibly needy and weird, and Hunter most likely wouldn't reply at all because he wouldn't know what to say.

Chase groaned and checked the time. He'd need to head inside in a minute or two. Then he'd have to leave his phone in his locker and agonize over his stupidity for the next few hours.

To his immense surprise, his phone dinged again. Peeking cautiously through one squinted eye, he opened Hunter's reply.

Aw I can't tonight I'm afraid. But are y'all free tomorrow night? One of the nurses told me about a pizza place called Rocket that does great food. It's supposed to be good for kids :) My treat.

Chase stared at the text until he realized he was going to be late. He almost fell out of the car in his haste, locked the door, then ran to the back of the store. He had about thirty seconds to reply before he needed to throw his personal items in his locker and dash to the shop floor.

Hunter was being so generous it was unnerving. What did he want? Did he actually like Chase and want to get in his pants? Or was he just a nice guy? Chase found it hard to believe that someone would be that kindhearted and not expect anything in return. But so far, Hunter had been seemingly genuine.

Rocket was kind of cheesy, but Chase loved it. He'd only been a couple of times. Ironically, one was his and Amanda's first date when he was trying to convince himself he could date girls. It was a retro place decked out like a fifties diner with spaceships and bright colors. Lyla would absolutely adore it.

That was what swung it in the end. Hunter was offering. Chase could stress over his motives, or he could be gracious and accept, knowing his little girl would have a great time.

He skidded to a halt in front of his locker and opened the message again.

That would be great! If you're sure? We can split the bill :) I'm just starting work. Talk later.

"This isn't a date, this isn't a date," he muttered as he swiped his ID card to start his shift and raced over to his checkout lane. He made it with no time to spare, calling over a customer to show he was open.

It may not have been a date. But he was going to see Hunter again and his little girl was going to have a fun trip out of the house. So long as Chase kept himself in check, like he'd promised he would, everything would be fine.

CHAPTER TWELVE

HUNTER

It wasn't like Hunter was struggling for friends. Everyone at work seemed to like him and he'd received enough invites out for an evening. His Marine buddy Connor had messaged him several times about catching up, which Hunter really wanted to do. Connor was the reason he'd moved to Hidden Creek in the first place, after all. They had shared a lot together out in Afghanistan.

So Hunter absolutely wanted to take him up on that. And go watch the Hidden Creek Bears with a couple of the doctors. And catch a movie with some of the guys he'd gotten to know at puppy training class. Hell, he might even get around to meeting Shelly's daughter and going on that date.

But despite all the offers, he still found himself spending Saturday afternoon at the park, sitting with Chase and watching Lyla and Trooper chase each other around the merry-go-round. He hoped he wasn't being too overbearing. But it was becoming obvious that every chance he got to hang out with Chase and his daughter, that was what he'd rather do.

Was that weird? They already had plans to get together for dinner. But when Chase had texted to say he was waiting for Lyla to finish up Little League practice, Hunter hadn't hesitated to invite them to meet him and Trooper at the playground.

Chase was slowly relaxing, though. The more time they spent together, the easier it became. It felt like he now believed what Hunter had told him. He could make up his own mind about who he wanted to be friends with, and Chase was fast becoming his best buddy.

They sat and chatted easily on the bench while Lyla tired herself out on the monkey bars, slides and swings. Everywhere she went, Trooper followed adoringly. He stood on the wood chips wagging his tail, patiently waiting for Lyla to come back down from whatever apparatus she was hanging upside down from.

"They make quite the team," Hunter observed.

Chase smiled at him. He looked so much better smiling than when he frowned in worry. "They do," he said. "Thank you."

"For what?" Hunter asked.

Chase shrugged. "For letting them be friends. She has kids at school she has play dates with. But...well, she really loves Trooper."

Trooper didn't ask questions, Hunter bet. He didn't ask about Lyla's mom or repeat any rumors about her dad. He didn't make her feel awkward or sad. He was just there for her, just like he was just there for Hunter when he woke up in a panic, thinking he was back in Afghanistan.

"He's a special pup, that's for sure," Hunter said warmly. "But she's a special girl. You're lucky to have each other."

"Do you think you'll have kids?" Chase asked.

Hunter shrugged. "I guess. Someday. I'm not even dating right now, though. So that'll probably be a while off."

Chase nodded and went back to watching his daughter scampering about, her red hair flying out behind her. Chase was so young to be a dad. Hunter couldn't have coped with that at twenty-three.

Chase still had plenty of time to meet a nice girl and make his family bigger. And Hunter still had years to start his own. But strangely, the thought didn't bring him as much comfort as he would have imagined.

A little while later they went their separate ways to head home for a couple of hours before dinner. Hunter forced himself to get through some chores like laundry and answering his friends' emails he'd neglected for a few days. But he was filled with a strange sort of energy, like crackling electricity.

For some reason, he felt a little nervous as well as excited for dinner that evening. That didn't make much sense, though. He had only just seen Chase and everything was fine. There was nothing to be apprehensive about. So why did he still feel like this?

Hunter shook his head and focused on picking an outfit. He didn't want to look like he was going to work, but he wanted to look smart. He bit his lip. He could copy Chase's style and wear a shirt over a T-shirt. That might be more appropriate? It wasn't a high-end restaurant, after all.

Since leaving the Marines, Hunter's hair was getting longer. It was very thick, so he was sure he'd cut it sooner rather than later to keep it manageable. But for now, it was a bit of a novelty to work some putty through it and make it have some shape rather than let it stick up however it wanted.

He remembered to use some of that aftershave his mom had gotten him for Christmas, then checked himself in the mirror. It was nice to get dressed up and go out for a change.

He turned to Trooper and spun around. "What do you think, buddy?" he asked.

Trooper barked and wagged his tail happily. Hunter laughed and rubbed the little guy's head and floppy ears.

"Aw, sorry, dude. This is a people only kind of place. I promise you can see Chase and Lyla next time." Trooper barked again, giving Hunter the illusion that he understood and wasn't mad at being left all alone.

Hunter left in plenty of time so he could stroll over to Rocket. It was a nice evening and by walking it meant he could have a beer or two without worrying. He hoped if he had a drink, Chase would feel comfortable as well.

Despite Chase's offer to split the check, Hunter knew he couldn't afford it. If Hunter picked up the tab then everyone could have what they wanted and enjoy themselves. That was all he cared about.

At least, that's the reason he told himself he was walking.

He sighed and aimed a kick at a stone on the sidewalk. It was so stupid. He'd been fine since returning to America. Well, not fine, as he still had regular nightmares. But with Trooper by his side, Hunter had found it easier and easier to pull himself back into the present after a particularly nasty dream.

His day-to-day life had been fine, however. He'd done his best to leave his time in service behind him, and on the whole, managed to allow the horrors of war fade into memory.

Until the plastic bag had blown across the street in front of his car two days ago, forcing him to slam the brakes and almost cause a traffic accident.

Logically, Hunter *knew* it hadn't been anything sinister. Certainly not an IED. But in that moment, his brain had convinced him that the bag had been a bomb, and every system in his whole body had gone into overload. It still made him feel sick even just thinking about it.

The trouble was, now, he didn't know how to turn those reactions off again. Every time he tried to sit behind the wheel of his car the panic took over almost immediately. It was paralyzing to the point where he'd given up trying to force it and had either taken the bus or walked everywhere.

Hopefully it wouldn't last. If he just gave himself a few days, there was every chance his brain would work out he was back in Texas, not Afghanistan, and things could go back to normal. Otherwise, he'd have to consider some kind of therapy. He didn't want his ghosts haunting his present.

For now, he resolved to enjoy his walk. Everywhere in town was reachable either on foot or by car. He'd just have to plan ahead and always make sure he had enough time to get where he needed to go.

He cut through Moore Wood, the park they'd been at earlier. It was a large green space in the center of town filled with all kinds of things to do and see. As well as the kids' playground, there were nature trails that he and Trooper had only just started exploring. The tennis courts were for everyday use, but Hunter had heard about a pro player who lived nearby and sometimes used them too, which was pretty exciting. As he walked, he passed a pretty waterfall in the distance. That was part of the creek that had given the town its name, and it fed into a lake filled with a flock of angry geese. He and Trooper had learned about those birds the hard way. Not wanting to get bitten or pooped on, Hunter skirted around that part of the park as he carried on his way.

Dusk wasn't quite upon them yet, but Rocket had its lights blazing all the same. Bright blue and yellow neon greeted Hunter as approached. There was even a gleaming Cadillac parked out front for show, and Hunter wondered if Lyla would like a photo next to it.

It was incredible how fast he'd adjusted his thinking to incorporate a five-year-old. But it felt natural to him rather than strange.

He stepped inside and took in the décor. Large black-and-white-checkered tiles on the floor, red leather on the booth seats, and a light blue bar with shiny silver swivel stools lined up in front of it. Along the walls were framed posters of old sci-fi B-movies. Another neon sign hung behind the bar that read 'Area 51,' and scattered all around the place were little green men and flying saucers.

Hunter smiled. If he thought this was great, he was pretty sure Lyla was going to go crazy. He'd have to thank his colleague for the recommendation.

"Hi there!" a server cried over the vintage rock'n'roll playing on the sound system. He snatched up a couple of rocket-shaped menus and marched toward Hunter. "Would you like a booth?"

"Table for three," Hunter said with a nod.

He'd barely gotten himself seated and glanced over the menu before a familiar, excitable little girl danced up to him. "Hunter, Hunter!" Lyla squealed. She hugged her stuffed dragon to her chest and stared bug-eyed at the diner's interior. "I love it, it's so cool. Look at the Martians, can you see?"

Hunter chuckled. "I did see."

He glanced up to greet Chase as he walked over at a more reasonable pace. He looked the best Hunter had ever seen him. He thought maybe he'd put on a bit of weight this past week, and he had good color in his cheeks. He was wearing a Henley shirt that clung to his body and the burgundy shade worked well with his eyes. He looked healthy.

Hunter wasn't sure why that should delight him as much as it did or make his mouth dry. Wasn't he pleased to see his friend looking well? He did his best to shake it off and smile back.

"You made it," he said, stating the obvious.

But Chase didn't pick up on it. He just helped Lyla into the opposite side of the booth to Hunter, then slid in beside her. "We did," he replied happily. "We've been very excited, haven't we?"

"Daddy said I could have a strawberry milkshake!" Lyla proclaimed excitedly. She fussed around with her dragon so he was sitting on the table, propped up against the wall at the end.

Chase raised his eyebrows and glanced at Hunter. "Um, if that's okay?" he asked.

Good. He was going to let Hunter pay.

Hunter beamed at Lyla. "You can have whatever you like, sweetie," he said. "Check it out. They have a kids' menu."

He watched on fondly as Chase didn't even look at his own menu. He leaned over and helped Lyla to pick what she wanted to eat first, reading out the options and pointing to the words she could decipher herself. It was sweet and made Hunter's heart ache. Would he ever do that with his daughter?

Eventually, they each picked a pizza, and Hunter added some potato wedges and chicken wings on top. Chase could always bag anything up that they didn't manage to finish. Lyla babbled cheerfully about her week at school as Hunter and Chase listened, sucking on their milkshakes.

The diner was pretty full. It was a Saturday night, after all. But service was fast and they had their food in no time. Lyla had a simple pepperoni pizza with the meat arranged to look like a face. She delighted in eating its eyes first.

Hunter caught Chase's eye and tried to silently tell him how well she was doing. Her whole life had changed, but she was still managing to have happy times among the sad. She was a credit to him.

Chase smiled back. Their gazes lingered. Hunter felt his cheeks warm.

"Hey y'all," a waitress said, appearing at the end of the table. Hunter started and snapped his eyes away from Chase. That was strange. "I'm Tammy. I'll be your server for the rest of the night. Is everything good with your food?" She was young, probably only sixteen or seventeen judging by the braces on her teeth. But she bubbled over with personality, making good eye contact with both Hunter and Chase.

They all nodded. "It's great, thank you," Hunter assured her with a smile. She must have just started her shift and taken over their section.

She beamed and went to move on when she looked at Lyla and did a double take. "Oh, gosh. You're Lyla Hart, aren't you?" Lyla blinked, then shyness overcame her and she hid behind Chase.

"Um, yeah," said Chase warily on her behalf.

Tammy waved her notebook in the air. "I think you play Little League with my kid sister, Geena Miller?" She turned to

Chase. "Gee, it's so great to see y'all out doing okay. I am so, so sorry for your loss."

Lyla didn't seem to catch what Tammy meant and went back to nibbling on her pizza. Hunter, however, stiffened slightly, on alert. Chase looked to do the same. "Thank you," he murmured.

Tammy rested her notebook over her heart. "My mom knew Amanda. She was a great gal. Really. It's Chase, right? Hopefully we'll see you around the field sometime soon." She glanced at Hunter. "Oh gosh, I'm so sorry, I'm interrupting your date. Where are my manners! I'll leave you be."

Date?

Chase spluttered. "Oh, no, um, this is my friend, Hunter. He's new in town and Lyla and I are showing him round."

Tammy gave him an embarrassed laugh. "Oh, no, it's fine. I co-chair the Gay/Straight Alliance at my school. Y'all don't have to worry. This is a rainbow friendly business. Otherwise I wouldn't work here." She hugged her notepad to her chest and rocked on her heels. "So, it's fine. Enjoy the rest of your night!"

She bustled off to another table.

"She was a nice lady," said Lyla, nodding as she picked up a potato wedge and carefully dunked it in barbecue sauce.

Chase was looking at Hunter in horror. "I'm so sorry," he said, stumbling over the words. "I...she's...I mean she must have just assumed. Because of me. I...I know this isn't a date."

Hunter continued to stare at him. The penny finally dropped.

Chase was gay.

The way he talked about Amanda. And himself. The way he said people treated him. Mr. Preston's behavior.

"Oh," said Hunter. It hadn't even occurred to him. But it

made perfect sense. "I see."

Chase had gone from deathly white to beet red. "This was a mistake. I said it was." He was scrambling for his wallet. "Here, I shouldn't...I'm sorry. I knew this was a mistake. Come on, honey."

He slid toward the end of the booth and dropped a twenty on the table.

"Wait, what are you doing?" Hunter said.

Lyla looked at them in confusion. "Daddy?"

"We have to go, pumpkin," Chase said. His breathing was ragged and he was avoiding looking at Hunter.

"Wait a minute. No, you don't," Hunter cried. He could feel people in the booths around them turning to stare. "Chase, what's wrong?"

Did he really think that Hunter was that much of an asshole? That he would be repulsed by finding out Chase was gay? Christ, Hunter didn't give a damn about that!

But Chase looked close to tears as he reached over and pulled Lyla toward him. "Come on, baby. We have to go home now."

"No," Lyla squawked. "No, Daddy! We're not done!"

"I'm sorry, hun," he said. "Hunter, thank you. I'm sorry."

"Chase, calm down," Hunter said, also getting to his feet. "You're being ridiculous. Why are you leaving?"

"Because this was a mistake," Chase said again. He hauled Lyla onto his hip despite her protests. People were openly staring now and Chase glanced back at them. "I'm not...I don't want people thinking you're..."

He gulped and shook his head. Lyla was squirming and started to cry.

"Daddy, stop! I want to stay!"

"Chase, please," said Hunter. He reached for him but Chase flinched away. "This is crazy. Sit down and we can talk!"

Chase backed up into a waiter. Luckily, he wasn't carrying more than his notepad, but the two spun around, putting Chase further away and the waiter in between him and Hunter.

"I'm sorry," Chase said again, dashing for the door.

Hunter knew he should have run after them. But he didn't have any cash on him and he needed to settle their check. Besides, he was so stunned, he wasn't sure what to think or do.

So he asked the waiter in front of him to fetch Tammy to run his card, then sunk back into his seat. He was aware of people whispering around him, but he didn't care.

Chase had looked terrified. Like he might puke. Hunter hated that he'd treated him like he was going to get his pitchfork out and condemn him. Hunter had nothing but support for the LGBT community. It cut deep that Chase would assume he'd hate him just because of his sexuality. For crying out loud, Connor was gay and he was the whole reason Hunter had moved to Hidden Creek in the first place.

Hunter looked over their half-finished meal. Then he noticed Lyla's stuffed dragon still sitting at the end of the table. Hunter reached across and brought it over to his lap where he held it in both hands. He rubbed his thumbs over its soft, purple belly.

The idea that Chase thought Hunter was mad at him physically hurt, like a knife in his chest. They were friends, goddamn it. Hunter looked down at the dragon and knew he couldn't leave things as they were.

He had to fix this.

CHAPTER THIRTEEN

CHASE

Lyla cried the whole way home. Chase was glad he'd driven, as walking would have been a hundred times more miserable. But it still wasn't a fun journey.

"I want to go back!" she wailed. Her little hands were in fists and fat tears rolled down her face. Chase glanced in his mirror at her and felt like a terrible parent.

"I'm sorry, baby," he said. "It's not your fault. Daddy messed up."

"Then go back and say you're sorry!" Lyla kicked the back of the passenger seat.

"Hey!" Chase yelled. "No, you don't kick Daddy's car."

"Go back! Hunter was sad!"

Something contracted his Chase's chest. He ground his teeth. "I know, baby. That's why we had to leave. Daddy made him sad."

"Say you're sorry!" Lyla sobbed. "I like Hunter. I like him!"

"Me too," Chase said around the lump in his throat. "But he doesn't like Daddy anymore. Daddy did something bad."

"But I like him. I like Trooper!"

Chase bit his lip. "I don't think we can see Trooper anymore, baby."

Lyla went volcanic. Her face was the same shade as her hair. "I hate you!" she screamed and kicked the seat again. *"I wish Momma was here!"*

Those words broke something in Chase that he'd been desperately clinging to for weeks. He burst into tears and cried as hard as his little girl the whole way home. "I'm sorry," he whispered several times. He didn't think she heard him.

He parked the car in the drive. But he had to wait a few minutes before he calmed down enough to get out. Lyla was snuffling quietly too. Thankfully, she let him get her out of her booster seat and carry her up to the house.

"I'm sorry, darling," Chase told her again once they were inside.

Lyla hiccuped. "I'm sorry, Daddy," she said. "Tell Hunter you're sorry too, please? I want you to be his friend. I'm Trooper's friend."

Chase rubbed her back and carried her to her bedroom. "I'll try," he said. He wasn't sure he could, but it was better to tell her a white lie now so she stayed calmed down.

Slowly, he helped her brush her teeth and get into her pajamas. But when she crawled into her bed, he faced a second melt down.

"Bo-Bo," she said in horror. "Bo-Bo! Daddy, *I left Bo-Bo!*"

Chase realized she was right. In his rush to leave, they had left her dragon on the table.

"It's okay, sweetie," he said, trying his best not to panic.

"I'll call the diner right now. They'll have him. I'll get him back."

But she was crying too badly for him to leave her. He got into bed and cuddled her up to his side, allowing her to sob noisily. He stroked her hair and rocked her, telling her everything was going to be all right.

He couldn't guarantee that. But as her dad, he had to try.

Slowly, she quieted down again. Once she began to suck her thumb, he knew it wouldn't be long before she nodded off. But even when she was fast asleep, he couldn't find it in him to move, despite the fact he needed to call the restaurant.

This was all his fault. He was a shitty dad. Not only had he upset his baby, but he'd also completely blown it with Hunter. Forget their friendship. He'd more than likely tarnished Hunter with the same homophobic brush that Chase had suffered most of his life.

Chase closed his eyes and tried his best to breathe and not panic. Why did everything he touch turn to crap? He couldn't do anything right.

He started dozing off, hugging his daughter to his side. Which is why he almost missed the knock at the door.

Blinking, he roused in time to hear the knock come again. He was muddled in his sleepy state, so didn't stop to consider who it might be as he gently disconnected himself from Lyla and went to the front door.

Hunter was on the other side.

Chase was suddenly fully awake. Hunter held his gaze as Chase stared. Then Hunter wordlessly held up Bo-Bo the dragon for Chase to take.

Chase wanted to cry again. He probably looked a mess. "Thank you," he whispered as he took the toy.

"May I come in?" Hunter asked.

Chase looked at the carpet and nodded, allowing Hunter inside. He felt so ashamed it was like acid washing over his skin.

"I'm sorry," he said again.

Hunter walked in and sat on the sofa. He had a to-go bag in his other hand that he placed on the coffee table. "If you're apologizing for running off, I accept. If you're apologizing for not telling me you're gay, I don't. Can we please sit and talk this through?"

Chase closed the door and tried to swallow, but his throat felt too constricted. He nodded and shuffled to the opposite end of the couch, sitting as far away from Hunter as he could and hugging Bo-Bo to his chest.

"I told you I was no good," he protested weakly.

"And I told you I can pick my own damn friends," Hunter said. There was a harsh edge to his voice. Chase looked up at him, scared. But Hunter's expression was nothing but sympathetic. "Chase, please stop pushing me away. I like you. You're my friend."

"Why?" Chase asked into Bo-Bo. He couldn't stop more tears slipping free and he angrily rubbed them away. "I'm nothing."

"You're a great dad and a kind friend," Hunter said without pause. "You're driven and fun to be around, and when you're not being a jackass, I actually really like hanging out with you."

Chase managed a small smile which Hunter reciprocated tenfold. "Even though I lied?"

"You didn't lie," Hunter said quickly. "It never came up.

And if you'd have stuck around, I would have been able to tell you that I don't care."

"That I'm..." Chase trailed off.

He'd never, ever said it out loud before. He couldn't finish the sentence. He closed his eyes, unable to look at his dad's house. But the words that had rung against the walls echoed in his mind. Cruel, relentless words. He realized he was crying again. Quietly, into Bo-Bo.

Then he felt a strong hand slip around his back.

"Shh," said Hunter.

He pried the dragon from Chase's hands, then pulled him into a hug. Chase knew he should be stronger, he should pull away. But he didn't have it in him. Instead, he melted into Hunter's side, allowing himself to be cradled just like he'd done for Lyla.

He hated himself. Why couldn't he just have been normal? Then he could have married Amanda and the three of them would have been a proper family together. Who knew? Maybe if they'd lived that life, Amanda would be still with them today.

That made him cry harder. He shook against Hunter's chest while Hunter rubbed his back and murmured words of support to him. Chase didn't deserve this. Not his patience nor his understanding.

But, much like Lyla, he managed to cry himself out after a while. "I'm sorry," he said yet again.

"Please stop apologizing," Hunter said. He produced a tissue from god only knew where and Chase gratefully blew his nose. "You don't have to say you're sorry. I like you, Chase. Otherwise, I wouldn't be here. Can you believe me on that?"

Chase felt composed enough to sit up and look at Hunter.

He was very close. Their faces were only a few inches away. Chase sniffed again, self-conscious of how blotchy he must look.

"I guess," he said. He laughed nervously. It was so hard to shake the feeling that Hunter was either lying, or if he did really like Chase as much as he said, there must be something wrong with him.

He looked back at Hunter but he was surprised by the expression he found on his face. It was like Hunter was seeing Chase for the first time. His hand was still on Chase's back.

Within a breath, something changed. They were staring at each other again, but it was like all the air left the room. Hunter was frowning slightly, his chest rising and falling as he looked unflinchingly into Chase's eyes.

What was going on? Chase licked his lips. Hunter's gaze darted down to look at them.

Was Chase insane? Or did it seem like Hunter wanted to kiss him?

He didn't dare move. Hunter had said he didn't care Chase was gay several times now. But he hadn't divulged what his own orientation was. Hope blossomed in Chase's heart and he stopped breathing.

Hunter moved. It was only an inch. But it was closer to Chase, bringing their lips almost together.

Chase didn't have much else to lose. If this backfired, he'd just be back to where he was before Hunter had knocked on his door.

So he closed his eyes and pressed his mouth to Hunter's.

CHAPTER FOURTEEN

HUNTER

SOMETHING HAD COME alive in Chase.

Hunter honestly thought he'd lost his mind as he held Chase on his sofa, their lips inching closer together. But perhaps this was what he'd been feeling all along, just not understanding. Yes, he wanted to be friends with Chase. Because he was attracted to him.

Hunter would have thought such a deep, personal revelation about his sexuality would have rocked his foundations far more than it currently was. But it was as if discovering the truth about Chase had unlocked a door for him. Caused the dam to break. Because now that he knew that he *could* kiss Chase, that was all he wanted to do.

And dear lord, it was easy enough to believe that was all Chase wanted, too. His kisses were assertive, confident, commanding. He slid his fingers through Hunter's hair and held tight, swinging his leg over Hunter's lap to straddle him as his kisses grew more fervent. His tongue dueled with Hunter's like he'd been desperate for this.

It turned Hunter on.

Chase wanted him. He wanted Chase.

But the shock eventually did creep in as they broke apart and gasped for air. He was kissing a man. In all his twenty-eight years, Hunter hadn't ever felt the urge to do that. But now, he couldn't remember ever quite feeling this electrified kissing a woman either.

It was like any making out he'd done in the past had all been a warm up for this moment right there and then.

He held on to Chase's slim waist as they panted and stared at each other. Chase really did have the most beautiful green eyes.

"Are you all right?" Chase asked, his voice little more than a whisper. His confidence melted away, that uncertainty creeping back in again. Hunter didn't want that. He was tempted to kiss him again to bring back the fire.

Instead, he rubbed his thumbs against Chase's flanks, feeling the T-shirt move between his hands and Chase's skin. Hunter realized he wanted to touch Chase like that. With no barriers.

Was he gay?

That seemed a huge leap. He'd been with women in the past, and it had been fine. He'd never really understood the big deal about sex. He preferred dating. But as he'd been stationed abroad so much over the past decade, he'd never been able to make anything last with anyone.

He wasn't going anywhere now, though. It occurred to him that he and Chase had sort of been dating already. He'd loved it. And right now, the prospect of getting more intimate with his new friend was tantalizingly appealing.

But that was a lot, and fast.

He realized he hadn't answered Chase's question. "Um, yeah," he said slowly. "This is a bit of a shock. But I think I am all right."

Chase fiddled with the buttons on Hunter's shirt. He was glad he hadn't gotten off his lap. He felt perfect there, and not just because certain parts of their anatomy were getting excited and rubbing together. Hunter wanted to hug Chase. To cradle him to his body and look after him.

"So...are you...uh," Chase said, clearly struggling. "I mean...I didn't think you were...into dudes."

"Neither did I," said Hunter with a faint chuckle. "I don't know. This is all pretty new."

"Oh," said Chase.

From what Hunter had been able to piece together, it was pretty obvious Chase was ashamed of being gay. He didn't seem to even be able to say the word. That made Hunter sad. He decided to be bold and take a chance. So he reached up and cupped Chase's jaw. His stubble was rough against Hunter's palm. It felt nice. Different.

"I wish I had a better answer for you," he said. "But...well, I do know I like you. More than just as a friend. I didn't really appreciate that's what was happening until now."

Chase's green eyes widened in hope. "Yeah?"

Hunter's heart swelled. He would have expected him to deny it, to tell Hunter that he was no good. But he clearly wanted Hunter to like him. That must mean he liked Hunter enough to outweigh his insecurities and doubts.

"I know your life is completely up in the air right now," Hunter said. "But is this something you might want?"

Chase looked down at where he was sitting in Hunter's lap. "You mean...something between us?"

Hunter nodded. He was too apprehensive to give it a name or any kind of label yet, so Chase would almost certainly be skittish about that, too. But they had to start somewhere.

"If you want," Hunter repeated. "You call the shots."

Disappointingly, the look on Chase's face suggested he wasn't comfortable with the idea of being in charge. But Hunter could understand that, at least.

"How about," he ventured, "we just continue as we were? Hanging out and stuff. And any time you feel like kissing me again, I'd like that."

Chase blushed. It was adorable. Hunter stroked his cheekbone with his thumb and Chase responded by nuzzling his face against Hunter's palm. It caused warmth to blossom all through Hunter's chest. Seeing Chase made so happy and content at his hand was immensely satisfying.

"Okay," Chase said softly.

Hunter's heart skipped a beat as Chase carefully leaned forward and pressed his lips gently against Hunter's. Hunter ran his hands up Chase's back, skimming over his T-shirt. His smaller body felt like it slotted in with Hunter's larger form like two puzzle pieces fitting together.

They kissed chastely. There wasn't the urgent blazing desire from before, but an exploratory meeting of mouths. Hunter felt Chase's stubble scratching against his face. Rather than being uncomfortable, it was a persistent reminder that Hunter was here with Chase, a man, even though his eyes were closed.

This was new and unexpected. But it was also wonderful.

However, Hunter had more than just himself to consider. Everything in Chase's life had been turned upside down over the past few weeks and he had a lot of pressure on him. Hunter had to think responsibly.

They pulled apart again and Hunter brushed back Chase's hair. "Okay?" Hunter asked. Chase nodded and bit his lip. Hunter smiled. "Me too. But I think I should head home. Give us both some time to think about everything."

Chase's eyes dropped. "Oh, yeah, sure," he said.

Hunter almost caved. It would be so easy to suggest he stayed. But as much as Hunter knew this was what he wanted, he had to give his mind time to wrap around the concept of being intimate with another man. He felt strongly it would be a bad idea for them to jump into bed together, much to the disappointment of his cock.

"Hey," he said softly, rubbing the back of Chase's neck. "Don't be sad. I think this is important. You're important. So we shouldn't rush it."

He was relieved when Chase perked up at that. Hunter wasn't sure how many people had told him he was important in his life. Hunter felt the urge to do it every day if it lit up Chase's face like that.

"So, you want to meet up again this week or something?" Chase suggested tentatively.

Hunter beamed up at him. "Of course. Whenever is good for you?"

Chase dropped his head and smiled with his eyes closed. Hunter thought he was maybe holding back tears. "I really thought I'd blown it with you."

That made Hunter grin. "Naw," he said kindly, but there was an edge of playfulness as well. "You can't get rid of me that easily." Chase smiled bashfully then stood up, allowing Hunter to get off the couch. "Make sure you put that in the fridge," Hunter said, pointing to the bag he'd brought in with him. "I got Tammy to box up all the food we left."

Chase sighed. "You didn't have to do that," he said.

Hunter rolled his eyes. "Don't be silly. No sense letting it go to waste. It was good pizza."

It seemed Chase couldn't argue with that. So he followed Hunter's suggestion and put the food in the fridge so he and Lyla could have it the following day. Then he walked Hunter to the door.

"I'm glad you swung by," he said, nodding to Bo-Bo the dragon.

Hunter snagged Chase's hand with his and entwined their fingers. "Any other reason you're glad I swung by?"

He almost felt guilty for teasing him. But then Chase blushed again and it was so gorgeous Hunter didn't regret a thing.

"I suppose there might be *one* other reason," Chase said. He bit his lower lip and looked up at Hunter through his long eyelashes. Something flipped in Hunter's stomach.

Whatever he was discovering his sexuality was, Hunter had to admit he was definitely not straight. His thoughts immediately turned wicked.

It felt perfectly natural to lean down and capture Chase's mouth for another kiss. Hunter could practically feel the happiness radiating off Chase. That was all because of Hunter. It felt amazing.

He eased away before things could get too heated again. "Goodnight," Hunter said, his voice hoarse.

Chase rearranged his jeans slightly. "Uh, yeah. Goodnight," he said.

Hunter wondered if Chase would do anything about that

boner once Hunter had gone. The thought made him extremely hot and bothered.

"Sleep well," he said. He then stepped out the door before he changed his mind and offered to help Chase fix his not-so-little problem.

The spring night air was a little cooler on his skin, helping him to calm down as he began his walk home. He considered what seeing Chase's hard-on meant. Did he feel able to touch that? He'd have to if he wanted to take things further. But it hadn't really ever occurred to him before. What would it be like to hold another guy's cock in his hand?

Could he take it in his mouth?

Hunter rubbed his lower lip with his thumb as he made his way in the dark along the sidewalk. He expected to feel repulsed at the idea of blowing another guy. But he simply felt mildly curious. What would it taste like? Would he enjoy it? Or was it something you suffered through because your partner liked it so much?

He was out of his depth. He needed help.

He took his phone from his pocket and pulled up Connor's number. He'd been eager to see his buddy again anyway after all the developments with Chase. But now, Hunter needed more advice than he ever would have imagined.

He fired off a quick text asking when was the soonest Connor could meet for a drink. To his surprise and relief, Connor answered right away asking if everything was all right. Hunter nibbled on his lip.

Everything's great, he typed as he walked. *I was just hoping for some advice. I met someone. A guy.*

He added the See No Evil monkey emoji and hit send with a grimace. Well, there it was. He'd come out for the first time to someone that wasn't Chase or himself. Despite knowing full well that Connor was gay, it was still terrifying. Having to admit something so personal about himself when he wasn't even sure what it all meant yet.

His phone didn't take long to alert him to a reply. He opened the message from Conner with a small amount of trepidation. But he didn't need to worry.

No way! That's awesome, dude. We could meet Monday evening for a beer?

Perfect, Hunter wrote back. He let out a long breath and pocketed his phone again. He wasn't far from home now. If Trooper was still awake, he might take him out for another extra walk around the block. Hunter thought he might need to clear his head some more.

Part of him was over the moon. He couldn't remember the last time he felt this happy. He was almost giddy with it. But he was still sensible that this was a huge lifestyle change, and he couldn't afford to run into it recklessly. Chase's heart was on the line as well as his own. Whatever the outcome, Hunter would never want to hurt Chase if he could manage it.

But for now, he was quietly hopeful that this could be the start of something truly exceptional if he was just brave enough to seize the moment.

CHAPTER FIFTEEN

It took Chase a long time to get to sleep on Saturday night. He had too many thoughts whirling around in his head. But thankfully, they were mostly happy ones.

He was struggling to actually believe the last couple of hours had taken place. The relief he'd felt when Hunter had appeared on his front doorstep – with Bo-Bo no less – to make sure their friendship wasn't about to fall apart had been huge.

Chase still felt ashamed of the way he had run out of the restaurant. He was lucky that Hunter was so understanding.

But then...

He grinned to himself in the dark of his bedroom, tears pricking at the corner of his eyes. Hunter may not be sure what his sexuality was yet exactly, but he kissed like he was into Chase enough to reassure him plenty. Fuck, Chase's entire body tingled at the memory of it. He hadn't really rated kissing before. It was like a handshake before you got down to actually fucking. But he felt like he could have snuggled on the couch and made out for hours.

From the sounds of it, Hunter had thought he was straight his whole life. But the way he had kissed and held Chase made Chase hope that they could experiment further, soon. For now, he would be happy to just kiss again. He'd take anything Hunter wanted to offer him.

Once Chase finally did pass out, he fell into a deep, uninterrupted sleep until morning. But the ecstatic scream that came from Lyla's bedroom sometime around six o'clock woke him with a fright.

"Daddy! Daddy!" she squealed as he was throwing himself out of bed, worried something was really wrong. Before he could make it out the door though, she came tearing into his bedroom. "Daddy! It's Bo-Bo!"

She thrust the purple dragon toward him, absolutely overjoyed.

Chase smiled and picked them both up so the three of them could sit back in his bed. He had tucked the dragon into her arms before going to bed last night, hoping she would be as pleased as she was now when she woke up.

"It is," he said. "Guess who rescued him and brought him to the house last night?"

Lyla's eyes went wide. "Hunter?" she asked. Chase nodded and she clapped her hands. "Are you friends again?"

Chase bit his lip. He wanted to be extremely careful how he handled this. Lyla had enough change in her life and there was no guarantee of where his and Hunter's relationship would go. But on the other hand, he wanted her to be prepared.

"We are. Daddy said he was sorry, and Hunter said he forgave him. He even brought our pizza back for us, so we can have it for dinner tonight."

Lyla sighed and hugged her dragon. "Hunter's so kind, isn't he?"

Chase smiled. Sometimes she sounded so grown up it caught him off guard.

"Lyla," he said carefully. "I know you like Hunter. But...I think he might be Daddy's best friend now. Like...a special friend. Is that okay?"

She frowned at him and used her whole hand to push back her wild hair where it had fallen all over her face. "Of course," she said. "Trooper is my special friend. So we each have a best friend."

He rubbed her arm and squeezed her into a hug. "Thank you," he said. She played with Bo-Bo's arms for a bit, making him dance. "Do you have any people best friends?" he asked.

Lyla shrugged. "Some," she said.

Her tone had gone a bit frosty though. Chase became a little worried. "Do you have kids you play with at recess?"

Lyla carried on playing with Bo-Bo some more. "Yeah," she said after a while. "I like Becca and Alexis. We play jump rope. And Noah let me play soccer, even though some of the mean boys said girls can't play soccer, but I said girls can do anything that boys can, and Noah said I was right, and I kicked the ball three times so I was right."

She curled a lock of hair around two of her fingers and tugged at it.

"You're absolutely right, pumpkin," he said with pride. "Girls can do anything boys can. And boys can do things girls like doing too, can't they? It should all be fair."

She nodded emphatically.

"What about dance and Little League?" he asked. "Are the kids nice there?" He thought of Tammy from last night. "Do you know the little girl, Geena Miller? The one our waitress said was her sister?"

Lyla looked up at him, excited. "I like Geena," she said, nodding some more. "She shared her gummy bears with me and said my hair was nice and she likes dogs too." From her serious tone, Chase thought maybe liking dogs was the best compliment Lyla could give to somebody.

"That's great," said Chase, feeling a little better. He'd been worrying that perhaps Lyla was having a hard time with other kids. It would explain why she appreciated her time playing with Trooper so much. But he figured she probably just loved the little puppy a lot. "Maybe we could organize a playdate with Geena's mom sometime soon?"

"Yes please, Daddy," Lyla said. She cuddled Bo-Bo to her chest. "Thank you."

He kissed the top of her head. "And what about Little Ladies' Etiquette?" he asked. "Are you looking forward to the parade?" The Princess Leia costume he'd ordered had arrived a couple of days ago. Their plan today was to try it on and practice how to tame her hair into the cinnamon rolls Carrie Fisher wore in the movie.

Lyla shrugged. "It's okay," she said with decidedly less enthusiasm.

Chase couldn't say he blamed her. He didn't really see the point in paying for a kid to go learn manners. Surely that was a parents' job to do that?

But Chase's upbringing had hardly been sophisticated and neither had Amanda's. He understood that she had wanted her little girl to have every advantage in life. These classes taught her how to address people correctly and formal dancing and the different knives and forks you got at fancy restaurants. If

Lyla knew that stuff, she wouldn't feel out of her depth in situations that made Chase want to curl up into a ball. So, that he could support.

But it wasn't hard to hear the lack of eagerness in Lyla's voice. "Don't you want to be Princess Leia on the float?" Chase asked. "We can always change it still," he assured her. He really didn't want to waste the money on a second costume. But he would rather his little girl was happy.

She snapped her head up to look at him though. "Oh, no. I want to be General Leia," she said firmly. "But..."

She trailed off and turned her gaze back to her dragon.

"But what, honey?"

Lyla sighed. "Brianna-Grace said she's not a *real* princess."

Chase knew who Brianna-Grace was. She was the girl who had snatched up Merida for her costume, despite being blonde and able to pick half a dozen more traditional Disney princesses if she wanted.

"Well, Brianna-Grace is wrong," said Chase. "Leia is a princess *and* a general. So that makes her awesome."

Lyla sniffed. Chase couldn't see, because she'd let all her hair fall forward around her face. But he was worried she was crying.

"Has Brianna-Grace said anything else to you, baby?" he asked delicately.

Lyla sniffed again. "She says I'm poor," she mumbled. "And poor girls can't be Little Ladies."

Anger boiled inside Chase, but he bit his tongue until he calmed down enough to speak. "It doesn't sound to me like Brianna-Grace knows much about anything," he said, attempting to lighten the mood. "Just because you don't have a lot of money doesn't make you poor. If you have people that love you, that makes you rich."

He managed not to let his voice catch, but he had a lump in his throat. That was something Amanda used to tell him when they were younger.

Lyla turned her glassy eyes up toward Chase. "But we *don't* have a lot of money, do we?" she said. "Even less money than Momma had."

Chase tried not to let that upset him. She was just being honest, the way kids were. "Yeah," he said heavily. "I'm sorry, darling. Daddy doesn't have as good a job as Momma had. I'm going to try and get a better one, though."

Lyla nodded. "Thank you," she said. Then she sighed. "I miss Momma."

Chase closed his eyes briefly and took a deep breath. "I know, me too," he said once he'd found his composure. They sat in silence for a while, both of them lost in thought. "I'm sorry that girl is being mean to you, honey. Does she go to your school, too?"

Lyla nodded. "Although, she's in first grade, so I only see her at lunch and recess and stuff. So, it's not so bad."

"Do you want me to talk to her mom?" he asked, hoping he sounded more confident than he felt. The idea of confronting one of those Little Ladies parents filled him with dread.

But Lyla shrugged. "Nah, it's okay," she said. "I don't want to be a tattletale."

"There's a difference between telling tales and being bullied," said Chase crossly. "You're not a tattletale, sweetie. This girl is a meanie and it's not okay."

Lyla shrugged again. "It's okay. I don't see her much. And I have my secret base where I'm safe."

"A secret base, huh?" he said.

She nodded. "It's like Batman's cave. No one knows about it and it has all my secret weapons in it like my ray guns and my invisible guns and it's hidden by a waterfall, so no one will ever, ever find it!" She got more and more excited as she spoke. "You have to press the special buttons to get inside and I'll only allow my best friends in like Noah and Geena and Trooper." She patted Chase's knee. "You can come in too, Daddy," she said. "Because I like you."

Chase laughed, wondering if he ever had such a good imagination when he was a kid. "I like you too, sweetie."

"Do you think Hunter would like to come too?" she asked.

He smiled down at her. "I think he'd *love* to," he said.

Chase had no idea what he could hope for his and Hunter's relationship. It was all so new he was too scared to even *call* it a relationship. But if Lyla was accepting of Daddy's special friend, then that meant Chase was braver going forward.

He still had Mr. Preston and his prejudices to worry about. But Chase could deal with that if and when it became an issue. He didn't even know if Hunter would really want to date a man, or sleep with one. It was a big leap for him.

So, for now, Chase promised himself he would just deal with one thing at a time as they happened. No sense worrying about the future when the present was tricky enough to navigate.

"Come on, then, *your highness*," he said in a high-pitched voice that made Lyla giggle. "Let's have some breakfast. Then we can try and make your hair look like Princess Leia's. Sound good?"

"Sounds great!" said Lyla, bouncing out of bed.

Chase watched her race out into the kitchen with her dragon. Then he reached for his phone. He didn't know what to say, so he just sent a single heart emoji to Hunter. He hoped that conveyed his happiness well enough.

He didn't want to scare Hunter away. But he also felt it was important for Chase to let him know that he was extremely excited about where this might be headed.

CHAPTER SIXTEEN

___

HUNTER

AT FIRST, Hunter wasn't sure if Connor was serious or not. But then he remembered Connor was always serious.

"You're taking me to a gay bar?" Hunter repeated as they drove through town.

It was Monday evening, as they'd planned. Hunter wouldn't normally go out drinking like this at the start of the week, but he'd wanted to see Connor as soon as possible.

Hunter was glad Connor had offered to drive. He still couldn't get himself behind the wheel and it was starting to really bother him. Maybe he'd mention it to Connor later, if he got the chance. Or maybe his anxiety would just fade away like he'd hoped, if he gave it more time. Lots of guys probably suffered from attacks like this. No sense in Hunter making a fuss if it would just sort itself out eventually.

Connor chuckled. *"The* gay bar," he said. "Might as well start at the top. Bottom's Up is the best place to go."

"Why?" Hunter asked.

Connor quirked his lips in a half-smile. "You'll see."

Connor wasn't one of those guys that was obviously gay. If he hadn't mentioned it a while back, Hunter might not have ever guessed. He'd said something about Hidden Creek being a great LGBT community when suggesting Hunter move into town as well. Hunter hadn't given it much thought before. Now, things made a bit more sense.

"So, you're not surprised?" he asked, referring to his coming out.

Connor shrugged. "Eh, maybe a little. Not so much you being into dudes. Most of the guys I end up being close to have the potential."

"Takes one to know one?"

"Pretty much." He smiled at me. "Plus I caught you checking out my ass more than once."

"No!" Hunter protested. "I – oh – really?" Connor chuckled and nodded. "Damn," said Hunter. Maybe he should have seen this coming?

"But seriously," Connor said and looked over from the driver's seat. "I'm proud of you. Coming out takes guts." He shook his head. "I owe you everything. If it weren't for you, man, I'd be dead. So, you need to go to a gay bar on a Monday night. That's what we're gonna do." Connor glanced at him with a devilish look. "Besides, I want to hear all about this guy. Must be someone special. I'm kind of jealous. You're not even here a month and you're already hooking up. I've been back four months and haven't seen any action. Well, not unless you count..." Whatever he was going to say faded away.

"Count what?" Hunter asked, curious. "Tell me."

"Maybe later," Connor said, sidestepping the issue. "You first. I want to hear all about this hunka burning man meat that's gotten you to consider switching teams. He must be a hottie."

Hunter rolled his eyes at the teasing and punched Connor's arm. "Shut up," he mumbled.

He knew Connor didn't mean anything by it though. Hunter had helped save a lot of lives during his service out in Afghanistan, but he and Connor had clicked during his recovery and stayed friends ever since.

Connor had received his compassionate discharge a few months before Hunter had left the Marines himself. His mom and step-dad rolled their car trying to avoid a deer, leaving Connor to come home and take care of his younger brothers and sisters. It was tough, but as usual, Connor was taking it all in stride. Or so Hunter had assumed.

His texts had sounded more and more tense lately. Hunter wondered if he wasn't the only one needing to get something off his chest.

Bottom's Up was a bar on the corner of an intersection. The outside of the building wasn't especially distinctive. It was just a big square made out of cream-colored bricks. But a rainbow flag was flying beside a Texas one over the front door, so Hunter had no doubt they were in the right place.

The first thing that struck him as they walked through the entrance was the size of it. There was a sleek bar in front of them with plenty of tables and chairs as well as booths lining the walls. To the right was a dance floor and above them was another story with a balcony that overlooked the dance floor. Air hockey, ping pong and pool tables were standing to the left of the room.

The house lights were down, and blue-and-purple spot-lights swirled around the dance area. As it was a Monday, the place was pretty quiet, but there were guys sitting at several of the tables along with some women. A gaggle of college-aged kids were crowded around one of the pool tables and looked to be placing bets on a game between two bigger guys.

There looked to be a little something for everyone. Hunter guessed it was the place to be simply because it was where all the queer guys came, regardless of tastes. He rubbed his hands on his jeans and tried not to feel out of place.

Connor placed a hand on his back and steered him toward the bar where a few people were waiting. "Nervous?" he asked sympathetically. "Don't be. Even if they do smell the baby gay on you, people will leave you alone. It's great here. Everyone's welcome." He leaned against the bar and raised his voice so the bartender could hear him. "I mean, sometimes they play a little too much Britney for my liking, but apparently I'm outvoted on that front."

The slim guy behind the bar gasped and pretended to clutch at his heart. "Did you just slander the Queen of Pop? Get out, you heathens."

Connor sagged down onto a barstool. "Please, Kris. Cut me some slack. I already got shit this week because I didn't know Lady Gaga's real name."

"What is it?" Hunter asked. Had he known she had a real name? Well, obviously her mother hadn't named her Lady Gaga.

"Stefani Joanne Angelina Germanotta," Connor said like a child reciting a poem they'd memorized.

Kris clapped. "You get a rainbow star. If you know Madonna's real name, I'll give you a blowjob on the house."

Connor leaned over the bar and reached for Kris's hands,

staring deep into the bartender's eyes. "You know you'd give me a blowjob for free any time I asked."

Kris actually blushed and looked down at the top of the bar.

"But for the record, it's Madonna Louise Ciccone." He leaned over the bar and gave the flamboyant man a quick peck on the cheek.

Hunter realized how much of his personality Connor had kept under wraps during his time in the service. And Hidden Creek might be liberal, but it was still Texas. They'd still had laws against sodomy on the books until 2003. It must be nice to have someplace to go where you could be yourself.

From what Hunter knew of gay lingo, he would call the bartender a twink. He sashayed his hips with every step and flicked his hands like a Broadway dancer. His white-blond hair had purple tips that Lyla would approve of. He wore a mesh T-shirt and sprayed-on skinny jeans, none of which left anything to the imagination.

"Hold the blowjob. You can owe me. Can I get two Coronas and a shot of Johnny Walker?"

Hunter was surprised. Connor wasn't usually a big drinker. "Whiskey? On a weeknight?"

Connor sighed. "After the week I've had, you're lucky I didn't show up on your doorstep with a bottle of Jim Beam and a straw."

Hunter patted Connor on the back. He wouldn't pry. If Connor wanted to talk about it, he would.

Kris batted his false eyelashes at Hunter. "Hello, tall, dark and handsome," he said. His lips were shiny with gloss. "Did Connor bring you to me for a present? I could hook you up with some sex on the beach rather than boring old beer."

He snatched two bottles from the fridge...and one promptly slipped out from between his fingers and smashed on the floor.

"Hey!" an older guy shouted from further down the bar. He placed the glass he was drying on the counter and pointed at Kris. "You drop any more drinks, it's coming out of your pay check."

Kris grumbled sheepishly as he fetched the dustpan and brush.

Connor and Hunter propped themselves up against the bar. Hunter tried to relax, but he'd never been one much for bars and clubs. Even if this weren't an LGBT space, he'd still be feeling uncomfortable.

Connor noticed and took pity on him. "We can leave if you want. Get that bottle and two straws?"

Hunter shook his head. "Nah," he said with a shrug. "I think we're a bit beyond that now. Might as well jump in with both feet."

"Here are your drinks," Kris said, placing the bottles in front of them. He sounded significantly subdued.

"Hey, Kris," Connor said. "Ignore that asshole. It's just one lousy beer."

That was what Hunter liked about Connor. For all his scowls and seriousness, he was a nice guy. The kid, Kris, was probably only a couple of years older than Connor's eldest sibling. Hunter appreciated seeing the protective side of him come out.

Kris preened, back to his showy self. "You're right. He's just old and grumpy. He can't tame my fabulousness. Right, gorgeous?" He winked at Hunter.

Hunter wasn't sure what to make of that. It wasn't like he'd realized he was gay or bi or whatever and now he was attracted to all guys. He was just attracted to Chase. He felt out of his depth.

Connor waved a ten in front of Kris's face. "Down boy, he's taken. Go find your sugar daddy elsewhere."

Kris wasn't put out. He plucked the bill from Connor's fingers with a snap of his wrist and licked his glossy lips. "You just watch me, baby. I have a man in every port." He flounced off to the cash register before coming back with Connor's change. "Have fun, boys," he said, dropping the coins into Connor's outstretched palm. "I'll be right here if you need me."

Shaking his head, Connor led Hunter upstairs where it was a bit quieter and they were able to get a table by themselves easily.

They looked at one another. "So..." said Connor, pushing the shot in front of Hunter.

Hunter laughed. "Well, this is isn't a conversation I pictured us having six months ago."

"Me neither," Connor agreed.

Hunter had to ask. "How are you doing?" He downed the whiskey and winced as the liquor burned down his throat.

Connor shrugged. "Hanging in there." He shook his head, fingers peeling nervously at the damp label. "It's been fucking tough, man," he admitted. "The kids are great. Well, Sean's a dick, but who isn't at sixteen? They're doing the best they can, but it's so hard. Their whole goddamn world has been turned upside down."

Hunter thought of Chase and Lyla. "Yeah, I get that," he said. "But so has yours."

Connor shrugged again, as if to say 'it is what it is.' "That fucking storm last night didn't help."

"Tell me about it," Hunter said with a frown.

The weather had been getting a little crazy of late. Not so much April showers as storms so bad they were practically tornadoes. Chase had texted during the night because Lyla got hysterical at one point after the thunder claps got too loud. They had both been in town during Harvey, after all. It was natural to panic that it was another hurricane.

Hunter wasn't surprised Connor's siblings were set off. From what he'd heard from Connor, Hurricane Harvey had hit the area hard. Lots of people had lost their houses and all their possessions from the flooding. Any storm had everyone on high alert. Trooper hadn't been impressed with all the noise either. He and Hunter had huddled on the bed together, trying not to flinch with every boom. PTSD was the gift that kept giving.

All of them were already emotionally on edge. So a massive storm would only make things worse. Thankfully, the sun had been back out today, drying up all the leftover puddles.

"How's money doing?" Hunter asked, changing the subject. Connor was a practical man and wouldn't mind him asking outright. Like with Chase, if there was anything Hunter could do to help out, he would.

Connor picked at the corner of the label on his bottle. "Tight but not terrible, you know. Kids get their death benefits. Insurance paid for the house with some set aside for college." he said with a nod. "Sean's been making noise about getting a job, but with football, track and what all, he don't really have time. Peggy took me back at the shop." He took a long swallow of beer. "It's not money. It's just there's so much shit that has to get done. And now social services is on my back about getting the house fixed up. And it seems like every kid has somewhere different to go every night."

Hunter tried not to sneer at the mention of social services. Thinking back to that visit with Mr. Preston still made him angry. "Sean must have his license by now, right?" he asked instead.

"He does, barely, but the kids are scared of cars right now. I don't want him driving them around. He's just a kid."

Hunter nodded. Between Amanda's death and Connor's parents, car accidents had taken quite a few people in town lately. "Maybe you could get a nanny or something. Do they still call them nannies if the kids are big?"

Connor pointed his beer bottle at Hunter. "Funny you should mention that. So, I, uh, kinda did get someone to help around the house. Mostly with the repair. He's gonna live in the RV in exchange."

"Where'd you find him?"

"He came into the shop. His van needed repairs." Connor rolled his eyes but couldn't hide a fond smile. "He fucking named his van Lady Gaga."

"Ah. Hence the Stephanie whatever whatever." Hunter chuckled. He also made a mental note to see about getting Chase's car into the shop. It was running fine now, but an overhaul of a vehicle that old would set Hunter's mind at ease.

"Exactly," said Connor.

"Do you like him?"

Connor pulled some more at the label. "He's got blue hair."

"Is that good or bad?"

"He helps around the house, too," Connor said, not directly answering the question. "And he's good with the kids. And he plays hockey. And...sings." The way he tacked on the last comment, Hunter wondered if it was a compliment or an insult.

It felt like there was more to this blue-haired mystery man than Connor was telling, but Hunter sensed it would be rude to pry again. Sure enough, Connor raised an eyebrow at him and switched up the conversation again.

"Enough about me. What the hell do you mean by 'I met a guy'?"

Hunter couldn't help but smile nervously. "Well, honestly I'm not sure. But I guess I'm not as straight as I thought I was." Connor simply kept his eyes on him as he swigged from his bottle.

"Okay," Hunter said, exhaling. "I met a guy. He's a single dad with a kid, and I got a puppy and we've all been hanging out a lot and I found out he was gay and it was like it flicked a switch where I realized I really liked him, like *liked* him, and then we made out on Saturday night and I think I want to do it again."

He inhaled and then downed half his beer.

Connor blinked. "All right. Once more, from the top, *slowly*."

Hunter sighed and resigned himself to explaining properly how he'd met Chase. He also asked if Connor knew him, as the way Chase talked, the whole town knew about his scandal. But Connor hadn't heard about him or Amanda's teenage pregnancy.

"I kind of know him from around now, but I was already long gone by then," Connor said. "So, I'm not hearing anything bad enough to get your panties in a wad. What's the problem? Freaked out that you might like the D?" He waggled his eyebrows at Hunter with an evil grin.

"Fuck you," Hunter said fondly. "And for the record, I actually think I might be gay. I've never felt like this about anyone before. It's like Dorothy going to Oz and suddenly everything's in Technicolor."

"Already with the Wizard of Oz references? That's pretty fucking gay," Connor teased.

Hunter punched his arm lightly. "Shut up."

"Seriously though," Connor continued. "What's the issue? Sounds like you and this guy have something going on."

Hunter rubbed his forehead. "It just feels like I'm taking advantage," he blurted out. "He's going through so much. And, yeah, I think he is absolutely gay. But he doesn't seem comfortable with it at all. I don't think he's officially out. So, while I really like him and want...stuff to happen-"

"You want to fuck him," Connor interjected wryly. "Or have him fuck you. Either way is good. I don't judge. Switch it up. Keeps things fresh."

Hunter flinched at the crude language. Sure, he wanted that, but it sounded so dirty when Connor said it.

"Hey," Connor said seriously, leaning toward Hunter. "If you can't say it, you can't do it. As I tell the kids. Or will tell them when the situation comes up. Which, if there is a god, will be never."

Hunter made an exasperated noise. "I'm putting pressure on him, aren't I? He's in a vulnerable position. It's selfish for me to come barreling in when I don't even know what I'm really feeling."

Connor tilted his head. "You just told me you reckon you're gay."

Hunter shrugged. "Maybe?"

"One make out session and you're barreling full speed down the gay highway. Do not pass bi, do not collect two hundred dollars," Connor pressed. "But you still think you might change your mind about him?"

It was Hunter's turn to pick at his beer label. "I don't know that I will. I mean, as much as anyone can guess when they get with someone. I don't feel like this is a fling."

"Sounds like you're all in to me, buddy," Connor said kindly.

"But," said Hunter, not willing to cave just yet. "He's so young and he's got so much on his plate. He doesn't need some guy trying to work out his feelings and sexuality with him."

Connor placed his beer down and folded his arms. "How young is young, exactly?"

"Twenty-three," Hunter said.

Connor scoffed. "Don't give me that shit. Half the guys you patched up over there or stuffed in body bags were younger than that. No," he said as Hunter tried to interrupt. "He's a grown-ass man. A father, even. Have you asked him directly if he wants to date, wants to fuck? Whatever."

The idea of just fucking Chase made Hunter shudder. This wasn't a hook up. Although making out had been incredibly hot. Hunter was interested in more than sex.

"Sort of," he said. "I left after we kissed. I told him we needed to think about this seriously. But I'm sure he wanted me to stay. I mean, we've said we like each other."

Connor nodded and gripped his shoulder. "Ask him. Don't dance around it. That's the best thing you can do if everything really is as complicated as you say for him. Tell him how you feel and what you want. If he's not on the same page, hopefully he'll be honest and let you know. But you've got to be honest first."

"That sounds far too logical," Hunter said with a smile. Connor chuckled.

"Sorry, man. I just bring the truth."

Hunter knew he was right. He sighed in resignation. "Life's too short," he admitted.

"That it is, my friend."

They clinked their bottles together.

Hunter pulled out his phone while Connor watched approvingly. *Hey,* he texted Chase. *Are you free tomorrow night? I thought I could come around and we could talk :)*

That was it. With the decision made, Hunter felt like a weight was lifted off him. There was no going back now.

It made him realize that he didn't *want* to back out, though. He was in this with both feet. All he could do now was hope Chase felt the same.

He would soon find out.

"Feel better?" Connor asked.

Hunter nodded.

"That's because you think you're going to get laid," Connor said, nodding sagely. "Always cheers a man up. Lifts your spirits."

"Some of us don't just think with our dicks," Hunter objected. A guy at a nearby table snorted a laugh, and Connor lifted his bottle at the guy. Hunter shook his head. "Fine. Let's talk about your dick for a while then. Tell me about the singing, blue-haired hockey player who's living in your house."

"Not in my *house,*" Connor objected.

Hunter stared him down.

"Fine," he said with a sigh. He took a pull from his beer and looked up with the smile in his eyes Hunter remembered from Afghanistan. "He's fucking hot, dude."

Hunter laughed, and they spent the next couple of hours talking about everything from hockey, which they both knew nothing about, to raising kids, something else they knew nothing about, to Hunter's new job and what repairs Connor's house still needed.

They ended the night as they always did, with a toast to friends and brothers-in-arms lost but never forgotten. They hugged each other hard before splitting up with a promise to get together regularly from now on.

CHAPTER SEVENTEEN

CHASE

Chase was trying not to pace. Hunter had asked to come over and talk. *Specifically,* he said it would be best to come later while Lyla was asleep so they could get some time to themselves. So Chase had spent the last twenty-four hours wondering just exactly Hunter wanted to do when they were alone.

It had been three whole days and Chase still couldn't get the kiss out of his mind. He and Hunter had been texting, so Chase tried not to feel too nervous. But what if he'd had an epiphany that he was straight after all and was coming over to let Chase down gently? Or maybe he was mad that Chase forced himself on him and never wanted to see him again?

By the time the soft knock came on the door, Chase had convinced himself that Hunter wanted to file charges against him for his inappropriate behavior. He was practically shaking as he opened up the door.

But then Hunter smiled at him. He was in jeans and a navy-blue button-down shirt and looked absolutely gorgeous.

"Hi," he said shyly, offering up a medium-sized cloth bag. Chase accepted it with trembling fingers. The flowers were already visible poking out of the top. But inside as well were a bottle of red wine and a box of chocolates.

"Oh," said Chase, completely stunned.

"I wasn't sure what to bring," Hunter said, slipping his hands into his pockets. "But it seemed safe to go with the classics."

The classics. For a date. Chase's heart was acting like it might thump itself right out of his chest. "Yes, no," he stammered. "Uh – this is perfect. Thank you."

"May I come in?"

Chase snapped his head up from the bag and almost tripped over in his haste to move backward. "Sorry, of course, come in."

He wished he had a nicer place. If Lyla weren't in the picture, he would have been more than happy to spend time at Hunter's home. It almost certainly had to be better than Chase's. But ironically, thanks to Lyla, it at least had a lot more character than it had before.

Hunter followed him inside and gently closed the front door. Chase fussed around, putting the flowers in water and getting glasses for the wine. He was so nervous, he wasn't even sure he could drink anything. But it gave him something to do for a few minutes which, didn't involve looking at Hunter.

When he turned around, two glasses in hand, he found Hunter standing very close to him in the kitchen. "Hi," he squeaked.

Hunter smiled and his eyes sparkled with something Chase hadn't seen before. "Hello," he said, his voice low and melodic. "Thank you."

He slipped the glass from Chase's hand to his, their fingers brushing as they wrapped around the stem. Chase gulped. "Uh, so," he said. He took too big a mouthful, then did his best not to splutter. "How have you been? Since Saturday." *Since we made out.*

Hunter nodded. "Good. I met up with an old friend last night. We went to Bottom's Up."

Chase knew his eyes went wide. There wasn't a much gayer place in town than there. Not that he'd been brave enough to ever go out that close to home. He preferred to venture into Houston for his very occasional hookups.

"Oh, um, well, that's good," he said. Real smooth. Wait. Was he trying to tell Chase he'd been on a date with another guy? That he wasn't interested?

Something must have shown on his face because Hunter raised his eyebrows. "Uh, no, I mean. He talked some sense into me. About you."

Chase looked down at his wine. Was this a breakup? Could you break up if you weren't even together? "Oh," he said, swallowing down his disappointment.

Hunter sighed. "I'm doing this all wrong." He slipped his hand into Chase's. The skin to skin contact sent immediate chills down Chase's spine. "Come sit with me?"

Chase nodded and allowed himself to be led over to the sofa where they'd kissed like horny teenagers only a couple of days ago. Chase purposefully left some space between them when he positioned himself on the cushions.

"Okay," said Hunter, taking a deep breath. "I've been thinking about us."

Chase wasn't sure if he dared breathe. "Okay," he said. He

sipped his wine again, uncertain if it was nice or not. His whole mouth felt numb.

"I've been worrying about what you're thinking," Hunter continued. Then he laughed. He placed his wine down on the coffee table, then leaned over to take Chase's free hand again. Chase copied him and also put down his glass. His pulse was so loud in his ears he had to concentrate to keep listening to what Hunter was saying. "So my buddy told me to stop being such an idiot and just ask you how you feel."

"Me?" Chase said stupidly. "Um, well, how do you – I mean – what do you think?"

He knew Hunter had kissed him and said Chase could kiss him again any time he wanted. But that felt like a lifetime ago now. Hunter rubbed his thumbs over the back of Chase's knuckles, though. It made his entire body quiver.

"I like you, a lot, Chase," Hunter said. He seemed nervous but determined to push on. "I've never been with a man before, but I'd like to be with you. To, um, date you and stuff."

Why? was Chase's immediate reaction. If Hunter Duke wanted to try dating men, he could have anyone he wanted. He could have stayed at Bottom's Up and left with his pick of dozens of guys. And yet he was here, sitting on Chase's couch. Again.

"I know you have a lot going on," Hunter said. His eyes dropped to look at their connected hands. "So if this is overkill, if I'm putting too much on you, we can just go back to the way things were-"

"No!" Chase blurted, causing Hunter to snap his gaze up. "Um, I mean. No, thank you. I like the part where you're my friend, but you also kiss me now." Chase felt like an absolute fool, so he closed his eyes in an attempt to make himself keep talking. "I can't believe a guy like you would be interested in me. But if you are, then I like you very, *very* much and I'm definitely not too busy. For you. Us."

He didn't know what else to say. Did Hunter want to be boyfriends? Was that a step too far?

Chase felt a ghost of a breath on his lips. "Can I kiss you again?" Hunter murmured, his voice extremely near.

"Oh, god yes," Chase replied, his eyes still closed.

Hunters lips were soft against his, gently probing as they touched Chase's again and again. Slowly, Chase slipped his fingers into Hunter's hair, pulling him closer, encouraging him. Hunter's large hands took hold of his waist and the back of his neck. More and more of their bodies were touching. Chase felt like he was on fire.

"I want you to be mine," Hunter said into his mouth.

Chase melted, almost literally. He sank onto the couch, encouraging Hunter to lay on top of him. "Yes," he whispered back. "Fuck, yes. All yours."

Hunter may not have made out with a guy before him, but he wasn't exactly shy either. He crawled on top of Chase's body, pressing him into the sofa with just the right amount of pressure. He ground down, making Chase gasp as his rigid cock dug into his thigh. Their kisses were urgent now, desperate.

Chase couldn't ever remember being this hard before. His dick was painful as his jeans tried to hold him back. "Take me to bed," he rasped.

He only had a second to marvel at his own bravery. Then Hunter was standing up, hauling Chase after him and practically dragging him to his room. Chase glanced worriedly in the direction of Lyla's room along the corridor. Hunter closed the door behind them, then cradled Chase's face in his hands.

"We'll have to be really quiet," he said. Chase nodded. As anxious as he was not to disturb his daughter, he was also elated that Hunter's first thought had been the same thing.

They kissed again as they walked toward the bed together. Chase had never shared it with anyone else.

Hunter let him go so Chase could sink into the mattress. He backed up against the pillows as Hunter pulled his shoes off, then crawled up alongside Chase. They lay side by side, arms locked around the other as their tongues met in exploration. Chase shuddered in pure bliss.

"You really want to be with me?" he asked, his insecurities getting the better of him.

Hunter brushed his hair back, his fingertips tracing over his jaw, the edge of his lips, the shell of his ears. "Yes," he said simply. "Tell me what you like. I want to make you feel good."

There was a possibility Chase could have come there and then. He screwed his eyelids shut and moaned as quietly as he dared. Fuck, he wanted everything from Hunter. But he'd been too afraid to pick up condoms because of some ridiculous thought that he might jinx this if he did.

He almost cursed himself. But if he was honest, full anal was a lot of preparation and psychologically a fair amount to wrap your head around. For Hunter's first time, he didn't want any unnecessary stress or hassle.

"Naked," he panted. "Good place to start."

Hunter laughed and sucked on his earlobe. Chase trembled and whimpered. "Solid plan," Hunter whispered.

His hands found their way under Chase's T-shirt, his fingers tickling up his sides. Chase did his best not to squirm, but the way Hunter's eyes widened in the gloom suggested he quite liked feeling Chase wriggle under him.

"Tell me if you like it," he said, placing open mouthed kisses down Chase's throat.

"Uh huh," Chase said, unable to string real words together.

Hunter laughed, low and delicious. "Which bit?"

"All of it," Chase said with a gasp. "Oh my god."

Hunter captured his lips for another kiss, then studied Chase's face in the dark. Now his eyes were getting used to it, Chase could make out most of Hunter's features. "I don't know what I'm doing," he said.

"I very much disagree," said Chase. He ran his hands over Hunter's chest, shoulders and arms. The man was built like a powerhouse.

Hunter grinned and kissed Chase a couple of times. He was very generous with his kisses, Chase was beginning to appreciate. He hadn't rated them at all before, but they were becoming Chase's favorite thing.

"No, I really don't know," said Hunter. "So you have to make sure I'm doing it right. Ask me for what you want."

Chase was more inclined to just let him carry on and correct him in the unlikely event he messed up. But it seemed important to Hunter that Chase have the reins. So Chase simply nodded. "Okay," he promised. At least he had an easy place to start. "I *want* you to take your shirt off, please."

He grinned and squirmed, feeling devilish. Hunter growled.

"Absolutely."

He was already straddling Chase's hips, so he sat back and began undoing the buttons on his navy shirt, one by one. Chase gulped as he watched. Gradually, Hunter revealed an expanse of smooth muscled flesh, dropping the shirt to the floor.

His arms were usually hidden by long sleeves, so Chase was surprised to find several tattoos along them and his chest. He reached up and touched them reverently with his fingertips.

"Wow," he said.

Hunter watched him exploring his flesh. "You don't have any ink?"

Chase bit his lip and looked at him through his eyelashes. What was it about Hunter that made him so bold? "You'll have to see for yourself," he goaded. He didn't. But he loved the idea of making Hunter search every inch of his body just in case.

Hunter licked his lips and slid his hands under Chase's T-shirt again. Obediently, Chase lifted himself up so Hunter could pull it over his head. Now they were both only in their jeans and when Hunter lowered himself down again to bring their mouths back together, the meeting of skin was heavenly. Hunter ran hot compared to Chase, who always seemed to be cold. His belly rubbing against Chase's was divine.

Chase was usually quite passive when it came to sex, allowing the other dude to go ahead and call the shots. But he felt safe with Hunter. So he pushed him away slightly and wrapped his lips around one of his nipples, sucking and licking with his tongue.

"Holy fuck," Hunter hissed.

Chase grinned. "Never had anyone do that before?"

Hunter blinked and shook his head. "Thought it was just something chicks liked."

"It depends," said Chase, licking and kissing the little nub. "Some guys aren't particularly sensitive." The way Hunter moaned again made Chase think he was pretty sensitive and he loved it. It got him thinking. What else could he do? "Roll over," he instructed, feeling like a minx. He couldn't remember sex ever being this fun and they hadn't even gotten to the good stuff yet.

Hunter grabbed his hips and tumbled them around so he was lying on his back with Chase looming over him. Chase didn't imagine he made much of an imposing figure. But he was having fun, so he didn't care.

He attacked Hunter's body, kissing along his collarbone and down in between his pecs. He spent time on each nipple, licking, sucking and even nibbling on them until they were tight as rocks. The whole time Hunter kept running his hands up and down Chase's flanks, along his spine and through his hair.

"Yes, baby," he whispered over and over. "Like that, so good."

Chase never liked staying over with random guys, so he'd always felt hurried when he had sex. There was never any time to smell the roses. He realized he had all night with Hunter. Unless...

He paused as he was nuzzling and kissing the fuzzy happy trail on Hunter's stomach. He looked up at him. "What?" Hunter asked, sensing something was off. He cupped Chase's jaw with his large hand, encouraging him to come back up the bed to talk to him face to face.

Fear ran through Chase's body like ice. Did he have the balls to ask? "Will you stay?" he whispered, afraid to speak too loudly. As if that might limit his chances of rejection. Hunter gave him a puzzled look, so Chase cleared his throat. "The night," he clarified. "Will you sleep here?"

The relief from the big smile that broke out over Hunter's face was immense. "Of course," he said, tugging Chase down for a kiss. "I'd love to."

Chase sighed happily. "Great. Because I don't want to rush this."

The look Hunter gave him was smoldering. "Take your time, sweetheart," he said.

Chase kissed his way back down Hunter's body, loving the way his impressive muscles moved under his hands and lips. Hunter quietly groaned and gasped, letting Chase know just how much he was enjoying his ministrations.

Then Chase reached his intended destination. The fly on Hunter's jeans.

He looked up, feeling like the best kind of slut. He watched Hunter watching him as he slowly pulled down the zipper. Hunter bit his lip and moaned. When the fly was all the way undone, Chase tugged on the jeans a little to give him more room, then nuzzled his nose against Hunter's big cock through his underwear.

He wasn't so large he was scary. Chase had been with a guy hung like a porn star once before and it had been painful more than anything else. But Hunter looked just right. Chase would certainly feel it when he sank onto that glorious pink monster and he salivated to get it inside his mouth now.

It strained against Hunter's expensive-looking briefs, tenting the material as far as it would go. "Please, baby," he begged down to Chase.

Chase mouthed his cock through the cotton. "What is it you want?" he asked, teasing.

"Mouth, there," Hunter said. His brain seemed to be

stalling. Chase was doing that. This big, gorgeous guy was coming unraveled because of him. "Naked?"

Chase liked that plan.

He looped his fingers over the briefs and jeans waistbands and tugged them carefully over Hunter's straining erection, freeing it. Hunter kicked, trying to shake the clothes off, while also reaching for Chase's buttons.

It was easier for Chase to strip himself, though. He wriggled free of his jeans, then practically jumped back on top of Hunter.

It took a moment to register they were both naked.

"Oh," he said. He looked down at Hunter as Hunter studied him with equal intensity.

Chase would have assumed it to be awkward. But their hands traced naturally along the other's skin and their cocks strained to touch one another. Not yet though. Chase had designs on that delicious-looking prick.

He stroked it first, feeling the velvety flesh over a steel-like rod. Hunter panted and babbled sweet nothings, petting Chase's hair as he kissed his way up Hunter's thigh and along the shaft. Just a taste, that was all he needed to keep him satisfied for now.

He lapped up the leaking precum like a melting popsicle on a hot summer's day. Then he sheathed his teeth and suckled at the thick, cut tip of Hunter's magnificent cock. If Hunter wanted to put his faith in Chase, had chosen him when he could have had any guy he wanted, Chase was going to do everything he could to impress this Adonis in his bed.

Hunter was muttering "Oh my god," over and over again. So Chase figured he must be doing something right. He swallowed more down, cocooning the hot cock with his tongue and rubbing the tip against the inside of his cheek.

He was tempted to keep going and make Hunter come down his throat. But for their first time, he wanted them to do it together. It was probably totally stupid, but Chase hadn't had much romance in his life. For once, he figured he could indulge.

So he enjoyed Hunter's cock for a little longer, stroking himself too so he could stay rock hard. Then he released him and moved up the bed to find his lover's mouth again.

"Hi," he said, feeling cute as he stole chaste kisses.

Hunter's eyes looked totally blown wide from what Chase could see in the dark. He panted and pawed at Chase's face and the back of his neck. "Hello, darling," he said.

Chase positioned himself on Hunter's body so their dicks were aligned. Then he could reach down and circle them both with his fingers. Hunter gasped and squeezed his eyes shut. His hand drifted down to find Chase's so they were both creating a channel for them to thrust into.

"Holy fuck," Hunter hissed. "Chase. Not gonna..."

"Me neither," said Chase. He was rutting wantonly as his orgasm built at a rapid pace. Hunter gripped the back of his head to kiss him and stare into his eyes as their climax peaked together.

"Fuck," Hunter cried. His body jerked along with Chase's as pleasure tore through them. Their stomachs became slick with hot mess as they both spilled hard and fast.

Chase's trembling arms finally gave way and he collapsed on top of Hunter who hugged him tightly. Their breath mingled as they both panted and Chase wondered if Hunter felt as dizzy as he did. His whole world was swirling around him like a fairground ride.

"Was that okay?" he mumbled.

Hunter chuckled and for a moment Chase panicked. But then he stroked Chase's hair and kissed his cheek. "That was wonderful, darling," he said. "I loved it. As long as you loved it?"

"Oh, no, yes," said Chase as quickly as he could in his sleepy, fucked-out bliss. "Lovely, great, awesome, thank you."

Hunter laughed again but kissed him on the mouth. It was gentle and unhurried. It made Chase feel cherished.

Unfortunately, the problem with frottage was that it left a big old mess and that mess was rapidly cooling on Chase and Hunter's bodies. "Um," said Chase. He awkwardly peeled himself off Hunter. "Sorry."

Hunter caught Chase's chin between his thumb and finger. "Baby," he said patiently, kissing him. "Please don't apologize for a gorgeous fuck like that. I can go get tissues or a wash cloth."

Chase kissed him back. "I'll get it," he said.

As nice as Hunter's offer was, he probably hadn't considered the slim possibility that he might run into Lyla. That wasn't appropriate. But Chase didn't mind pulling his boxers back on and dashing to the bathroom across the hall. He dampened two cloths and made it back without getting caught.

Once they were cleaned up and comfortable Hunter reached over and slipped his own briefs back on as well. Then he hooked his arm around Chase's middle, pulled him into the bed, then yanked the comforter over them both.

"I think I have to sleep now," Hunter said, kissing behind Chase's ear.

"Me too," he replied.

It was so silly. But in that moment, all Chase could think was that this had been his father's room for so many years, and he'd just had sex with the most stunning man he'd ever had the good fortune of getting into bed. *Take that, Dad,* he thought in savage triumph.

"What's so funny?" Hunter asked, nuzzling his nose into Chase's damp hair.

"Nothing," Chase said and lifted Hunter's hand up to kiss the back of it.

It was nothing. This night wasn't about getting back at his dad for all the unforgivable things he'd said to Chase when he was alive. It was about deepening his connection with Hunter. Developing something special and precious between them.

Chase remembered to set his alarm for the morning, then enjoyed being the little spoon against Hunter's warm, strong body. Sleep came easily after that.

Maybe things in his life were finally starting to look up?

CHAPTER EIGHTEEN

HUNTER

It was probably the unfamiliar bed that did it. That, and being away from Trooper.

Hunter had no idea where he was when he woke up thrashing and yelling. He battled with the sheets, trying to break free as his panic rose.

"Hunter," a voice called out to him. "Hunter! It's okay!"

There were hands gripping his face. Hunter's own hands flew up to grab at the wrists, his eyes blinking in the dim morning light. What the hell was going on?

"Hunter," the voice said soothingly. "Hunter, baby, it's me."

The word 'baby' broke through the fog. He stilled, gasping for air as he focused on the worried face looking at him.

"Chase," he croaked. He allowed himself to be hugged. But Hunter felt so ashamed. Chase had trusted him enough to let him into his home, his bed. And Hunter had probably just scared the shit out of him. "I'm so sorry."

"It was just a nightmare," Chase said. He stroked his damp hair and kissed his cheek. "You're okay."

Hunter shook his head. How did he explain they weren't just nightmares? "I'm sorry if I frightened you."

Hunter squirmed uncomfortably as Chase leaned back and studied him in the pinkish pre-dawn light. "My alarm's going off soon anyway," Chase said, kindly avoiding the issue. "Are you all right?"

Hunter took a deep breath and ran his hand down his face. "Yeah," he said flatly. The adrenaline was still leaving his system. "I'll be fine."

Chase nibbled on his lower lip. "Is it...?" he began to ask, sounding unsure. "Uh..."

Hunter took his hand and urged him to lay back down next to him. Their heads rested on Chase's pillows as they looked at each other. "You can ask me anything," Hunter said, playing with Chase's fingers. "But if you were wondering if it was a PTSD thing...yeah. A little."

Chase swallowed and stroked Hunter's cheek. "I can't imagine what things you might have seen."

"I don't want you to," Hunter said quickly. He had a strong constitution. He wasn't freaked out by blood or bodies. Otherwise he never would have signed up to be a combat medic. But no one should have to see some of the horrors he had witnessed.

Chase shook his head. "You can talk to me if you need to," he said. "Anytime. But aren't there groups for guys like you? People who know what you've been through. You can get together and talk."

Chase was so sweet. Hunter shifted so they could cuddle close. "Yes," he admitted. "There are support groups. But I've been doing okay. Trooper's helped me a lot." He didn't mention the driving thing. He was still hoping that would go away by itself eventually.

"Really?" asked Chase.

He was running his fingers along Hunter's arm and placing little kisses on the skin. It was incredible how easily they had become acquainted with each other's bodies.

"Yeah," said Hunter. "It's easier to calm down and come back to reality if someone else is there. It's...it's not just bad memories. When you get a flashback, your brain thinks you're actually there again. So your heart rate is elevated and the adrenaline gets released."

Chase held him tighter. Hunter breathed out long and slow, allowing his body to relax.

"Do you feel better now?" Chase asked.

"Much," Hunter told him honestly.

"You know, um," Chase began. He pulled away from their embrace so Hunter could fully see his face. "Next time you stay over...Trooper could stay, too. If that would help?"

His cheeks went bright red and he struggled to look Hunter in the eye. Hunter understood it was brave of Chase to make the offer, but if he'd just look up, he would see the joy on Hunter's face.

"Next time, huh?" he said impishly. He nuzzled his nose against Chase's so he could maneuver in for a kiss. Chase had to feel how big his grin was. "I like the sound of that."

He wasn't sure he would rush to bring Trooper over. Hunter had walked him right before he'd come over to Chase's house and would do so again before going to work that morning. He'd also left puppy pads down, so hopefully he wouldn't have had too many accidents. It was important for Hunter not to rush Chase into this. So maybe he would wait before bringing his dog over and making an even bigger deal out of this than it was already.

Speaking of which, he was waiting for the big crisis to kick in. He'd had sex with a man last night. At twenty-eight, he had been foolish to think he'd known everything there was to know about himself. It turned out, he had no idea how much he loved rubbing his cock against another guy's until now.

He studied Chase's happy, sleep-rumpled face. "What?" Chase asked.

Hunter shook his head. "Nothing. Nothing bad," he amended. "I think I might be gay. It's kind of awesome."

Chase's face broke into a wide grin, his eyes sparkling. "Yeah?"

Hunter nodded. "Talk about a late bloomer."

But Chase shook his head back and hugged him close. "I'm glad I was your first."

So was Hunter. What they'd shared last night was precious. He'd always treasure it. But he hoped it was just the start of something even more wonderful between them.

It didn't go unnoticed by him that Chase still hadn't called himself gay. Or bi. He'd had sex with at least one woman, after all. Lyla was proof. But still, Hunter was slightly disappointed he still didn't feel comfortable to open up about that side of him, not even to Hunter.

He didn't address it though. Chase's alarm went off and they needed to get going with their morning if they were all going to make it to work and school on time.

Chase offered Hunter the first run through the shower and he sped through as fast as he could. He knew how not to hang about in the bathroom thanks to his years of service and strict timetables. He also had the added pressure of not wanting to get in the way of Chase and Lyla's morning routine.

By the time Chase came back into his bedroom, dripping wet with a towel wrapped around his waist, Hunter was dressed and ready to leave. He was momentarily distracted by the sight of Chase's almost naked body. How had he not known he was gay before? He'd seen plenty of naked guys during his time in the military. None of them had elicited this kind of response in him before.

He hurriedly pulled his mind out of the gutter. They didn't have time now for any more making out.

"Did you want me to sneak out?" he asked, remembering what he originally wanted to ask before Chase's lithe body distracted him. "Before Lyla wakes up?"

Chase slipped some boxers on underneath his towel before dropping it to the floor. Hunter got a glimpse of his ass before the underwear covered it. Thanks to internet porn, he'd had a crash course in the kinds of things two guys could do together in bed. Despite his naivety, he was already imagining what he and Chase could get up to next time.

Chase pulled on socks and black work pants. "Actually," he asked, his cheeks a little pink. "I did ask Lyla already if she would mind you being my, uh, best friend. How she felt about you being around more. She really likes you." He yanked his JJ's polo shirt over his head and briefly hid his face. "So, um, if you *were* planning on staying over again...more than once... well, maybe it would be best to be honest with her and say hi now?"

He was properly blushing again by the time he turned to face Hunter. In spite of his promise to himself they wouldn't make out again, Hunter had to cross the room and slip his arms around Chase's slender frame.

"I'll follow your lead, Daddy," he said.

"Ew, no," Chase said. He laughed and batted at Hunter's chest. "Not my kink." Hunter laughed too and stole a kiss.

"I'd be more than happy to stick around for breakfast, though," Hunter said. "Honesty is always good in my book, too."

Hunter was surprisingly nervous as he sat at the table waiting for Chase and Lyla to come out of her room. He sipped at his coffee, hoping the caffeine would make him feel more confident.

Halfway through his cup, Hunter heard a shriek come from Lyla's room. She came racing out into the main open-plan area of the house. Hunter recognized the stuffed dragon she held in her arms.

"Hunter!" she yelled, running over to him.

Her hair was a riot of red curls. Hunter was a bit alarmed at how Chase was supposed to get a brush through that. Now the very early start made more sense to him.

She was wearing pajamas with unicorns all over and the words 'I believe in humans' written on the top. She flew to Hunter's side with her arms open and launched herself and Bo-Bo into his lap. He had little choice but to grab her and settle her on his legs. He immediately looked to Chase to make sure that was okay. But he just smiled warmly at Hunter.

"Daddy said you're friends again!" Lyla said, bouncing up and down. "I'm so happy. Please don't fight anymore because he really likes you and he was sad and so was I. Is Trooper here? I want to show him my bedroom because I was silly and forgot to show him last time, but I think he'll like it."

She stared at him with big green eyes that Hunter now recognized right away as being Chase's. He rubbed her back, then lifted her to sit in her own seat. "It's just me today. I'm glad Daddy and I are friends again too. He said you wouldn't mind me having breakfast with y'all."

He deliberately didn't imply that he'd slept over. Sure enough, it didn't seem strange to a five-year-old that he might have gotten up at the crack of dawn to come over and eat with them.

"Of course," she said earnestly. "What cereal do you like? We have all kinds."

Hunter allowed Lyla to pick the most ridiculous and sugary breakfast for him while she chatted on about her school day ahead. Hunter looked up at one point to see Chase just watching them with a smile.

It felt right in a way that warmed Hunter's heart. He wondered how many more mornings with this little family he could look forward to.

He hoped the answer was 'a lot.'

CHAPTER NINETEEN

CHASE

Chase was frustrated that he spent the next few days waiting for the bubble to burst. He couldn't seem to help it. Rather than basking in the glow of new-relationship bliss, every time Hunter's name flashed up on his phone, he panicked that he was calling or texting because he'd changed his mind and remembered he was straight after all.

But it was never the case. Hunter texted him at least once every day. Sometimes they'd have conversations that spanned hours, sneaking moments throughout the workday or across the evening. By Saturday, Chase finally began to trust that this wasn't all going to go up in smoke.

They made a plan to all meet at Moore Wood to walk Trooper around the park. Chase was so nervous he put Lyla's T-shirt on inside out and almost tried to force her feet into the opposite shoes.

"Daddy," she said with a giggle as he knocked his spoon out of his breakfast cereal and splattered milk across the table. "You're being funny."

"I'm being silly," he said with an exaggerated eye roll, making her laugh more. He was. What did he think was going to happen? He couldn't enter into every date thinking Hunter was going to break up with him. Hunter would get pissed off.

So he did his best to take deep breaths while he finished getting them ready. Finally, he managed to wrangle himself and his daughter out the door.

They parked in the public lot not far from the tennis courts. Trooper went berserk on the end of his leash when he saw the two of them approaching him and Hunter.

Chase looked around, but he didn't spot Hunter's Toyota. Odd. It seemed like he never drove anywhere anymore. Maybe it was because he had Trooper so he was taking every chance to walk him he could. He certainly was an energetic little fellow.

"Trooper!" Lyla cried and sprinted toward him.

She had never once remarked on the fact the little pup only had three legs instead of four. As far as she was concerned, he was absolutely perfect, just the way he was. Chase watched her throw her arms around him and couldn't help but feel proud.

Chase walked up to Hunter and smiled. He wasn't sure they should kiss hello in front of Lyla, or indeed, in front of anybody. Luckily Hunter picked up on his vibe and just smiled as well.

"Hi," he said. That one single word sent a quiver down Chase's spine. He needed to get a hold of himself.

They began a slow stroll around the park's perimeter. Lyla and Trooper happily chased around any other dog they met, making friends with them all.

"Have you had a good week?" Chase asked, almost tripping over his tongue. He wasn't sure why he asked. They had been talking every day. But still, it was different in person.

Hunter nodded. "Yeah. I'm settling into work now. My colleagues are nice, friendly. I'm even starting to recognize a couple of the patients."

Chase nodded. "That's good," he said. "My work was... uh...well, work. It never really changes. Nobody shouted at me this week," he added with a laugh.

Hunter's hand twitched and he swayed closer to Chase briefly. But then he looked around them at all the people milling about in the park. He sighed.

"I'd really like to hold your hand," he said.

Chase stared at him. "Oh," he said dumbly. "Um, really?"

Hunter nodded. "But I don't want to make you uncomfortable."

Chase scanned the area. He didn't know anyone he could see. "How are you so good at this already?" he asked. He tried to make a joke out of it, but he was serious. "Aren't you afraid of what people might think? You hardly know anyone yet."

Hunter shrugged. "If someone's going to have a problem with me being with you, with being gay, then they're not worth knowing."

Chase admired his spirit. But he was also sad at his naivety. He wondered if Hunter would still feel that way after people had been dicks to him several dozen times for no better reason than disagreeing with his sexuality.

At the same time, though, Chase couldn't help but feel like he had the right attitude. If they had each other to rely on, what did it matter what anyone else thought?

He had spent his whole life trying to hide from this town. Trying to disappear from everyone around him. But now he had Hunter, who for some inexplicable reason wanted to stand by his side. Hold his hand.

What did he have to lose?

Chase frowned. His job. His home. His *daughter*. But then he looked back over at Hunter, who had such a fond look on his face for him. Hunter made him feel safe. Like he would protect him against anyone trying to take those things from him. Chase couldn't really imagine Hunter letting anyone do that to himself, after all.

Chase bit his lip and carefully pulled the hand closest to Hunter out from his pocket and extended it over in silent invitation. He looked ahead, too afraid to fully acknowledge what he was doing. But then Hunter's large, strong fingers slipped around his, and Chase felt vaguely faint.

The grin was unstoppable on his face as he peeked over at Hunter. He was equally smiling back at him, his joy clear.

"Well done." He whispered it so quietly Chase wouldn't have known what he'd said if he hadn't been watching his mouth move. Chase felt his cheeks get warm. He glanced down at their connected hands, then out over the park.

The world hadn't stopped. No one had tripped over themselves in horror. Nothing had been set on fire.

More to the point, Chase marveled at how *amazing* it felt to simply hold hands with someone he cared about. Hunter's skin was warm as always, but where Chase usually ran cold, his entire body now felt like a furnace.

He grinned wider, feeling giddy.

Then Lyla noticed them.

She stopped in her tracks several feet away from where she had been throwing a stick for Trooper. The puppy continued to dance around her legs, but she stayed still as Chase and Hunter approached.

"Do you want to let go?" Hunter asked out of the corner of her mouth.

But Chase shook his head. "No hiding, remember?" Even as he said it, though, his heart was going crazy in his chest. If this upset Lyla, he wasn't sure what he would do.

She continued to stare at their joined hands as they came closer, a frown on her little face.

"Hi, sweetie," said Chase, trying to sound more confident than he felt. "Is everything okay?"

She curled a strand of her hair around two of her fingers and pulled as she continued to think.

"Hunter," she said, dead serious. "Do you love my daddy?"

Chase spluttered and Hunter laughed. They came to a halt in front of her. "Um," Hunter said. "I like him very much."

"Like other mommies and daddies?" Lyla asked. Chase felt a bit sick. This was a mistake. It was too much for her to understand. She had enough to work through with Amanda being gone without taking this on as well.

He went to pull his hand away from Hunter's.

"You could be my other daddy."

Chase and Hunter both froze at the same time.

"Oh, no, honey," said Chase. "No one's trying to replace your momma."

She tugged her hair again. "No," she said with a hint of impatience. "Not like Momma. Momma said you were my daddy but not her..." She struggled for the word. "...her husband. Because you were best friends. Momma said you needed 'a nice man to love like Noah and Becca's moms love their dads.' So Hunter can be like that, can't he?"

She stared up at them with her mouth hanging open. She squinted against the sun and continued to frown, assessing them with her young mind.

Chase didn't know what to say. He was such an inexperienced parent he didn't know how best to handle this. Shame was creeping into his gut. He shouldn't have been so selfish.

But Hunter squeezed his hand. "So...you know some daddies like boys and not girls, hon?" he asked Lyla.

"Sure," she said with a shrug. "Mindy in my class has two moms. And Tyler doesn't have a mom *or* a dad. He lives with his nanny and pops."

"So, you don't mind me and Hunter holding hands?" Chase asked, his heart in his throat.

She looked at him with confusion. "No," she said. "You should have just said he was your boyfriend. You're so silly, Daddy."

She flicked her hair and skipped off, Trooper galloping behind her.

Chase and Hunter stood for a moment, both equally stunned.

"Well," said Hunter eventually with a laugh. "I guess that's that then?"

Laughter bubbled out of Chase like it was making an escape. Relief flowed through his whole body. "Um, I guess so?"

Cautiously, they began walking again. Chase was scared to say anything in case it broke the spell. But gradually, he began to relax. If Lyla really didn't mind, then all he had to worry about was other people giving them a hard time.

That, and Hunter himself. Chase still had all his hangups about whether or not Hunter truly liked him. Or was even really gay. And if he was, why would he settle for Chase?

But the longer they held hands, the more Chase started to actually have faith. Hunter kept smiling at him and rubbing his thumb over Chase's knuckles. If Chase suspended reality, he was able to imagine that was what normal couples felt like.

Opposite-sex couples, he corrected himself. Because if there was one thing he was *finally* starting to understand, it was that there was nothing abnormal about him.

They came upon a farmers' market. Chase thought it was maybe in the park every Saturday, but he hadn't visited enough to know for sure. There were stalls displaying all kinds of fresh fruits and vegetables, and even a few with hand crafted goods. Naturally, Lyla went running up to the first stall in wonder, grabbing something that looked like a turnip.

"Lyla, honey," Chase called. "Be careful." He didn't want her to drop anybody's produce. But she was conscientious as always.

The guy standing at the booth snapped to attention. Chase recognized him. Was he one of the guys that delivered goods to the store, maybe?

"Afternoon, gentlemen. Oh, and young lady!"

Chase fought the urge to release Hunter's hand as they came to a halt in front of him. He was so terrified of being judged. But the guy had clearly seen them and didn't even bat an eyelid as he waved them over.

"Bottom of the food pyramid, vegetables," he said to Lyla. "You want to grow up big and strong?"

"Like a princess!" she declared, staring at the unusual items on display. Since they had organized her Leia costume, she was all about princesses again.

"Those are weird, aren't they?" the seller carried on. Then he spotted her wild red mane. "Oh, a princess! An archer, by chance? With hair like yours?" He grinned when she nodded hard. "Well, rutabagas will help!"

He presented Lyla with the turnip-like thing with a flourish. Chase smiled while Hunter laughed, squeezing his hand.

The seller was gay, Chase realized with a lurch. He wasn't covered in glitter, but Chase had no doubt. The guy winked at them and popped his hip with natural ease. He wasn't shy to present as a little fem, the way Chase knew he did if he didn't keep himself in check.

Wasn't he afraid of people not coming over to his stall if he acted like that? Clearly not.

His eyes sparkled as he turned from Lyla to address Chase and Hunter. "What about you?" he asked. "Carrots? Potatoes? Or something more exotic?"

"I think we're good," said Hunter in a friendly manner. He glanced at Chase, his gaze warm. Chase knew the seller clocked it, but he actually seemed to sigh wistfully at them. That they were a real couple he was...what? Jealous of? Chase couldn't imagine anyone ever being envious of him for anything.

But Hunter was gorgeous. Who wouldn't want him? And here he was on Chase's arm. That was pretty incredible.

He turned back and smiled at the guy, who was still doing his best to charm his way into a sale.

"Oh, you don't want to wither away without your vitamin K."

The guy clicked his tongue. Like expensive, fresh vegetables should obviously be on the top of Chase's shopping list.

He clearly didn't know Chase, which was actually a comforting thought.

"That would be bad," Chase admitted, throwing the guy a bone.

But he did have a point. Chase would love to be the kind of dad who got only the best for his little girl. Hunter would be that kind of dad, he realized. That was way too far ahead to be thinking. He did give Hunter a little nudge though, briefly imagining a future where they came to the market every Saturday.

Trooper put his front paw up on the table, only just big enough to sniff at the vegetables.

"Oh!" the seller cried. "And an adorable dog. Does the adorable puppy like fresh vegetables? Of course he does! Because he's adorable!" He scratched the dog's ears and then straightened up. "He recommends lots of everything."

Chase really did laugh at that. It was hard to argue with that logic.

Hunter started picking up leeks and onions. "I could get something for dinner tonight?" he suggested.

Chase's heart melted at the idea Hunter just assumed they would be spending the whole day together. Chase hadn't told him yet that Lyla was in fact due to go for a sleepover at Geena's house later. Chase had been brave and reached out to her mom after he promised her he would. She'd seemed delighted to get the girls together.

Chase bit his lip. "That would be great," he said.

Eventually, they thrilled the seller by buying several items. Lyla gave him a wave goodbye and blew him a kiss, which the guy reciprocated. Chase would have to say hello the next time he came into the store.

They walked on, idly looking at other stalls as they passed. Chase felt a little dizzy from everything that had happened in the last hour. His brain was whirling.

When they were out the other side of the market the crowd quieted down considerably. Chase felt something bubbling up inside him that he'd never experienced before.

"I'm gay," he blurted suddenly, startling a jogger as she went past. But Chase ignored her. He turned and looked at Hunter. "I guess you know that, but I've never, ever actually said it out loud, but I am. So gay. I knew since I was tiny. I really liked Amanda as a friend, and I wouldn't change a single thing that happened between us. But I...I'm gay." He ran out of steam and wondered if he was going to cry.

Hunter stopped and stared at him for a good ten seconds, his smile getting bigger and bigger. Then he pulled Chase into a hug. "You're amazing."

Chase laughed, the last of his nerves breaking free. He really wasn't, but if Hunter thought so, that was worth something at least.

He felt a small arm wrap around his leg. Lyla was hugging him and Hunter at the knees. "Cuddles, Daddy," she said.

Chase laughed and bent down to pick her up so the three of them could have a hug all together. Trooper hopped about at their feet.

In that moment, Chase thought he knew what being part of a family might feel like.

CHAPTER TWENTY

HUNTER

CHASE SURPRISED Hunter by telling him that Lyla had a play-date for the evening. A sleepover in fact. He went adorably pink as he stammered through the explanation of how Lyla knew Geena from Little League like the waitress Tammy had told them. They were good friends and her mom was only too thrilled to have Lyla come over. So he and Hunter could be alone. All night.

Hunter had only teased him a little by pretending he might have other plans, but Chase was a bundle of nerves. So it was more fun to see his face light up when Hunter admitted he was only teasing and he'd been really hoping they could spend the night together.

Hunter found it strange. He was essentially announcing he wanted to have more sex with Chase. In his limited experience with second dates, he usually played it coyer than that. He liked the illusion that some-thing may or may not happen depending on the mood. But the way he and Chase were looking at each other, it was pretty clear what direction they wanted the night to head.

Seeing as they didn't have to stick to Lyla's usual routine, Hunter suggested Chase come over to his house. Hunter had been making a real effort to straighten up his new place the last couple of weeks. Now he could admit it was partly because he was waiting for the opportunity for Chase to visit again.

He was taking some spare boxes out to the garage when his neighbor Shelly came home. With her was a cute young woman with short hair, several piercings and tattoos, and a small carryon that she pulled out of the car.

"Hunter!" Shelly called, waving to him. He placed the boxes down and wandered over the yard with a slight amount of apprehension. "How lucky we caught you. You know I've told you so much about my daughter." She extended both her hands out toward the young woman standing beside her. "Ta-da! This is Ginger."

Ginger rolled her eyes but gave her mom a good-natured smile. "Hi, Hunter," she said with an air of a person who was indulging someone they loved. "It's nice to meet you."

She reached out her hand so they could shake, which Hunter obliged. She had a slim, boyish figure which made her seem young, although now they were close up he'd guess they were about the same age. Her hair was dark and her eyes blue underneath the thick black liner she'd applied. She gave off an alternative sort of vibe.

Strangely enough, Hunter felt himself warming to her right away. Although he was glad he'd never agreed to a date for obvious reasons.

"Hi there," he said. "You visiting for the weekend?"

Ginger nodded. "I live in Houston, so I like to come home

when I can. To see the dogs," she added, raising her eyebrows. "Mom's just here to feed me."

She patted her mother on the head while Shelly scoffed. "I'll put you right back on that train," she pretended to grumble. Then she switched her attention to Hunter with a devilish grin. "Say, how about you bring that adorable puppy of yours over and have some iced tea with us?"

Hunter could see where this was going a mile off. So could Ginger by the way she shook her head slightly. Hunter didn't want to offend anyone, but he felt he had to nip this in the bud now.

A cold shiver ran over his body, despite the heat of the spring day. This was his first time coming out to someone he didn't really know. He'd known deep down that Connor would accept him as he was. But if Shelly and her daughter didn't like him being gay it was going to make living next to each other very awkward.

"Um, thank you, ma'am," he said with a nod. "But I'm afraid I'm short on time. My boyfriend is due over soon."

He couldn't really blame Chase for being so terrified to come out of the closet in that moment. Knowing that these people could change their opinion of him over something he couldn't control was pretty darn petrifying.

"Boyfriend?" Shelly repeated.

Her and Ginger's faces transformed into matching expressions of disappointment. This was it. Hellfire and brimstone. Hunter winced in anticipation.

"Oh," Shelly said, throwing up her hands. "Why didn't you say so? I could have introduced you to my *son*. He lives right here in town!"

Ginger shook her head. "You're just Koby's type and all,"

she said with a sigh. "All big and handsome and caring like. Ain't that a shame."

"A real shame," Shelly said with a smile.

Hunter blinked. "Oh," he said, still processing his shock. "Oh, okay. Well, I'm terribly sorry."

Shelly blew a raspberry. "Nah, don't you worry about it. So, who's the lucky fella? We'll be expecting an introduction."

They both looked at him eagerly. Hunter faltered for a moment. Was Chase really ready to come all the way out of the closet?

His instinct told him he could trust the Duvalls, however. Especially if they had a gay relative themselves. "Well, his name's Chase, ma'am. Chase Williamson. He's been kind enough to take a chance on the new guy in town."

"The Williamson boy?" Shelly asked. Her expression softened. "Oh, that's just wonderful he's met someone like you. I swear, I thought he'd never come out."

"You know him?" Hunter asked, curious.

She nodded. "You remember, Ginger?" she asked her daughter. "He was a couple of grades below Koby. I think Koby tried to make friends a few times, but the poor dear was too scared to say boo to a goose." She turned back to Hunter. "His daddy was a mean old piece of work. Ain't nobody around here missin' that son of a bitch."

Ginger raised her eyebrows, making Hunter guess she didn't cuss often. "Oh," he said, unsure how else to respond.

Shelly shook her head again. "Well, I'm just pleased as punch for you boys. You come say hello sometime. I'll be glad to see Chase looking happy for a change."

"I'm sure Koby would like to see y'all too," said Ginger

with genuine affection. "This is a great neighborhood for the queer community. He'll introduce you to folks."

With that, the two women bade Hunter good day and headed inside Shelly's house to face the excitable pack of dogs.

Hunter stood outside for a moment. "Wow," he said to himself. That went about as well as it could have possibly gone. He felt proud of himself. Taking a chance and being brave had paid off.

He couldn't wait to tell Chase.

CHAPTER TWENTY-ONE

Dinner went extremely well. Hunter had called his mom for another recipe he could make for their date. He'd dusted and vacuumed and tidied any bits away that hadn't found permanent homes into the garage or under his bed.

He'd also been to the drug store and bought supplies. It was ridiculous how much he'd felt like a guilty teenager at the checkout. But luckily, the clerk hadn't looked twice at Hunter or the enthusiastic number of condoms and lubricant he'd purchased.

Chase had worn a dark gray shirt that really made his eyes shimmer. Hunter's stomach flipped every time he looked over at him. It didn't help that it caused Chase to blush and smile shyly with increasing frequency. Hunter's mouth watered for him.

But first they made it through two whole courses of dinner without jumping each other. They talked about shows on TV, local history and a little light politics. Whatever Chase said about being a high school dropout, he was a smart, interesting guy. He certainly held Hunter's attention.

"Koby Duvall?" Chase repeated when Hunter told him about meeting Shelly and Ginger earlier. He rubbed his stubbled jaw. "Yeah, I remember him. I can't believe his mom's your dog breeder and she knows who I am." He laughed. "What are the chances of you moving in next to her?"

Thankfully, he wasn't mad at all that Hunter had outed him. It seemed he was warming up to the concept of coming out of the closet. Hunter was glad. He wanted Chase to be living a more honest, happier life. He reached over and took Chase's hand.

"Ginger said there are a lot of LGBT people around here," he said, probing gently. "She seemed pretty certain Koby would want to meet us."

The way Chase had talked in the time they'd known each other made it sound like the whole town was homophobic. But the more Hunter had seen here, the less accurate that seemed. He was starting to wonder if it wasn't just Chase's dad who had been the asshole, making Chase feel like everyone else hated him and thought he was a freak.

Chase smiled at him. "Um, as long as Shelly doesn't want to set you guys up anymore, then yeah. Sure." He looked apprehensive at the idea of reuniting with Koby or trying to make new friends. He'd been on his own for so long, Hunter guessed. But he was so proud of him for trying. For taking a chance.

Hunter lifted Chase's hand and started kissing his fingers. He'd never been this bold, physically, with any of the women he'd dated. It added to his theory that he'd been gay all along, just waiting for the right guy to come along and open the door.

Chase bit his lip and mumbled something. He appeared to be having trouble taking his eyes off Hunter's lips on his own fingertips. Hunter grinned. They'd eaten enough of their dinner to move on to dessert as far as he was concerned.

"Maybe I should call Geena's mom," Chase stammered. "Check on Lyla."

"Lyla's fine," Hunter said. "Let's look after you for once, hmm?"

"Uhh," said Chase. His pupils were getting bigger, darkening his lovely green eyes. His breathing hitched, too. Hunter took that as a yes.

Hunter tugged on his hand, encouraging him to stand up from his chair. He stumbled the couple of steps over so he was by Hunter. Hunter put his hands on Chase's slim waist and looked up at him. His lips were wet as he panted. His hands trembled on Hunter's shoulders.

"Mr. Williamson," Hunter said, his voice low in what he hoped was a seductive tone. "I would very much like to take you up to my bed and keep you there until morning."

"Uh huh?" Chase said.

Hunter licked his lips and rubbed his fingers in little circles on Chase's hips. "How do you feel about that?"

"Yes?" Chase squeaked. He cleared his throat and swallowed. "I mean, yes please, Mr. Duke." He blushed a gorgeous shade of crimson.

"I've been thinking up all kinds of delicious things I could do to your beautiful body," he said. He ran his hands up Chase's flanks then down again to grip his tight ass. Seeing as his crotch was level with Hunter's face, it was pretty easy to spot he was already perking up in his pants. "Would you like me to tell you? Or show you?"

"Show," spluttered Chase with a fervent nod. "Show and talk and touch and...um..." His eyes were drifting shut.

Hunter stood, then leaned down to capture his mouth in a sweet kiss. His hands gripped a little tighter around Chase's waist. Chase let his hands slide down from Hunter's shoulders to rest on his chest.

"I want to make love to you," Hunter said. Chase trembled from head to toe in his arms.

"Please," he mumbled into Hunter's mouth.

Hunter kissed him a little while longer. Then he pulled back, taking Chase's hand. Chase blinked as if he was coming out of a daze. But he soon nodded at Hunter, giving him the go-ahead.

Hunter led Chase up the stairs. Trooper was sound asleep in his dog bed and Hunter hoped he wouldn't mind him shutting the door on him, at least for a few hours.

His heart was pounding in his chest, but more from anticipation than nerves. He still wasn't wholly convinced he knew what he was doing. But he was excited to fumble his way through with Chase as his teacher.

In anticipation of the evening ahead, Hunter had set up his room a little differently. He'd switched the main lights off and had half a dozen flameless candles on to light the room. He'd splurged on some new throw pillows and a fluffy rug to drape across the end of the bed so it looked like a fancy hotel one. Then he'd placed a bouquet of red roses on his dresser standing in a vase, a bottle of Champagne chilling in an ice bucket with two glasses, a bowl of strawberries and some chocolate dipping sauce that he had several intended uses for.

He let Chase walk in first and take in the scene. Hunter had to say he was pretty proud of himself. But when he slipped his arms around Chase's waist from behind, he felt him stiffen, not in a good way.

Hunter paused. "Is it too much?" he asked.

Chase gripped onto his hands that were resting on his stomach. "You did this...for me?"

Hunter was tempted to break the sudden tension by joking he'd done it for his other boyfriend, and that Chase would have to do. But he sensed something was off. So instead, he hugged Chase's back to his front and kissed his neck gently.

"Of course," he said. "I thought my boyfriend needed to be extra spoiled." *To make up for a bunch of other shitty things that he's been through,* Hunter added mentally.

Chase's grip on his hands got tighter. "Boyfriend?"

Hunter kissed his neck again. "That's what I told Shelly," Hunter admitted in a murmur. He nuzzled his nose against Chase's hair. "If that's what you want?"

Chase looked over his shoulder. His eyes were glassy and he chewed on his lip. It made Hunter's heart ache. "I'd love to be your boyfriend," he said in a whisper. "No one...no one's ever done anything this thoughtful for me before."

Hunter touched his lips to Chase's. It wasn't like a lot of kisses they'd shared before. It was reserved but full of promise. Tender. Chase turned in his arms and cupped his hands on either side of Hunter's face to kiss him more intensely.

"I'm all yours," he assured him.

Hunter closed the door and turned his music system on quietly. He'd found a romantic playlist before that was several hours long. Perfect for the night ahead. "I'm all yours too," he said, leading Chase over to the bed with him.

Chase allowed Hunter to slowly unbutton his shirt while they kissed. Hunter's lips devoured Chase's, then strayed along his jaw up to his earlobe, sucking on it as he eased the shirt over Chase's shoulders, letting it drop to the floor.

"You taste so good," Hunter whispered.

He'd been wondering since Tuesday if he had the guts to go down on Chase like he'd done for him. Now the moment had come, he found he was salivating at the thought of swallowing his pretty cock. Hunter marveled yet again how he could possibly have not realized he was gay for so long.

Chase swayed under his touch. Hunter ran his hands over his slim, firm body. He tweaked his nipples, wondering if Chase was as sensitive as he was. The way he gasped suggested he wasn't far off.

Hunter sucked on Chase's neck as his fingers worked the fly of his pants. Chase trembled, allowing Hunter to touch him however he wanted.

There was something extremely erotic about having someone completely naked while you were still dressed. Chase's cock strained upward as soon as it was freed, begging Hunter to touch it. He wanted to admire Chase for a while longer, though.

"Lay on the bed, baby," he murmured into his ear.

Chase nodded, dropping to the mattress and resting his head on the pillow. He watched Hunter with wide eyes as he crawled up next to him. Hunter propped himself up on one elbow and ran his free hand over Chase's body, loving how he quivered at each touch.

"I want to make you feel so good," he said.

Chase turned his head, his wide green eyes serious. "You do?" he said. He took hold of Hunter's wrist and moved his hand so he could kiss his palm. "It's so nice just to be held."

Hunter considered Chase for a moment, then cuddled him

close, their bodies lining up from head to toe. How touch-starved had Chase been for most of his life? His dad sounded like an absolute asshole and his mom had left fifteen years ago. From the sounds of it, he'd never dated, only hooked up with guys. So how much had he actually been touched in a meaningful way during his life by another human being?

No wonder he always had Lyla on his hip or was kissing her hair. It wasn't about anything sexual. It was showing love through physical connection.

The realization made Hunter's heart hurt. Chase was made to be cuddled. To be cherished. He was sweet and pure and should feel like that every day.

Without saying anything, Hunter gently released Chase to strip as quickly as he could. Chase watched him silently. He'd wilted somewhat, but Hunter wasn't worried about that. They had plenty of time for them both to get hard again. Hopefully more than once if Hunter got his way.

Chase gasped as Hunter joined him once more, bringing their naked bodies together. "I want to be inside you," he murmured between kisses.

"Yes," Chase whispered back.

His hands were roaming nonstop all over Hunter's body. They were both damp already with a light sheen of perspiration. Hunter wanted Chase dripping and panting, hot and enveloped by Hunter's entire body.

"How do you like it?" Hunter asked. Chase was regarding him with such wide eyes. He wished he knew what was going on in his lover's head.

"Uh," said Chase. Hunter assumed he would be nervous to ask for what he wanted, but Hunter was determined. "I don't mind."

Hunter smiled indulgently. "No, baby," he said gently. "You're teaching me, remember? I want to master all your favorite positions."

Chase bit his lip and still looked unsure. So Hunter stroked Chase's cock and nibbled on his collar bone, sucking and kissing a mark there. Chase inhaled and shuddered.

"On your back?" Hunter asked. "On your stomach? All fours?" He grinned and kissed his way up Chase's throat. "I could pin you against the wall or bend you over the dresser. Make you scream."

He didn't really want this time to be rough. Tonight was meant to be sensual, loving. But he would do whatever Chase desired.

Chase was already a beautiful mess, gasping shallow breaths and thrusting his cock into Hunter's hand. "Hands and knees," he managed to say. "Good angle. Feels so good."

He grabbed Hunter's face and kissed him with fervor. Hunter's cock was coming back to life with force, throbbing between his legs, aching for Chase's hot, tight hole. Hunter reached for the chocolate sauce he'd left on the dresser.

"I read rimming is a great way to stretch," he said, wiggling the tube of body paint.

His cheeks felt a little warm. He wasn't used to much dirty talk. But he had decided he wanted to take on the role of Chase's provider, his caretaker. He was in charge right now and his job was to make Chase feel as amazing as possible. If that meant discussing things more explicitly, he was determined to do it.

Chase giggled. It was a gorgeous sound. "You got chocolate paint for us to play with?" he asked, still laughing. "You're not messing about, are you?"

"Actually," Hunter said, pretending to be serious and study the tube's label. "I'm hoping to get *very* messy."

Chase howled with laughter and covered his face. Hunter used the opportunity to grab one of the strawberries from the bowl. He drizzled some of the sauce onto the tip then nudged Chase's side with his elbow.

"Here, try it," he said with a grin. "It's all organic and the chocolate's fair trade and stuff."

Chase snorted, but obediently let Hunter feed him the fruit. He licked the sauce from Hunter's fingers and it made shivers run all over Hunter's body.

He was surprised when Chase reached over to get a strawberry himself. He was a little clumsy, but he diligently spread some of the paint on the tip, then fed it to Hunter. He loved it.

Was it bad he was having so much fun when they had barely even touched each other's cocks yet? Let alone asses. Seeing the happy glow on Chase's face as he licked fruit juice from his fingers made Hunter decide things were only going to get better.

He stole a few kisses, tasting the sweetness on Chase's mouth. "Lay back," he told him again.

When Chase was snuggled against the pillows, Hunter squeezed a little of the paint onto each of his nipples and rubbed it over the hardening flesh. Chase moaned and screwed his eyes shut, writhing when Hunter then proceeded to lick it all off.

"Jesus, fuck," Chase said, gnashing his teeth. "Whoa, good – very good."

Hunter laughed. But as soon as he was done, Chase pushed him onto his side and went on to return the favor. Hunter had never realized how sensitive his nipples were. He was in danger of letting his neighbors know exactly how much as well. He stuffed his fist in his mouth and tried to hold on to a shred of composure.

He was getting needy for more. So was Chase by the looks of it. Chase dropped back amidst the many throw pillows, then coated his cock with a good portion of the chocolate. Tossing the tube aside, he then licked the sauce from his fingers as his gaze bore into Hunter's.

"Still hungry?" he asked.

It was one thing to receive a blow job. It was another to give it. It didn't get much gayer than that. But as Hunter kissed his way down to Chase's straining, glistening erection, all remaining doubt evaporated. He was as gay as a rainbow, and he wanted to suck every smear of that chocolate off Chase's cock.

Chase moaned and grunted and thrust into Hunter's mouth as Hunter sucked and swallowed him down. Hunter, in turn, did his best not to splutter or cough and focused on his breathing.

Despite Hunter's misgivings, giving head was incredible. Chase's cock was hot and heavy on his tongue. Hunter could have stayed down there and made Chase come down his throat quite happily. But he'd promised to do this properly and take them all the way.

"Turn over," he said, wiping his mouth and repositioning himself. Chase hurriedly flipped so he was on trembling arms and legs, his entrance in the air, waiting for Hunter to tend to.

He began slow, rubbing some more of the paint against Chase's tight ring with his fingers, pushing a digit inside. He hadn't realized there were certain kinds of paint you could get that would work in harmony with condoms and lube, but luckily, he'd picked a good one by accident. So he used the chocolate to begin to stretch Chase out, first with one finger, then two.

He still wasn't entirely sure how he felt about putting his mouth on someone else's most intimate area. But Chase really did look appetizing in that moment. Hunter decided he would give it a try and see how he felt. If it was unpleasant, he'd just continue with his fingers.

It was worth it for the utterly sinful noises that escaped Chase's mouth. He wailed and cursed and whispered the most delicious things to Hunter as he kissed and licked the chocolate from his hole. It was surprisingly enjoyable, especially knowing it was causing Chase so much pleasure. He relaxed beautifully for Hunter, too. Soon he knew he was ready for him.

Being a medical professional, Hunter had ensured he had tissues and wet wipes within reach. He wanted them to be as comfortable as possible. He hastily cleaned off his hands and face, then concentrated on suiting up and dousing his cock and Chase's hole in plenty of lube. The research he'd read couldn't stress enough how much a lot of lube helped everything go smoothly.

Still, when Hunter began to press the tip of his dick into Chase, it felt impossibly tight. Amazing for him, but he worried it was uncomfortable for Chase, even hurting him.

"Is that okay?" Hunter asked. His whole body was trembling, as was Chase's. He found it difficult to talk.

Chase nodded. "Big," he said, a laugh bubbling out of him. "But good. It's okay, go slow."

Hunter did as he was told and took his time. Gradually, Chase allowed him in. His cock pushed further and further into that incredible tightness. He felt like his eyes were going to roll into the back of his head.

"Holy fuck," he stuttered. "You feel so good, baby. It's amazing, you're amazing."

Together they worked until Hunter bottomed out. Chase had fistfuls of the comforter in his grasp, his knuckles white from the effort. They both sucked down lungfuls of air.

"Oh my god," Chase whispered over and over.

Hunter reached forward, wrapping his arm around Chase's middle and pulling him to his knees. Hunter kissed his lips gently while they both gasped for air. "You're doing so well," he told Chase. He stroked his weeping cock and kissed along his jaw. "So well for me, baby."

"Want to move," Chase said. "Fuck me, oh my god, Hunter."

Hunter nodded and kissed his cheek once more before releasing him. Chase dropped back on all fours and pushed his ass back against Hunter's groin. It was all the invitation Hunter needed to begin pounding him into the mattress.

It took an embarrassingly short amount of time for them both to come, but Hunter was more than ready for it. It didn't take him long to find Chase's prostate and make him squeal. He managed to babble that he was close, so Hunter reached around and jacked Chase off in time to his thrusts. As soon as he started spurting over the sheets, his body went rigid and his ass clenched around Hunters cock sublimely. A heartbeat later, Hunter was coming too.

They collapsed together on the bed. Hunter was sticky with sweat and lube and chocolate and cum, yet he couldn't have been more content. "Holy fucking Christ," he managed to stammer a few moments later. That had easily been the best sex of his life.

Chase pawed clumsily for his hand, then linked their fingers together, kissing Hunter's knuckles. "Thank you," he rasped, his voice hoarse. "Perfect."

Originally, Hunter had planned for them to stumble into the shower in his en suite and have some more fun washing the chocolate off each other. But he was utterly exhausted. Chase was almost asleep in his arms.

Carefully, he eased out of Chase and discarded the condom. Then he plucked a few wet-wipes from the packet and gave them both enough of a clean that they could get under the sheets. He'd have to wash all the bedding no doubt, but for now, they'd be comfortable enough to sleep.

Chase draped his whole body over Hunter's, spooning up to his side like a koala. He planted a couple of kisses on Hunter's chest and stroked his arm. Chase looked so peaceful it made Hunter's heart swell.

Almost immediately, Chase's breathing evened out as he fell into a deep sleep. Hunter stayed awake a while longer. He ran his fingers through Chase's soft hair and along his back. This was total bliss. And the best part was, they were only just getting started.

CHAPTER TWENTY-TWO

CHASE

It was amazing the difference a few weeks could make.

Chase stood in the middle of his living room, looking around at his home. There was so much color and character to it now. He was startled to realize how drab it had been before Lyla.

And before Hunter of course.

Chase felt his cheeks get warm like they always did when he thought of his boyfriend. But he had gotten enough of a handle on it by now that he hoped he didn't blush. Loving, generous, *sexy* Hunter. Being a medical professional, it wasn't all that surprising that he had come along and breathed life into Chase's broken heart.

Between him and Lyla, Chase never really stood a chance.

His daughter was everything to him. Chase deeply regretted not being a bigger part of her life before. He understood it had been because he didn't think he was worthy. But now he was beginning to appreciate that maybe that wasn't actually true. When Lyla had no other options, he *had* to step up and be good enough. Luckily, Hunter was helping him to appreciate his own worth more every day.

Because the truth was, if he really wasn't good enough, there were other drastic options that could be taken. Amanda's parents were still making rumblings about petitioning for custody, or if social services wanted to take it even further, they could put Lyla into the system immediately.

The thought made Chase physically sick. He would never let that happen. Not while he had an ounce of fight left in him.

He had to remind himself that there was no reason for that to happen, though. He and Lyla might have gotten off to a slightly rocky start. But all things considered, Chase had gone from zero to a hundred on the parenting scale in the blink of an eye. A little whiplash was bound to be expected. Now that the two of them were settled, he had no doubt Mr. Preston would see Lyla was exactly where she should be.

A lot of that was due to Hunter's stabilizing influence on Chase. For that, and so many other things, he was incredibly grateful.

They just had to get through this visit. With any luck, it would be the last.

Lyla herself was in a winner of a mood when the day came. It was vastly different to the last time Chase had faced Mr. Preston. She'd helped pick out an outfit herself, one of her favorite T-shirts with robots all over. They'd picked it from the 'boys' section at the store. Chase still smirked about how affronted the woman on the checkout had been when she realized it was for Lyla.

Lyla had sat and allowed her hair to be brushed and braided again after school. She had even helped Chase tidy the place up so it was as neat as could be.

A selfish part of him had almost asked Hunter to come over again. But Mr. Preston clearly had issues with same sex couples and Chase didn't want to aggravate that. Besides, it was a Wednesday evening and Hunter would have been at work all day. The last thing he wanted was to deal with this shit on top of all that.

He would though, Chase knew. That was one of the things that made Hunter so wonderful – his generosity. But Chase didn't want to abuse his kindness. He could manage this alone.

He'd keep Hunter by his side in his mind. Knowing he was there whenever Chase needed him was almost as good as having him there for real. Until he could see him again in the flesh, Chase would try and use his motivational words over the past several days to keep his head on straight.

It had been a week and a half since the chocolate date. Chase still shivered every time he caught a whiff of any candy. Hunter had destroyed him in the best possible way. They had been able to squeeze in a couple more less extravagant nights together since, but Chase knew he'd remember that date for the rest of his life.

Chase was starting to trust that Hunter wasn't going to change his mind and back out of this. In the past, it hadn't mattered to Chase if he got with a guy struggling with his sexuality. It didn't affect the hour or two they spent together. But Chase was very invested in whether or not Hunter was going to realize he was dating a man, not a woman, and freak out. The more time they spent together, though, the less likely that seemed to be.

He needed to file Hunter away for now and focus on getting through Mr. Preston's visit. "You've got this," Chase muttered to himself as he polished the coffee table.

There was no reason for social services to take Lyla away from him. She had a stable, loving home. She was getting into fewer fights at school. And although Chase didn't earn a lot, his pay check was just enough to get them through each month. This was going to be fine.

Hunter believed in him. So for once in his life, Chase was going to try and believe in himself.

"Are you ready, kiddo?" he asked Lyla.

"Sure!" she cried. She struck her 'superhero pose' with one fist in the air and the other on her hip and she jumped her feet apart. Chase imitated her.

"Good job!" he said before dropping back into a normal stance. "Okay, so, Mr. Preston might seem a bit scary, but he's a nice man. And if he likes us, that means you can stay living with Daddy. We're very likable people, aren't we?"

She nodded keenly. "We're awesome."

He gave her a high five. "So, nothing to worry about." He almost believed it. "Hey, do your pose again," he said, getting his phone out. "Let's take a video to show Hunter."

"Cool," said Lyla as he pressed record on his camera. He laughed as she did it a couple of times then spun around and held out her shirt. "Look, Hunter, robots!" she said.

The knock at the door made them both jump. Chase quickly dropped his phone on the coffee table and stood up with Lyla by his side. "Okay, you ready?"

"Ready," said Lyla. She nodded and crossed her arms.

The two of them went over and opened the front door together.

"Good evening, young lady," Mr. Preston said in a simpering voice from the porch.

She smiled shyly and stepped back to allow him in. Chase

nodded and offered his hand out to shake. "Good to see you again, Mr. Preston," he said. He managed not to grimace at touching his sweaty palm, but subtly wiped his hand on his jeans afterwards.

Chase watched as Mr. Preston scrutinized his home. "Do you think it's appropriate to have so many photos of the child's mother present?" he asked, making notes in his file.

Not even a hello or chance to offer some coffee. Of all the questions Chase expected him to ask, that wasn't one of them. "Uh, yes," he said. Then he cleared his throat and vowed he wasn't going to stammer again. He didn't have anything to hide here. "Absolutely. We find it very comforting knowing she's watching over us."

Mr. Present sniffed and raised an eyebrow. "I would have thought she would find it distressing."

Lyla moved to Chase's legs and clung to them. Chase rubbed the back of her head and did his best not to scowl. He would appreciate it if Mr. Preston wouldn't talk about Lyla as if she wasn't there. Or worse, like she was some sort of thing. A number in a file.

"Not at all," he said with a smile. "I hope you've seen from Lyla's report cards that she's doing much better now."

"I'll be the judge of that, Mr. Williamson," Mr. Preston muttered, not even bothering to look at him as he scanned his notes. "Did you know my niece and your daughter are enrolled at the same school?" He did look up at that, giving Chase a smile that chilled his blood. "They even attend Little Ladies together. Isn't that nice?"

Chase swallowed. "Lovely," he said, hoping he sounded sincere.

Mr. Preston slid his gaze down to Lyla. "You know Brianna-Grace, don't you sweetheart? She's a wonderful girl."

Chase was very proud that Lyla didn't immediately call the other child out for the bully she was. She just stared at Mr. Preston without responding.

Mr. Preston sighed. "I find your daughter to be very withdrawn and unresponsive, Mr. Williamson," he said, shaking his head. "It's concerning."

"She's not like this normally," Chase said, trying not to get rattled. This was going terribly. "Usually she's very chatty and happy."

"And why isn't she now?" Mr. Preston asked.

Because you're an asshole, Chase thought to himself.

"I guess she's just shy," he said vaguely.

Mr. Preston wrote something down in his notes. "Brianna-Grace has informed her mother, my sister, that Lyla struggles with socializing. That she's an odd child. Does this bother you, Mr. Williamson?"

Chase wanted to punch him. How *dare* he call his little girl odd. He'd had to put up with people in this town thinking he was a freak his whole life. There was *nothing* wrong with Lyla. He'd be damned if he was going to let her be put down like that.

"I am confident my daughter is a healthy, happy girl," Chase said. "I don't believe your niece and her are in fact friends, so maybe Brianna-Grace just doesn't know her very well. But I can assure you that I have no worries that Lyla is doing spectacularly after such a difficult time in her life." He took a breath and tried to stop himself shaking.

Mr. Preston closed his file. "I've had numerous reports that she is struggling, Mr. Williamson. Not just with socializing, but with her studies and controlling her temper. It is my belief that an unstable home-life is the root cause."

Chase's eyes widened and he briefly glanced around his near-immaculate little home. "Unstable?" he repeated.

"What is your relationship with Mr. Duke?"

Chase blinked and his heartrate leaped up a notch. "Mr. Duke?"

"Hunter Duke," Mr. Preston elaborated. "He was present the last time I visited. How would you describe your relationship with him?"

Heavenly. Divine. None of your fucking business. "We're good friends," Chase said. He refused to let his gaze flinch away from Mr. Preston's.

"The two of you were apparently seen together in Moore Wood the weekend before last," Mr. Preston continued. "Holding hands at the market. Is it safe to say you are...*romantically* involved?" He practically sneered the word 'romantically,' like he was gagging on it.

Chase glanced down at Lyla. She was looking at him with a frown, like everything about this conversation was confusing her.

But he knew she wasn't troubled by him dating Hunter. If anything, she had more faith in their relationship than Chase.

"We're partners, yes," he replied, trying not to sound defensive. "Lyla is aware of the situation and comfortable with it. Obviously, she is my priority above all else."

Mr. Preston looked amused but there was also a cruel glint in his eye. "I would think if that were the case," he said softly so Lyla would struggle to hear, "you'd think twice about flaunting your persuasions in public."

Chase's blood ran cold. "I don't-" he began.

"It's not healthy for a child to be subjected to this kind of mockery," Mr. Preston said. He seemed to be enjoying himself. "It isn't in their best interest for their sole guardian to be humiliating them in such a manner. If I were you, Mr. Williamson, I would take a serious look at your priorities and decide what you want."

What the hell was he suggesting? That if Chase wanted to keep custody of Lyla, which of course he did, he would have to stop seeing Hunter?

He could have screamed if he wasn't concentrating so hard on not crying. Hunter was the best thing that had ever happened to him. There was nothing wrong with their relationship. They weren't a threat to Lyla in any way.

He had considered if a new relationship might add another unstable element to her life when it was already going through so much change. But Hunter and Trooper had been an undeniably reassuring presence for Lyla and Chase.

If Hunter was a woman, they wouldn't be having this conversation.

Chase knew, deep down, that he would always bring shame to Lyla because of who he was. The other kids and their parents would always gossip about him. Especially if he had a public relationship.

The only way to protect her would be to keep his love life private.

Or stop it all together.

"She shouldn't be sucking her thumb," Mr. Preston steamrollered on. Chase looked down to see Lyla had indeed popped her thumb in her mouth.

"She only does that when she's tired, or..." Or deeply upset. He thought that wouldn't be good to mention now.

Mr. Preston rubbed his mustache and sniffed loudly. His eyes were narrowing at Lyla, making her shrink back behind Chase's legs. "Mr. Williamson," he said, a touch of scandal to his words. "Is that a *boys'* T-shirt?"

Chase's blood ran cold. "It's a robot shirt," he said faintly. "Lyla's new favorite."

"Are you denying it's from the boys' clothing section, though?" Mr. Preston demanded. He was shaking with anger. "As if your kind weren't bad enough, you have to inflict this on the children as well?"

Chase felt hot tears at the back of his eyes. "What?" he stammered.

Mr. Preston advanced and jabbed a finger against Chase's chest. "This is disgusting," he said. "She's a girl, not a boy. I'll be damned if I let you pervert her with your sick ways."

"I – I know she's a girl," Chase said. What was he implying? That he was hurting Lyla by letting her pick a shirt from a different section of the store? Lyla was hugging his leg and he reached down to cradle the back of her head.

"Mr. Williamson," Mr. Preston spat. He was a couple of inches taller than Chase and loomed as much as he could over him. His breath smelled of stale coffee and cigarettes. "You and your kind disgust me. I don't care what the law says. I believe you are unfit to care for this child and will make it my personal mission to see her removed from your custody. I am giving you *one last chance* to clean up your act and behave like a responsible parent." He sneered, his lip curling under his whiskers. "We'll see if you choose your perversions over your flesh and blood."

Chase was trembling and he could feel Lyla was too. He couldn't believe this was happening. It wasn't fair. Mr. Preston was a prejudiced asshole, yet he held the power to destroy Chase and Lyla's lives.

"I...I..." Chase stammered. But Mr. Preston flashed him a nasty grin and turned on his heel.

"You have one week," Mr. Preston called out over his shoulder as he wrenched the front door open. *"One week."* He slammed it behind him, leaving Chase and Lyla stunned and silent in his wake.

CHAPTER TWENTY-THREE

A storm was brewing.

Hunter looked up into the gray sky and hoped the rain would hold off at least until the parade was done. It would be absolutely miserable for everyone to get soaked in their costumes. The bystanders wouldn't appreciate it either.

The route had already been changed because the insurance building on Victory Boulevard had caught fire. Someone had told Hunter at work that there had even been an explosion. It was therefore probably sensible to keep large numbers of the public away from that area, but the last-minute re-arrangements had caused a good deal of stress for a lot of people.

It wasn't especially cold at least, even with the winds that whipped up every few minutes. The crowd was still in good spirits, eagerly cheering on the floats as they passed. Particularly the ones with the kids on them.

The Spring Festival was quite a big deal around Hidden Creek, Hunter had gathered. They had talent shows that the schools put on, beauty pageants for the girls, vegetable growing contests and charity drives. It felt like a great community project to someone who had never felt all that connected to the towns they'd lived in. Hunter took it as a sign he was finally settling in.

There was just one thing troubling him as he waited for Lyla's float to come slowly down the street.

Chase.

Something wasn't right.

Hunter tried not to worry, but Chase was being extremely quiet. He was reluctant to meet Hunter's eye and his smiles were distressingly sparse. Maybe he was anxious about how Lyla would do. But all she had to do was stand and wave as the float took her down the street. Her costume had looked awesome this morning, so even if some of the other girls were mean about her looking different, she should still be okay to stand up for herself.

"Hey," Hunter said warmly into Chase's ear. They'd not been able to meet up all week, but as it was a Saturday, Hunter was hoping they could make the most of the full day together. Only if Chase wanted to though. He turned and looked at Hunter. "Are you okay?" he asked him directly.

"Fine," mumbled Chase.

His hands were stubbornly in his pockets, which was a shame as Hunter really wanted to hold one. Trooper pulled on his leash in the other, trying to get Hunter's attention because that was what puppies generally did.

"You seem tense," Hunter said, not giving up. "Are you worried about Lyla?"

Chase shrugged, making Hunter think he was partially right. "Kids can be jerks," Chase said by way of confirmation.

Hunter felt his hackles raise, quite literally. "Is someone picking on Lyla?" he asked. "Do we need to talk to someone?"

"There is no *we*," Chase blurted, flashing an ugly look at Hunter. "She's *my* daughter."

Hunter felt like he'd been slapped in the face. "Okay," he said slowly. "I was just trying to help."

"Well, you can't," said Chase. He was determinedly staring out over the parade, but his voice was trembling. "You can't just swoop in and fix everything all the time, all right? Some things can't be fixed."

"Have I done something wrong?" Hunter asked with a sinking feeling. He felt completely blind-sided. As far as he was aware, everything had been going great.

Chase scrubbed his face. The crowd was jostling around them and he glanced at the bodies pressed against him like he was worried who was listening.

"No," he said in a small voice. Hunter felt a little relief at that, at least. "Of course not, I'm sorry. I've just got so much running around in my head."

Hunter also looked at the people in the throng, but nobody seemed to be paying any attention. "Do you want to talk about it? Later, if you don't feel comfortable?"

"Why do you have to be so nice?" Chase lamented, shaking his head.

Hunter was starting to get seriously concerned. He didn't like the way Chase was talking. He placed his hand on Chase's back as he leaned in to speak to him again...but he felt Chase flinch at his touch.

Sickness washed through Hunter as he dropped his hand again. "Chase," he said, trying to stay calm. "You're freaking me out."

Chase chewed his lip and looked tearful. The noise of the parade and the heaving crowd was claustrophobic. At least Lyla's float was coming up soon. Hunter could see the little princesses all waving about thirty feet away.

"Can we just watch the show?" Chase asked, obviously seeing it too.

Hunter knew he should probably say yes. This day was about Lyla, after all. But this thing with Chase was still so new to him and he didn't know what he'd done wrong or how he could fix it. What had changed between now and last weekend?

"I'd love to," Hunter said. "But I'd really like to hold your hand as well. Is that not possible?"

Chase clenched his jaw. "People can see us," he said simply.

Coldness washed over Hunter's skin. "Are you ashamed of me?"

Chase made a frustrated noise and turned to look Hunter in the face. "It's not you, okay?" he all but snapped. "You're fucking perfect. But people talk around here, all right. I know being gay is all new and shiny to you. But for those of us that have suffered all our lives, we know there are consequences to being out." He turned back to face the street. "I should never have done this."

Lyla's float was upon them. Hunter was too stunned to do anything but wave at Lyla along with everyone else. She was the only non-cartoon princess on the whole thing, but she didn't seem to care from the way she laughed and waved at the crowd.

Thunder rumbled overhead. Trooper pulled on his leash and whined.

"Should never have done what?" Hunter asked. He wasn't sure he wanted to hear the answer.

Chase's shoulders were so tense Hunter was worried they might snap. "Look," said Chase through gritted teeth, "I have to think about Lyla first. I can't be selfish. So, maybe this wasn't such a good idea."

"What wasn't?" Hunter asked, trying not to get mad. But he wanted Chase to be the one to say it. Hunter wasn't going to jeopardize anything.

"Us," Chase said. His voice was tiny and his eyes glassy. "At least, not right now."

Hunter's heart plummeted. He clung onto hope, though. All wasn't lost.

"What does us being together have anything to do with Lyla?" he asked gently. Shouting would only push Chase further away. "I don't get in your way looking after her, do I?" He'd be mortified if that was the case.

But Chase shook his head. "Hunter," he said, sounding pained. "This isn't about you. You haven't done anything wrong. But I need to be the best dad I can for Lyla or they're going to take her away from me. Amanda's parents are still debating my suitability and so are social services."

Hunter remained flummoxed. He knew Mr. Preston was an ass, but what could he object to so strongly? Chase was a fantastic father.

"Do they think you being in a relationship is damaging for Lyla?"

Chase chewed his lip, watching Lyla's float disappear from view. "Being in a relationship with a man. Yes."

Hunter did very well not to explode, but he did clench his fists and close his eyes for a few seconds. "Those homophobic, bigoted, narrow-minded *dinosaurs.*" He reached out and grabbed Chase's arm. "No. Do *not* let them poison you like this! There is *nothing* wrong with you!"

Chase pulled away and began pushing his way out of the crowd, heading toward where the floats finished up. Hunter and Trooper followed right behind.

"Mr. Preston disagrees," Chase said bitterly over his shoulder. "That's all that matters. Please, just try and understand."

Hunter understood. That didn't mean he had to agree. "Chase," he said. He tried to get his attention as they marched down the street behind those still watching the parade. Thunder rumbled overhead again and Hunter thought he might have felt a drop of rain. "Chase, stop. *Are you breaking up with me?*"

He jogged in front of Chase to see his face. It was anguished.

"I don't want to," he whispered.

He side-stepped around Hunter, staring at the ground. Hunter fell into step with him, his heart pounding. "Then don't," he said. "Mr. Preston can't discriminate against you like this. It's illegal."

"Yes, he can," Chase said. "They can all make my life as difficult as they like. But more to the point, they can make *Lyla's* life miserable too. That's not something I'm willing to risk."

"So, what," said Hunter, finally getting angry. "You're just never going to date? Hide away from the rest of the world, forever?"

Chase shrugged. "Maybe?"

"That's not a life!" Hunter cried. "That's not fair!"

"Life isn't fair," Chase snapped. "I'm not a kid anymore. I

know this. Sometimes, you just have to get over the crappy hand you're dealt."

"You're being rash," Hunter insisted. "You're too close to it all. We just need to talk about it. Baby, come on," he said, trying to smile despite his worry. "We're a team, we can get through this."

For a moment, Chase looked like he wanted to believe that was true. Then he shook his head and began marching down the street again. "I have to make sure I'm there to pick up Lyla," he said. "Can't give them a single excuse to call me irresponsible."

"Fine," said Hunter, still walking beside him. "But I would like to come with you and discuss this some more. Rationally," he added with emphasis.

"I don't know what to say!" Chase cried, flinging his arms out. "Mr. Preston thinks that me being gay is a danger to Lyla and a risk to her social standing. A lot of people agree with him. So if I don't date and just stay in the closet, doesn't that make everything easier?"

"For those bigoted assholes, yeah," said Hunter. "They'd love to stop any change in its tracks. Well, tough shit. I care way more about your happiness than their stupid prejudices. Lyla is a great kid and you are a *great* dad. They can't deny that!"

Chase crossed his arms and shoved his way through a particularly dense part of the crowd. The pickup point wasn't too far away and lots of parents were searching for their kids.

"Face it, Hunter," Chase said. "You can't fix everything."

Hunter wanted to tear his hair out. Trooper barked up at him from where he was running along at his feet. Hunter wasn't going to give up though.

"You're just so terrified that something good has finally come along in your life," Hunter said, staring at Chase's unhappy profile. "You think it's bound to blow up in your face, so you're trying to sabotage it before it can hurt you first."

"That's insane," said Chase, not looking at Hunter.

"Is it?" he shot back.

He had to make Chase see he wasn't talking sense. Hunter wasn't sure he could take the heartbreak if not.

They arrived at the pickup point. It was easy to spot where the princesses of Little Ladies' Etiquette were being corralled by all the pastel taffeta and glitter. Hunter followed Chase as he made his way over with single-minded purpose.

Hunter didn't want to come between Chase and Lyla. The mere thought horrified him. But he was damned if he was going to give up on him and Chase just because of a few bumps in the road. He was confident they could make this all okay as long as Chase gave them a chance.

Chase had come to a halt in front of the princess group, scanning them for Lyla. Even though it was in the Leia buns, her red hair still made her easy to spot. Except...Hunter couldn't see her.

"Lyla?" Chase called. He turned his head left and right. "Lyla!"

"Mr. Williamson!"

Chase and Hunter both turned to see two girls pushing their way through the crowd toward them. Hunter recognized Tammy, their waitress from Rocket. A girl a bit bigger than Lyla was holding her hand, leading the way. Lyla was so small for her age this girl was probably also five or six.

Hunter remembered Tammy saying she had a sister,

Geena. That was who Lyla had gone to visit for a sleepover two weeks ago.

"Girls?" Chase said as they approached. They both looked extremely worried.

"Mr. Williamson," Tammy said again. She appeared much younger in jeans and a kitty cat T-shirt than she had looked serving at the restaurant. "Geena, tell him."

The little girl looked up tearfully at Chase. "Mr. Williamson," she said, wringing her hands. *"Lyla ran away."*

CHAPTER TWENTY-FOUR

CHASE

As the heavens opened, Chase felt like the world fell out from underneath him.

"What do you mean she ran away?" he stammered and the cold rain hit him. Nausea rolled in his stomach and a wave of dizziness threatened to buckle his knees.

"You're not in trouble, sweetie," Hunter said to Geena as the girls huddled together.

None of them had an umbrella. As always when there was a storm now, Chase's heartrate doubled. He tried not to think about the hurricane from last summer. Hunter placed a hand on the small of Chase's back. This time, Chase didn't shrug him off. He felt like it was the only thing keeping him standing.

"Can you tell us what happened," Chase asked, shielding his eyes from the deluge. "Where's Lyla?"

"We don't know," said Tammy. Geena shook her head, the wind whipping tendrils of dripping hair around her face.

"She was crying," the little girl explained. "She said she wanted to hide away."

Chase spun in a circle, his hands in his dripping hair as he desperately looked through the throng of soaked people buffeting around them. "LYLA!" he bellowed over the thunder.

"Why was she crying?" Hunter asked. He still had his hand on Chase, anchoring him. "Who was she talking to. They might know where Lyla went to hide."

Little Geena stuck her nose in the air and scowled. "Brianna-Grace made her cry," she said, making it clear how she felt about Mr. Preston's niece. "Lyla said she didn't want to stay and she wanted to go to her secret base."

Geena pointed through the crowd at a very pretty girl in an expensive looking wig that gave her hair just like Lyla's, hiding away her blonde locks. She was looking bored under an umbrella that a man was holding above her while he and Brianna-Grace's mother screamed at one another. The umbrella holder was presumably her dad. Brianna-Grace caught Chase looking and gave him a sly smile accompanied by a slow wiggle of her fingers.

Chase turned away from her and whispered a string of profanities that the girls were definitely too young to hear. His panic was causing little black spots in front of his eyes. He couldn't see straight or get enough air into his lungs.

"Lyla," he whimpered. "Oh my god, where the hell is she!"

Hunter gripped his shoulders and looked at him with stern brown eyes. "We'll find her, it's okay," he said.

But the place was heaving as people tried to escape the sudden storm. Anyone could pick up tiny Lyla and walk off with her and no one would notice. Even if she screamed, chances were people would think she was just having a tantrum.

"It's not okay," Chase said, trying to wipe the water from his eyes. His teeth were chattering and he thought he was maybe going to vomit. "Oh god, my baby girl, fuck. She's...I can't..."

"Geena, did Lyla say anything else?" Hunter asked, still holding onto Chase. "Anything at all sweetie?" Geena looked guilty. "Hon, you're not in trouble. You've been an amazing help. Please, can you tell us anything else?"

"She was really mad," Geena said, pulling at her fingers. "She, um, hit a few people."

That sounded like Lyla all right.

Hunter squeezed Chase's shoulders. "Chase," he said. "Think. To you know where she might have gone?"

"No!" Chase wailed. "No, I don't, because I hardly know my own daughter and I'm a terrible parent!"

Hunter yanked him into a fierce hug, the water in their clothes squelching. "You are a wonderful parent and we're going to get through this together," he insisted.

Chase shook his head and choked back a sob. "I'm so sorry," he said. "I didn't mean any of those things I said to you. I don't want you to leave me."

Hunter kissed his cheek. "I'm not going anywhere." He let Chase go and gave him a searching look. "Now, does Lyla have a favorite place in town. Would she go to a friend's house?"

But Chase was frowning as a memory came back to him. "Wait. Wait," he said. "We were talking about Brianna-Grace the other day. Lyla was upset then too and she said something about a secret base..."

Why couldn't he remember? He thought she was using her imagination. But what if it was a real place?

"Girls, which way did she go?" Chase asked.

Geena stuck out her tongue and thought about it before pointing to the right. Tammy was shivering uncontrollably. They needed to get into the dry.

"That's the way to Moore Wood," Hunter said with a frown.

They could just about see the entrance to the park in the gloom from where they stood. People were still jostling around them, making it hard to see clearly.

But Chase felt his eyes go wide. "She mentioned a waterfall," he said. "I thought she'd been watching too many superhero cartoons. But...could she have been talking about somewhere that really exists?"

It was a long shot, but hope blossomed in his chest. At least they had a possible direction to head toward.

"A waterfall. Are you sure?" Hunter asked.

Chase nodded. He wished he'd listened to her properly now. She'd talked about what friends she'd allow inside. She said he could come in if he wanted. But as for a location...

"That's all I have," he said, blinking back the tears. She was going to be okay, she had to be.

Christ alive, what if social services found out about this? Even if they got her home safe and sound, he'd never be allowed to keep her. He'd *lost* her. He wasn't fit to be her guardian, he was a disgrace.

"Chase!" Hunter said firmly, giving him a little shake. "There's a small waterfall in the park. I spotted it near the tennis courts and angry geese. Maybe she's there?"

"Really?" Chase asked.

Hunter nodded. "Come on. She can't have gotten far. If we hurry, we might catch her if that's where she's gone."

Chase nodded back, trying to pull himself out of the fog of panic. Hunter was right. He was always right. "Yes, okay. Yes, let's go."

Hunter looked at Tammy and Geena. "You girls did a great thing. Are you here with your folks?"

Tammy shook her head, water droplets flying off from her hair. "We're supposed to meet them at the ice cream parlor."

Hunter smiled. "Okay. Well, you go on and find them. Then Chase will call your mom as soon as we find Lyla. Sound like a plan?"

The girls nodded.

"Thank you, mister," Geena said to him. "Good luck, Mr. Williamson."

They turned and made their way through the rain and the thinning crowd. Chase didn't realize how badly he was shaking until Hunter pulled him in for another hug.

"It's okay," he said. "We need to go now. Do you feel up for that?"

Chase nodded and rubbed his back. "We have to hurry." He took Hunter's hand and dashed toward the park with Trooper scampering along beside them.

He didn't give a flying fuck who saw them holding hands this time. Hunter was his rock. He was part of this damn family, no matter what Mr. Preston said.

"Thank you," he said.

Hunter frowned at him as they ran down the street. "What for?"

"For not giving up on me," Chase said, fighting down another sob. He could fall apart later. Lyla needed him now.

Hunter gave him a look of fondness mixed with sadness. "I'll never give up on you," he said, squeezing Chase's hand. "Now, let's go find our princess."

Chase nodded and picked up the pace. They would find her. Everything would be okay.

It had to be.

CHAPTER TWENTY-FIVE

HUNTER

Hunter had spent too many days in warzones. He knew how to use his adrenaline to his advantage. But he was entirely unprepared for the rage he felt when he thought about someone hurting Chase's little girl.

He had to remind himself as they sprinted through the heavy puddles that he had no real claim over her. But he cared for Chase, so he cared for her. It was that simple.

He was starting to suspect he didn't just *care* for Chase. That his feelings ran a lot deeper than that. But he could explore all of that once they'd straightened out this mess and found Lyla.

He didn't know who this kid was that had teased her, but he would be having stern words with her parents if Chase let him. He was so mad that they'd upset Lyla enough to make her run off he wanted to tear the world in two. She was so young, so tiny. What if something bad happened to her?

He couldn't think like that. Chase needed him. They had to stay strong. Together.

Hunter knew exactly where he'd seen the waterfall in the park from all his walks with Trooper. He just had to hope there was only one waterfall, and that was indeed where Lyla had gone. They just needed a bit of luck on their side.

Chase was whispering to himself as they raced through the entrance to the park, the American and Texan flags whipping violently against their poles as they passed. He was muttering reassurances that everything was going to be okay. "Hold on, pumpkin," he said. "Daddy's coming. It's okay."

Hunter realized he would do anything – *anything* – to take Chase's pain away.

Trooper barked as he ran by Hunter's feet, the grass beneath their feet muddy and slippery already from the rain. No doubt Trooper sensed their anxiety. He tugged on his leash, pulling ahead. "It's okay, good boy," Hunter said.

But Trooper kept pulling and barking. When Hunter looked up through the downpour he saw they were getting near the waterfall.

"I think she's here," he shouted over the rain as Trooper continued to go crazy.

Chase snapped his head to look at him. "Really?"

Hunter had learned long ago that intuition was a vital tool and he knew when to listen to his. Everything in his being was telling him he was right to keep running toward that waterfall, his dog leading the charge.

"Yes," Hunter said. Like a promise. He had to be right, he had to.

As the town's name would suggest, there was a creek that ran through its borders. This corner of Moore Wood had a brook that flowed by the trees, and at one point it cascaded down several feet over and around a cluster of boulders. They were green with moss and tree branches that crisscrossed in a natural canopy. The waterfall was pretty but not spectacular. Hunter had almost forgotten it was here at all.

As they approached, Trooper pulled him and Chase through the waterfall's spray across the slippery rocks. The creek had swollen already, threatening to take their feet out from under them as the water gurgled over the banks. The tree branches were slashing back and forth in the wind above their heads.

"Lyla!" Chase screamed over the rain and running water, his voice hoarse. "Lyla! Are you here? It's Daddy!"

Hunter continued to let Trooper pull him. Now he was close he could see there was an opening behind where the water was falling, big enough for a child to crawl inside. "Lyla!" he yelled.

"Lyla!" Chase wiped the water from his eyes and peered through the gloom. Hunter spat out the water that was continuously running into his mouth.

"Daddy?" a small voice drifted over the torrent.

Chase burst into tears. He threw himself into the churning water and reached inside the opening. "Lyla! Lyla, please come to me, please."

Hunter pulled a frantic Trooper back as he continued to bark and run in circles on his leash. The water was rushing past them at a terrific rate. He was scared Trooper could get swept away. Or Lyla if Chase couldn't grab her. He watched on with his heart pounding as loudly as the rain.

After several tortuously long seconds, Chase sagged with relief and stepped backward. In his arms was a shivering, bedraggled, crying Lyla.

"Lyla," Hunter bellowed. He seized hold of Chase to help

him get back out of the stream to safety and hugged them both so tightly he was in danger of leaving bruises. "Sweetheart, you scared us."

"I'm sorry," Lyla sobbed. Some of her hair had come out of her buns and was plastered to her face by the rain. She pushed it back over her face. "Trooper? Where's Trooper?"

Hunter bent down and picked up his drenched, ecstatic puppy to join in on the hug. Trooper wagged his tail like crazy and licked all over her face.

"Honey, you mustn't run away like that," Chase said, kissing her head. "You're very precious and Daddy was so worried."

"I'm sorry," she said again with a sniff.

"It's okay, pumpkin," Chase said.

Hunter wasn't sure if he should let them go to have some family time. But when he released his grip, Chase clung to him just as hard as he was with Lyla. So he decided he should stay.

The rain was cold, but the creek water had been icy, and they were all shivering horribly. After a while, Hunter decided they needed to get moving, or their body temperatures were going to plummet. They could still stay hugging and walk at the same time.

"We need to get you guys dry," he said. Chase nodded in agreement. He and Lyla were so small and naturally ran cold. It wasn't surprising that their lips were turning blue, but Hunter could warm them up quick enough if they all moved now.

They began heading back toward town where Chase had parked his car. Chase kept Lyla on his hip. Hunter placed Trooper back on the ground where he was happiest. With his leash in one hand, it meant Hunter could keep his other arm around Chase's waist.

Trooper was dancing around their feet. Every ten or twenty seconds he'd reach up with his front paw and scrabble at Chase's knee, spreading mud everywhere and trying to reach his beloved Lyla. Hunter thought maybe he'd suggest to Chase that Trooper sleep on Lyla's bed that night.

Lyla's white Leia dress was totally sodden and streaked with dirt. She looked down at it forlornly. "My princess dress is ruined," she whimpered.

Hunter shook his head. "We'll give it a wash. It'll be as good as new, I promise."

"Lyla," said Chase gently. He was rubbing her back with every step they took. "Can you tell us what happened? Did Brianna-Grace say something bad to you?"

Lyla's lip wobbled. "Yes," she whispered. She buried her face in Chase's neck. Chase threw Hunter a 'what do I do?' sort of look.

Hunter squeezed his side. "You've got this," he mouthed.

Chase nodded and stroked Lyla's dripping wet hair. "What did she say, hon?" he asked.

Lyla stared at Trooper for so long Hunter thought she might not answer. But then she screwed up her fists and eyes. "She said Leia isn't really a princess and it doesn't matter anyway because she's *dead* just like my *momma*."

Hunter felt his mouth drop open at the horribleness. How could a young child say something that nasty? Chase stumbled and stopped walking as thunder rumbled across the gray sky again. Lightning flashed, making Hunter flinch.

"Oh...sweetheart," Chase said. The emotion was thick in his voice.

"But Leia isn't dead, is she?" Lyla asked between sobs. "I saw her in the trailer for the movie. She's not."

A lump rose in Hunter's throat. Would it be better to lie to her? All he wanted to do was protect her.

But of course, Chase knew that wasn't the right way. "Oh, baby," he said heavily. "The character, Leia, is still in the films. But the actress who played her was an old lady. She died a little while ago."

Lyla hiccuped, her tears mixing with the rain. She pulled at her dress with her little hands. "I don't want her to be dead."

Hunter wasn't sure if she was talking about Carrie Fisher or her mom. Did it really matter? It was okay to be sad about both.

He reached around and cuddled father and daughter in sympathy. "Come on, y'all," he said. He bestowed a kiss on both their heads. "Let's go home."

It took them another ten minutes to get to the car. The parade crowd had largely dispersed thanks to the storm, so nobody looked twice as they sorted themselves out.

Luckily, Chase kept several towels in the trunk of his car to protect the seats when the sun got too hot. When he fumbled with his keys Hunter gently took them from him and got the towels out and unlocked the other doors. Together, they laid them down so their rain-drenched clothes wouldn't ruin the upholstery. Chase secured Lyla in her seat. She was already sucking her thumb and looked like she was ready to pass out any minute.

He closed the door and turned to face Hunter. He was soaked to the skin and looked totally drained. "Will you come back with us?" he asked.

With Trooper's leash around his wrist, Hunter wrapped

both hands around his boyfriend and hugged him tight, ignoring the rain still falling on their heads. "Of course," he said. "You don't even have to ask."

Chase gripped onto the back of his shirt and swayed. "I'm so scared," he said. "I don't want to lose you. But I *can't* let them take Lyla. I can't." He was trembling, both from the rain and the emotion of it all. Lightning illuminated the sky. Then a few seconds later, thunder rumbled overhead. "I hate this town. Why can't they just leave us alone?"

"Baby," said Hunter. He didn't want to upset Chase, but he knew he had to set him right. "It isn't the whole town. I absolutely promise you. I think your dad was a terrible person who brainwashed you into thinking everybody has the same prejudices as he did. And I have no doubt that Mr. Preston is the same kind of asshole. But from what I've seen already, I think most people here would support you, be friends with you, if you just gave them a chance."

For a while, Chase said nothing. He just let Hunter hold him as he presumably thought over what he was saying. "I thought the easiest way to protect Lyla would be to just let you go," Chase mumbled into Hunter's chest. "But I can't do it. I need you."

"I need you too, darling," Hunter said. "But I really don't think we have to choose. We can fight this together. If you want?"

Chase nodded. "I want you in our lives. So does Lyla."

Hunter couldn't help but smile, the rainwater running into his mouth. "Trooper wants that too," he said.

They laughed, two idiots standing in the rain, finding strength in one another.

"Let me take you home, sweetheart," Hunter said. "Let me take care of you."

Chase's grip on his shirt tightened. "Thank you," he whispered.

It wasn't until Hunter pulled Chase's car into his driveway several minutes later did he realize he had driven the whole way and not had even a hint of a panic attack behind the wheel.

CHAPTER TWENTY-SIX

CHASE

CHASE LET a drenched Hunter inside his small house with a sleeping Lyla in his arms and a dripping Trooper by their feet. Hunter remained by his side as they ran Lyla a bath and peeled her out of her sodden clothes. Then Hunter gave them some privacy while Chase washed the grime of the day off his little girl.

Chase pulled on some dry sweatpants and a sweater, but the best he could offer Hunter was his robe while he threw all the sodden clothes in the dryer. Chase felt bad, but Hunter was so much bigger than him. He struggled to even get into the robe and kept his damp briefs on so as to not risk flashing anything.

While Chase patiently dried Lyla's mass of red hair. Hunter dropped Trooper in the bath too and got all the river water, rain and mud off him as well. Between them they shared hairdryer duties, blasting dog and child until they were toasty warm and totally dry again.

"Are you hungry, hon?" Chase asked.

He hadn't bothered putting Lyla in new clothes, opting to dress her in her pajamas right away. But it was a bit early for bed and she hadn't eaten anything since lunch.

But she shook her head from where she was sitting on the end of his bed. "Reab be a stowy?" she asked around the thumb sitting firmly in her mouth. Without waiting for him to answer, she crawled up the bed and flopped in the middle of the pillows.

"You want a story in here?" Chase asked. He glanced at Hunter who had been drying Trooper's fur. The puppy was already asleep on the carpet, snoring softly. Hunter just smiled back at him.

Lyla nodded. "Daddy read a story," she said. He'd noticed that her speech got more babyish when she was tired and feeling especially clingy. He didn't really want to deny her.

He leaned over to Hunter. "Do you mind waiting out in the living room? I can move her to her own room when she's asleep."

"Hunter stay too," Lyla piped up. Chase and Hunter turned to see her pouting at them. Then she patted the space to her left. "Hunter," she said, then patted the other side, "and Daddy."

Chase looked back at Hunter and raised an eyebrow. "Do you want to hear the story about the penguin and his teddy bear?" he asked skeptically. He'd intended to leave Hunter with the TV to watch hockey or something.

But Hunter scoffed. "Of course," he said, like that was a dumb question. He moved to sit beside Lyla, who immediately snuggled up to his side. Chase's heart melted at the sight.

"Um, okay," Chase said. "Give me a sec."

He dashed into Lyla's room and fetched her favorite book

of the moment. He stopped to take a breath and look around at all that she had filled his home with. So many toys and photos and drawings. Little bursts of joy between four walls that had seen so much misery. He hugged the book and allowed himself to feel the contentment he'd been so scared to let in.

When he returned to his room, he found Lyla still cuddled up to Hunter's side. He was singing softly to her. Some old Rolling Stones song, a ballad. Chase leaned on the doorjamb for a little while, just watching the peaceful scene.

Hunter looked up at him and smiled. "Hey," he said, his voice filled with kindness.

"Hey," said Chase back.

Lyla was struggling to stay awake. She would probably only last a couple of pages. That was okay though. After the day she'd had, Chase figured she deserved an early night.

So he sat himself on her other side on the bed and read aloud about the little penguin trying to find his lost teddy in the North Pole. The story was about how he looked for the bear all by himself. But in the end, he needed to ask his friends for help. Chase was starting to feel like he understood the penguin better every day.

Chase knew this book off by heart now. So did Lyla. Therefore, it didn't matter he only read five pages from the middle. What mattered was he was here with his family.

When she was sound asleep, he closed the book and looked at Hunter. He felt such a surge of affection it made his heart ache. "I'll put her to bed," he said, scooping up her little body, heavy with sleep.

When she was tucked in with Bo-Bo the dragon under her arm, he turned on her night light, then closed the curtains and door. Nerves threatened to creep into his belly as he returned to Hunter, waiting in his room. But he wouldn't let them.

This was how it was meant to be. He and Hunter were supposed to be together. He didn't want to fight it anymore, because there was nothing wrong about them being with one another. He didn't care what Mr. Preston said. He couldn't let the social worker's poison come between them.

After moving the sleeping Trooper onto the sofa, he closed the door and leaned against it, his palms pressed against the wood. Hunter had his legs crossed, his hands held loosely in his lap. He brightened at Chase's entrance, scooting over and inviting him to join him back on the bed.

As soon as Chase sat down, Hunter enveloped him in his strong arms. "You did great today," he said, kissing his hair and hugging him tightly. Chase turned into him, stroking his chest through the robe.

"You should have a drawer here," Chase said before he could think. "Some clothes and a toothbrush and..."

He trailed off. What the hell was he saying? That was moving way too fast. Hunter was going to freak out.

Except he wasn't. He was looking down at Chase with such fondness it scared Chase it might be something more.

Was he ready for that?

Did he love Hunter Duke?

"I'd really like that," Hunter said. "I'd be honored, in fact."

Chase bit his lip, physically stopping himself from asking if Hunter was sure. It was time to let go of his anxieties. He had to trust that this was real.

Instead, he moved to kiss Hunter's lips gently, trying to convey his gratitude, his affection.

His love.

"I..." he said, struggling to say the word out loud.

Hunter kissed him again. "Come here," he said, despite the fact they couldn't get much closer.

Chase took it as a challenge, though. He flipped his leg over and straddled Hunter's lap. He slipped his arms around his neck and rested their temples together. Chase took in a deep breath, tasting Hunter's cologne on his tongue. He smelled of fresh pine and warm timber and something spicy that was uniquely him.

Hunter had his hands under his sweater and was skimming his fingers over Chase's ticklish skin. "What do you want?" he asked. His lips were nuzzling their way along Chase's cheek, searching for his lips.

"You," he replied simply.

Hunter chuckled. "You have me," he said. "That's a promise."

"I'm so sorry I tried to push you away," Chase said. He shook his head and buried his face in Hunter's chest. "It was a shitty thing to do after you've been so kind."

Hunter captured Chase's chin between his finger and thumb. Chase let him gently move his head so they were looking at one another again. "You were trying to protect your family. There's nothing more important than Lyla. I understand."

You're my family as well, he wanted to say. But he was too afraid. But he could at least respond to Hunter's other thoughtful words.

"Thank you. I...you're amazing."

"I'm so happy I found you," Hunter said. The words broke something in a beautiful way inside Chase.

He couldn't continue being cruel to himself. He was worth

being loved.

"You too," he said sincerely.

There was less talk after that. Hunter moved his hands further up Chase's back, lifting his sweater over his head and discarding it on the floor. Their kisses were sweet and tender, but Chase still felt the possession in Hunter's touch. He was claiming Chase, declaring to the world that he belonged to him.

Chase allowed him to suck a mark onto his collarbone. It tingled as Hunter used his lips, tongue and teeth to darken the skin. Chase writhed in pleasure as he worked.

Chase never felt he'd belonged anywhere in his whole life. Not at school or work or even with his own daughter and her mother. But finally, Hunter had shown him he had a place in the world.

They worked in tandem, methodically taking all their clothes off. Soon they were naked and slipping under the covers together, joining their flesh in a beautiful union of body and soul.

Hunter laid back, his arms around Chase as he moved on top of him. Their hard cocks rubbed between their bellies as Chase kissed Hunter's lips over and over. Hunter cupped his hand behind Chase's head, holding him steady so they could look directly into each other's eyes while they undulated.

It was slow and intimate and full of simmering passion. Chase whimpered and gasped.

He wasn't entirely in control of himself. Which was probably why the words came tumbling out of his mouth.

"*I love you.*"

He felt Hunter still below him, alerting him to what he had done. Chase cringed and closed his eyes.

"I – I'm sorry," he said. "That's too much. I didn't mean-"

"I love you, too."

Slowly, Chase opened his eyes. Hunter was looking right at him. He reached up and cradled Chase's face with both his hands.

"You...what?" said Chase.

"I love you, too," Hunter repeated. He rubbed his thumbs against Chase's cheeks. "So much."

"Why?" Chase blurted.

Hunter didn't look annoyed like Chase feared he would. He smiled indulgently and brought Chase close for a brief kiss. "Because you're kind," he said. "And sweet and smart and really, *really* gorgeous. I love seeing your confidence grow every day with Lyla because you don't even know how great you are with her. I love every single little thing about you." He rolled his eyes and chuckled. "Even when you don't fold your laundry properly or leave dirty dishes in the sink. Because all those things make up who you are and what you are is perfect."

Chase's mouth was hanging open slightly as he let Hunter's words sink in. He could feel his cheeks going red and he was a little dizzy.

"Oh," said softly. "Um, well, you're totally perfect, too, you know. Smart and kind and um...all those things." It was like sensible words deserted him. "Wow," was all he could add in the end. Then, because he felt like trying it out some more, "I love you."

Hunter laughed, filling the room with warmth. "That sounds so good."

"Yeah?" Chase said.

Hunter nodded. "Say it as much as you like, baby. Any time you want."

Chase kissed his neck and squirmed, rubbing their cocks together again and bringing them back to life. "I love you, Hunter," he said as his boyfriend moaned in delicious contentment. "I love you."

Hunter pushed himself up and crushed their mouths against one another, the mood shifting from sweet to desperate in the blink of an eye. Hunter reached over blindly to the dresser, fumbling as he pulled at the drawer where Chase kept his supplies.

Chase took pity on him and broke the kiss for just a second to retrieve the lube and condom before Hunter tried to use pain killers or a sleep mask on his cock.

Although, actually, Chase paused a second on the eye mask. That might be fun someday.

Not tonight though. He didn't want to take his eyes off his gorgeous boyfriend while they made love. Chase closed the drawer and handed Hunter the rubber while he squeezed lubricant onto his fingers.

Hunter watched wide eyed as Chase reached behind and began to finger himself.

"You look *so* hot doing that," Hunter rasped.

Chase had obviously been watching too many cartoons because he thought Hunter's eyes were going to pop right out of his head with a *ba-dong* noise. Chase bit his lip and preened, loving the way Hunter devoured him with his gaze.

"Yeah?" he asked. "You like that, baby?" Hunter nodded. He ran his hands up and down his thighs, flanks and arms. The sheets were pooled behind Chase, leaving him exposed. It was scintillating.

Hunter rolled the condom on his cock and stroked it, putting on just as much of a show as Chase. Chase leaned down and kissed Hunter's mouth, knowing he'd been an absolute fool to think he could have lived without ever experiencing this again.

He wanted Hunter in his bed every night. He wanted to be by his side. He wanted to grow and achieve more with his life, because with Hunter next to him, he knew he could do anything, be anyone.

Chase wasn't as stretched as he should have been, but he'd waited long enough. He drenched Hunter's cock with lube and hoped it would be sufficient to get him inside. Chase wanted to feel everything.

They both gnashed their teeth and tried to stay quiet as Chase lowered himself down, impaling his body onto Hunter's thick, gorgeous cock. "Oh, baby," he whispered, trembling and sweating. "Baby, yes, baby."

"So good," Hunter said. "Just like that, sweetheart."

Slowly, inch by inch, Hunter filled Chase. The burn was just on the edge of pain, perfect as Chase's body accepted Hunter's. Chase gave himself some time to adjust by kissing Hunter's lips and neck, playing with his sensitive nipples. Hunter teased Chase's cock, stroking it just enough to keep him hard. Chase thought he was going to fall apart.

Of course, Hunter wouldn't let that happen. He held him every step of the way.

When he was ready, Chase rode Hunter hard. The bed rocked but Chase prayed it wouldn't be loud enough to wake Lyla. There was no way he could slow down now.

Hunter was a lovely mess below him. Panting and grunting and whispering sweet nothings. Chase never wanted the moment to end.

Naturally, it had to. But it was in the best way.

"Come for me, gorgeous," Hunter said as he thrust up inside Chase and worked his cock with his hand. "Come all over me. Show me I'm yours."

Chase was ready to explode, so it wasn't too difficult to climax on demand. His body arched as he came hard and fast, painting Hunter's broad, muscular chest with white stripes. Chase loved seeing his seed glistening all over Hunter's beautiful body art.

Hunter gripped Chase's waist tightly as his own orgasm hit. He filled the condom inside Chase, gritting his teeth as he rode through his wave of pleasure. Only then did Chase relax, collapsing on top of Hunter and the mess he'd made between them.

Hunter weakly ran his fingers through Chase's hair. "Amazing," he mumbled.

Chase couldn't agree more.

He'd learned from last time and had a packet of wet wipes also in the drawer, ready to mop them up enough that they didn't have to leave the bedroom in a disheveled state. Chase couldn't stop grinning as they cleaned up, clumsy with exhaustion.

"Stay the night?"

Hunter chuckled and pulled him into a hug under the covers. "As if you even need to ask," he said, shaking his head. "I've missed you so much. Promise me you'll talk to me the next time something upsets you."

Chase nodded. He didn't feel ashamed like he expected. He was extremely sorry to have put Hunter through everything he had, but he was done always blaming himself for everything.

"I missed you too. So did Lyla," said Chase. "It's been a

crappy kind of week. Oh, hey," he added as he remembered something. "I took a video I never showed you. Wanna see?"

Hunter smiled and kissed the back of his neck. Chase wondered if there was any better way to cuddle than being the little spoon. He felt so safe in Hunter's arms like that. "Of course," Hunter said. He ran his hand back and forth over Chase's belly as he reached for his phone.

"That tickles," he protested, wriggling as he thumbed through his phone. He hadn't even re-watched the video of Lyla doing her superhero poses again. He'd been too upset after Mr. Preston's visit.

They would still have to deal with that fallout at some point. But Chase was too happy now to let it spoil his mood. He could deal with that tomorrow.

Instead, he and Hunter chuckled as they watched Lyla enthusiastically showing off for the camera. Then Mr. Preston's knock could be heard at the door.

At which point, something very interesting happened.

"Oh," said Chase.

After a few more minutes, he and Hunter looked at one another.

"I think we've got something there," said Hunter.

CHAPTER TWENTY-SEVEN

WHEN SATURDAY MORNING ARRIVED, a week after the parade, Chase was a bag of nerves. Hunter had done his best to calm him down, but the truth was, there was a lot riding on this visit today.

Lyla knew it too and was acting out. She'd gotten mad when they'd insisted she wear 'real' clothes rather than run around in just her robe pretending to be Ginny Weasley. After tears and tantrums for fifteen minutes, they finally got her to understand that she could put her robe *back on*. She just needed to compromise with pants and a shirt underneath. Chase had the brainwave to make a wand out of a pencil and found an old notebook that she could scribble her spells in.

This was why Hunter was here. To remind Chase that no matter what social services tried to say, he was a brilliant dad. He pulled him in for a hug and made him breathe in and out with him. Hunter felt Chase's heart rate slow down. "It's going to be fine, I know it."

"I don't," said Chase, his voice wavering.

They weren't only facing Mr. Preston, but Dr. Felix and Lyla's principal, Ms. Adrienne Irwin as well. The purpose of the visit was to decide once and for all if Chase was fit to be Lyla's guardian, or whether to go ahead with Amanda's parents' petition for custody.

Hunter knew it was a huge deal and understood Chase's terror. But he also knew there was no court in the land that would take a child away from their loving, committed biological parent. Hunter had insisted on being present at the meeting so Chase had someone battling his corner. He could explain how hard Chase had been working to be the very best parent he could be.

A knock at the door made them separate as they looked toward the front of the house in anticipation. Lyla ran to hug her dad's legs, Trooper faithfully galloping by her side.

"Is that them?" she whispered.

Chase nodded and swallowed visibly. "I think so."

Hunter took a breath and strode toward the door, opening it to reveal the three people on the other side. He suspected they had met up beforehand to confer. Dark storm clouds were brewing overhead and he really hoped they weren't going to be facing another deluge.

Hunter didn't like the surprised look on Mr. Preston's face when he saw Hunter, nor the shark-like grin he gave him once he recovered.

"Ah, Mr. Duke. I'm delighted you're here. This concerns you, too."

Hunter smiled genuinely. He couldn't agree more.

"Come on in," he said, inviting them all into Chase's home. "Would you like some coffee?"

"I'd love a cup. Thank you, dear," said the woman he

assumed to be Principal Irwin. She was a tall African-American lady with closely shaved hair dressed in a light blue pants suit. She shook Hunter's hand with confidence as she stepped into the house, looking him in the eye with a smile. "Are you here for the meeting too?"

"Yes, ma'am," Hunter said. "I hope that's all right with y'all?"

"Certainly," said Dr. Felix, looking up at him through her bifocals. "Hello, Hunter. Good to see you again."

They had met briefly when Hunter had still been getting his bearings at the doctors' office. Part of his orientation had been to visit Hidden Creek Memorial, and it just so happened that Dr. Felix had been on duty that day. Hunter hoped their prior connection might go in his and Chase's favor.

Chase had already set down five cups of coffee on the table, having pre-warmed a pot of the good stuff Hunter had brought for him. He added a small jug of cream and a bowl of sugar cubes too while Lyla and Trooper watched on, quietly subdued.

"Thank you for coming," Chase said as they all settled around the room.

He placed himself on one of the sofas with Hunter. Lyla sat on his lap and Trooper lay at their feet. Principal Irwin and Dr. Felix took the other couch, whereas Mr. Preston chose to loom over them with his clipboard in hand. He rested his coffee cup on a bookcase shelf too close to one of Amanda's photos for Hunter's liking.

"I think it's time we put this all to bed," said Principal Irwin warmly. "Let you get on with your lives."

"Agreed," said Dr. Felix, nodding.

Mr. Preston just slurped his coffee and raised an eyebrow.

"Lyla," Principal Irwin said. "Would you mind if Dr. Felix took a quick look at you while I ask a couple of questions?" She smiled, kindness in her eyes. "Nothing too tricky, I promise."

Lyla looked at Chase who nodded encouragingly. "It's okay, honey."

She slipped off his lap and walked the few steps over to the doctor. Trooper obviously came with her.

"Looks like you've made a friend," Principal Irwin remarked, petting the puppy's head.

"He's my best friend," said Lyla seriously as Dr. Felix listened to her heartbeat and took her temperature.

Hunter could tell she was subtly looking for any physical signs of abuse. It upset him, but he knew it had to be done. He wished he had never, ever called social services and brought Chase's parenting skills into doubt back when they had first met. But it had been the responsible thing to do and he couldn't change his actions now.

"He looks like a good best friend," said the principal. "Did your daddy buy him for you?"

"No, silly," Lyla said with a giggle. She was clearly comfortable with her teacher. "Trooper is Hunter's puppy. And Hunter is Daddy's boyfriend. We hang out *all* the time."

"Really," said Mr. Preston. He had a smug edge to his voice, like he had an ace up his sleeve. Little did he know. "Mr. Williamson, I thought we had discussed this last time. Lyla needs a stable home to flourish in."

"We did discuss it, Mr. Preston," Chase said firmly. He fumbled for Hunter's hand and he held it tightly. "Hunter has had the best stabilizing influence on this family. We're very grateful for all his help during this very difficult time."

"Mr. Preston," said Dr. Felix with a frown. "I'm sorry, is there some concern we should be aware of?"

Mr. Preston wiped coffee droplets from his mustache and smiled insipidly at her. "Lyla is struggling greatly at the moment. Her temper and violent outbursts are a danger to other children around her. I believe she is being taunted because of her father's unorthodox relationship and suggested if Mr. Williamson were serious about keeping custody of his daughter, he would do something about it." He looked Hunter and Chase up and down, a sneer only just contained under his whiskers.

Hunter quashed the anger he felt and squeezed Chase's hand to help him do the same.

Principal Irwin frowned. "You believe Lyla is struggling socially?" she said. Dr. Felix had finished her examination and Lyla was now standing with Trooper watching the grownups talk. She looked worried. Hunter wanted to take that sad expression from her face, fast.

"My niece is also enrolled at your school, Adrienne," Mr. Preston said to the principal. "And she and Lyla also partake in some extra-curricular activities together."

"Used to," Chase corrected. "Lyla doesn't do Little Ladies Etiquette anymore. It wasn't the right environment for her," he explained to Principal Irwin.

"I'm a Daisy Girl Scout now!" Lyla explained happily.

"Yes," Mr. Preston scoffed. "She was asked to leave the group. Because your child *struck* my niece and several other girls on the day of the parade!"

"Lyla apologized for that," Chase said, his voice trembling as he struggled to contain his anger. "But she only did it because your niece and her friends were tormenting her over the recent passing of her mother."

"Oh," said Dr. Felix softly, glancing over at Mr. Preston with a less than impressed expression on her face.

"Well," said Mr. Preston, straightening down his waistcoat over his enormous belly. "Be that as it may, Brianna-Grace knows Lyla quite well."

"And I know Brianna-Grace," Principal Irwin said coldly. "My apologies, Mr. Preston. But my teaching staff have informed me that Lyla has returned back to her mature, enthusiastic and high-achieving self far faster than they might have expected. As far as we are concerned, we are happy with her home-life and see no cause for concern."

Warmth blossomed in Hunter's chest as he dared to hope. Chase clearly tried not to beam in delight.

"I see," said Mr. Preston. He took a moment to collect himself as he looked at his notes. "Well, I'm afraid there's more to it than that." He sighed and shook his head. "I believe Lyla is in danger if we leave her at the mercy of Mr. Williamson and his...persuasions."

Chase jerked in his seat, but Hunter kept hold of his hand and he stayed as calm as he could. They knew something like this was coming. They were prepared. But that didn't make the implication of something sinister any easier to swallow.

"What do you mean?" Dr. Felix said. She sat up a little straighter in her seat, concern clear on her face. Mr. Preston smirked and looked down his file.

"Oh yes," said Mr. Preston, shaking his head. "I've seen evidence that Mr. Williamson flaunts his relationship with Mr. Duke with no regard for how it is affecting Lyla. Even going so far as to push his 'LGBT' agenda unwillingly on the child." He used air quotations with his fingers when he said LGBT and rolled his eyes. Like it was a joke.

"I don't follow," said Principal Irwin, her eyes narrowing.

Mr. Preston took his time taking another sip of coffee. "On my last visit, Mr. Williamson all but gloated to me that he planned on turning Ms. Hart into a transgender boy. This is a very clear and dangerous threat to the young lady's safety."

"I...I'm sorry, I don't follow," said Principal Irwin.

Dr. Felix blinked a couple of times. "Chase, is this true? You want to force Lyla to be a boy?"

Hunter's heart swelled with pride as he watched Chase keep himself calm and centered. He released Hunter's hand and pulled his cell phone out from his jeans.

"No," he said. "I just bought her some clothes that Mr. Preston considers inappropriate because they aren't pink. Lyla likes all sorts of things, including robots, dragons and superheroes."

"I do," Lyla said, excitement clear on her face. "Can I go get Bo-Bo to show Principal Irwin, Daddy?" Lyla asked.

"Of course, sweetie," he said.

Lyla raced off. Chase didn't look at Mr. Preston as he opened up the right file on his phone. "I can show you what was actually said, though," he said to the principal and the doctor. "I didn't realize at the time, but my phone was actually recording the entire conversation. You can see for yourselves."

It was true. By some small miracle, when Chase had shot the video of Lyla posing in her robot T-shirt, he hadn't pressed stop when he put his phone down. It was audio only as the lens had been pointed at the ceiling. But with the volume turned up, it was a pretty good recording.

"Now wait just a second," Mr. Preston spluttered. "I don't think this is appropriate."

Principal Irwin held up her hand to shush him. "I would like to listen, if I may?"

They watched the small screen as Lyla did her superhero poses. Then Chase turned up the volume so they could hear the whole sordid exchange between him and Mr. Preston.

"You and your kind disgust me," his nasal voice carried through the phone's speaker. *"I don't care what the law says. I believe you are unfit to care for this child and will make it my personal mission to see her removed from your custody."*

The whole thing made Hunter feel sick to his stomach. But there was a savage triumph every time he heard Mr. Preston say he didn't give a damn about the law. He was all but admitting what he was doing was illegal and immoral.

By the time the recording finished, Mr. Preston had gone purple. "That's against the law. You can't record me without my knowledge."

"No," said Hunter getting to his feet. It wasn't often that he relished towering over most people in the room, but he certainly did now. "What's against the law in the state of Texas, is discriminating against a parent's custodial rights based on a prejudice toward their gender or sexual orientation." He smiled, feeling victorious. "I'm afraid being homophobic isn't enough to take Lyla away from Chase. In fact, it's my professional opinion that you have been grossly irresponsible throughout this whole case. Your personal beliefs have clouded your judgment and put this family through an unnecessary amount of stress."

"Mr. Duke," Mr. Preston boomed. "You overstep your place here!"

"I don't know," said Dr. Felix. "Sounds pretty solid to me."

"Look, look!" Lyla cried as she skipped back into the room brandishing her purple dragon. She held it up to Dr. Felix and Principal Irwin. "This is Bo-Bo. He likes marshmallows and rock climbing and magic tricks. He was my best friend before Trooper but now they're both my best friends, except when I'm at school, coz then Becca and Noah are my best friends, and Geena is my best friend at Little League." She frowned. "Wow, I have lots of best friends."

Principal Erwin looked up at Mr. Preston. "I find your behavior in this case quite unsavory, sir," she said. "I will be in touch with your supervisor. As far as I'm concerned, Lyla has a happy home with a loving parent and a firm support structure in place."

Dr. Felix nodded. "I have no concerns here." She slipped her purse over her arm and stood. Principal Irwin did likewise.

"Are you going?" Lyla asked, her green eyes wide.

"Well, that depends," said Dr. Felix warmly. "Are you happy here living with your daddy?"

Lyla gasped and ran to him with her arms open. He automatically picked her and Bo-Bo up. "Yes, yes I am! Don't make me leave!" Her eyes swam with tears, and before Hunter knew what he was doing, he was hugging both her and Chase.

"No one is making you leave, honey," Principal Irwin said with a pointed look at Mr. Preston. "Not if you don't want to."

Lyla shook her head and hugged Chase's neck tighter. "I want to live with Daddy and Hunter *all* the time," she said. "So does Trooper."

"We'll see about that," Mr. Preston said, puffing up his chest like a pigeon.

"I don't think Chase wants you here anymore, Mr. Preston," said Hunter, crossing his arms.

Principal Irwin stepped toward the door. "I think it's time we left y'all in peace," she said graciously. "Lyla, honey, I'll see you in school on Monday."

Lyla waved her and Dr. Felix goodbye, then shrank away from Mr. Preston. He huffed and puffed his way out. Hunter could only assume he was trying to convince anyone, including himself, that he was still important.

When the front door closed behind them, Hunter let out a sigh of relief as Chase practically collapsed against him. "Oh my god," he said, his voice thick with emotion. "Is it over? Is it really over?"

Hunter kissed the top of his head and hugged him even tighter. "I think so, baby. You did so great, both of you."

"I can stay?" Lyla asked.

Chase chuckled. "It looks that way. Does that make you happy?" Lyla nodded into his neck, her red hair bouncing all around their faces. "It makes Daddy very happy, too."

Lyla reached over blindly and pawed at Hunter's shoulder. "And Hunter can stay as well?" she asked.

Hunter smiled down at Chase, warmth swimming in his veins. His life was filled with so much love he could burst. "I'm not going anywhere, sweetie," he murmured.

As they hugged in Chase's small living room, a ray of sunshine broke through the storm clouds. Lyla's words got Hunter thinking. Chase had already set him up with a drawer, and Hunter was thinking of doing the same at his place. But it was such a big, empty house. That morning before he had headed over, he'd remembered how he'd dreamed about having a family to fill the rooms with love and laughter.

He had a family now. Chase and Lyla had accepted him into their lives with open arms and he knew he would never want to leave them. Chase's house was vastly improved with all the changes Lyla had brought with her. But it was still extremely small.

Today wasn't the day, but Hunter knew then he was going to ask them if they would like to come live with him. He wanted to wake up beside Chase every single day. He wanted Lyla and Trooper to grow up together. He wanted to be a dad and maybe even a husband and keep his family safe and loved however he could.

With Mr. Preston gone from their lives, they had nothing standing in their way. Hunter had been lost when he'd moved to Hidden Creek. Now, thanks to Chase, he was found.

He couldn't have been happier.

EPILOGUE

Hunter's backyard was full of people.

No. Not Hunter's. *Their* backyard. Chase smiled quietly to himself as he prodded the sausages on the barbecue. Laughter drifted through the air as the children played and the adults drank beers, basking in the sunshine.

The only reason it had taken Chase so long to accept Hunter's offer to move in was because he was worried about disrupting Lyla's life again so soon. It probably did them all good not to go rushing straight into a commitment. But now he and Lyla were here and had been settled for a couple of months, he had no doubt they'd made the right decision.

Even though Lyla had filled that old house with joy, it had still been the place where Chase had grown up. Where he'd had to suffer his father's torments day in and day out. Chase had convinced himself that he'd outgrown all those ghosts. That he could create new memories to paint over the bad ones. But sometimes, you just have to leave the past behind.

There was nothing to haunt him in Hunter's home. It was

only filled with love. In the year they'd been together, Chase had found himself growing in ways he never thought possible. He was working part-time at JJ's now while Hunter supported him studying for his GED. They'd even talked about him going to community college in the fall, if that's what he wanted.

Chase had stopped fighting now. He just accepted that Hunter would find a way to make him happy and pursue his dreams, not matter how unworthy Chase felt. At first, it was easier to go along with the flow. But somewhere along the way, Chase had truly started to believe he was worth all this fuss.

A year ago, Chase would never have believed that he would be hosting a party on a Sunday afternoon for no other reason than to simply see family and friends. Hunter had suggested it because Chase still wasn't used to socializing. Now he felt buzzed as he looked out over all the people he had in his life.

Lyla was playing knights and dragons with Geena Miller. Trooper was almost fully grown now, so was doing a good job acting as a mighty steed. He'd even allowed the girls to attach a unicorn horn to his head. Although he was no longer a puppy, he still followed Lyla around like she was his whole world. Chase could understand that feeling.

Tammy Miller was adorably trying to flirt with their next-door neighbor's son, Koby Duvall. Chase had to admit he was gorgeous, but he was absolutely gay. Tammy didn't seem to have picked up on this yet. Or maybe she wasn't flirting and was merely in awe of his edgy look.

He was some sort of sculptor if Chase remembered correctly. He certainly gave off a tortured artist vibe with his black hair and black eyeliner and black leather pants despite the balmy spring weather. The whole thing was certainly working for Tammy as she hung off his every word. Poor dear. She would work out she was wasting her time soon enough, Chase suspected. In the meantime, Koby was being very nice to her and talking to her like one of the grownups.

Koby's mom and sister, Shelly and Ginger, had brought over some of the new retriever puppies for people to meet. The small pack was currently delighting his and Hunter's guests by frolicking around on the lawn, snapping at dragonflies and chasing their tails.

Lucy and Paul Hart, Lyla's grandparents, were in attendance as well. Chase was extremely relieved that their relationship had improved a great deal over the past year. Once social services had deemed him fit to be Lyla's guardian, the two of them had taken a trip down to Florida to spend a week getting to know each other. Now that they understood Chase wasn't a terrible guy, both Lucy and Paul were happy for him to be the father he always should have been and keep Lyla with him.

They'd seen each other several times over the next year, but Chase was surprised they'd come all this way for a little barbecue. It was impressive, and a testimony to their new relationship.

Hunter's best buddy Connor was there with his younger siblings and his man, Beaux. He was hard to miss with that blue hair. Beaux had brought a couple of the hockey guys along as Hunter had hung out with them a few times in the past months.

There were also a couple of guys Hunter had met at the gym. As in, another *couple*. It made Chase happy to see so many people in love. The ginger guy, Fox, was easy to remember the name of thanks to his hair. Chase couldn't quite recall his boyfriend's name, but he looked like the kind to be pumping weights in his spare time.

All those muscly dudes would have had Chase drooling before. But now, he only had eyes for one hunk of a man.

He waved his tongs at Hunter across the crowd. He was talking to some of the only people Chase had invited. Typical. Hunter would know how happy that would make Chase. He always made an effort to be interested in all aspects of his life.

After meeting Gabriel at the farmers' market, Chase had finally worked up the courage to say hello the next time he'd made a delivery from the Miele farm to JJ's. It turned out the two of them had a lot in common and got on like a house on fire. Chase had nurtured a hunch his boyfriend, Orion, would be Hunter's kind of guy. They certainly seemed to be laughing a lot when Chase caught Hunter's eye.

Even after all these months, Chase's stomach still flipped when Hunter looked at him like he was the most important person in the world. He paused in his conversation to wave back. Gabriel clasped his hands together and made an 'aww!' face. Orion elbowed him in the ribs, but that only made Gabriel laugh.

Chase blushed and went back to the barbecue. The truth was he loved being surrounded by so many people. He hadn't quite realized how terribly lonely he'd been before Lyla and Hunter had come along and saved his life, quite literally.

Inhaling deeply, he rolled his shoulders and allowed himself to feel contentment. It was like his life was split into two parts that bore no relation to each other. There was Before Lyla and Hunter, and After Lyla and Hunter. The two Chases in those lives looked nothing alike, he was sure.

The Chase he was now wasn't afraid to laugh, to step out into the world and be himself. He was learning more every day that things weren't quite as scary as he had been led to believe.

Of course, bad things still happened. It wasn't all sunshine and roses. He'd discovered that with Mr. Preston and a few others that felt the same way he did. Occasionally, someone would have something bad to say to Chase or Hunter or, worst of all, Lyla. But Chase could weather any storm so long as he knew he had his family to come home to.

The last he'd heard, Mr. Preston had 'retired early' from his job with social services. Chase couldn't deny that brought him a large amount of glee. For once, he'd been able to stand up to one of his bullies and actually win. It felt incredible.

Mr. Preston didn't matter, though. What was important was his happiness and the happiness of his family. Chase kept glancing back up at Hunter as he plated up the meat as it was done, placing glazed chicken legs over the flames to cook next.

He'd been chewing over an idea for some time now. Maybe he should think about mentioning it sooner rather than later? Because the thing was, Hunter was essentially Lyla's other dad. Her papa. He had been since the moment he had entered their lives.

So why not make it official?

Chase was certain Hunter would want to adopt her if Chase asked. It was just such a big step.

His fears gotten the better of him yet again, however. It was still too early days to be thinking about long-term future plans. But maybe it wouldn't hurt to daydream a little in private. The last time he'd done that, he'd gotten himself a boyfriend.

"What did I miss?" someone asked with a dramatic sigh from behind Chase.

He turned with a smile to see one of his other new friends, Kris. Chase and Hunter regularly visited Bottom's Up now that Chase was no longer afraid of being seen there. Kris liked to tease them about being so in love, but after a while, Chase and Hunter had just started sitting at the bar so they could drink with him as well. Despite all his bravado, Chase knew Kris was an old-fashioned romantic at heart, too.

As usual, he looked more like he was about to go clubbing in Houston than he was going to hang out at a family barbecue. His lavender overalls were so short they were practically hot pants. He only had one of the buckles done up and underneath wore a white crop top that read 'Baby Doll' in the exact same purple as the tips of his hair. A starry bandanna, full face of makeup and glittery Converse completed the picture.

"Hey, man," Chase said, leaning over to kiss cheeks. No way he would have been confident enough to befriend someone like Kris before, let alone greet him like that. After so many years trying to hide his gayness, Chase was done with the closet. He loved how out and proud Kris was. "I have vodka in the freezer for you."

Kris blew him a kiss. "You're a saint. Then can I go prowl around those hockey boys?"

"You behave," Chase called over his shoulder as he disappeared back into the kitchen.

When he turned back around, Hunter was by his side, looking devilish. "Hello, gorgeous," he said.

"'Hello, gorgeous' to you too," Chase said, leaning in for a peck on the lips. "You met Gabe and Ryan?"

Hunter nodded and licked his lips. He seemed nervous.

That wasn't like him. "They're great," he said. "I can see why you like them. We should have them over for dinner some time."

Chase held back a grin. Hunter's main technique to care for someone was to feed them. It was adorable.

"I'd love that," he said instead.

"I love you," Hunter countered. He gently pried the tongs away from Chase and slipped his hands around his waist. Chase copied him, holding onto Hunter's hips. "Do you know what today is?"

Chase raised his eyebrow, wondering if that was a trick question. "Sunday?" he said.

Hunter smiled and bit his lip, looking down at Chase through his eyelashes. "Do you remember what happened a year ago today?" Chase frowned. Had he forgotten something? What the hell was the date? Hunter took pity on him though. "Here's a hint. It was after a slightly shaky start over a slice of pizza."

Chase's eyes went wide. Their sort-of-date at Rocket that led to... "Our first kiss," Chase whispered. He could feel himself blushing, wondering if anyone was watching them. He couldn't take his eyes off of Hunter for long enough to check though.

"Happy anniversary," Hunter said.

Was it? Chase figured it was a good a date as any to pick. They hadn't exactly had a simple start to their relationship.

"You should have said," Chase told him off, batting his firm chest. "I haven't gotten you anything."

"I haven't gotten you anything either," said Hunter, a twinkle of mischief in his eye. "Yet."

Chase huffed. "Babe," he said, feeling a bit deflated. "You don't have to get me a present. You already give me so much."

"Actually," Hunter said. He didn't sound put out in the slightest by Chase's shift in mood. "I was hoping I could ask you for something?"

That perked Chase up. Anything he could give to Hunter he'd do willingly. He felt like he could never spoil Hunter the way he spoiled Chase thanks to their vast differences in finances. "Of course," he said brightly.

Hunter leaned in close to whisper in his ear. "Your hand."

Chase frowned. That didn't make much sense. But when Hunter leaned back again Chase held it out for him to take with both his own hands. Hunter bit his lip, a smile playing on his mouth.

"I didn't mean literally," he teased gently. "But now that you mention it, it does look a little bare." He lifted Chase's hand up and kissed one of the fingers.

The ring finger.

Chase had given him his left hand without even thinking about it. He felt his eyes grow wide as dizziness swept through his whole body. "Hunter?"

Hunter glanced left and right, but everyone else seemed engrossed in their own conversations. Keeping ahold of Chase's hand with one of his, Hunter reached into his pocket and retrieved a small, old-looking box. It was dog-eared and faded and Chase couldn't take his eyes off it despite the fact the chicken might very well be burning.

"This was my grandfather's," Hunter said. He let go of Chase's hand to open the ring box. Inside was a simple gold band. "I checked and you guys wore the same size. I took it as a sign and my mom gave her blessing so..." He cleared his throat and plucked the ring from the box. It had obviously been recently cleaned from the way it gleamed in the sunlight. "Chase Williamson. I was very much hoping you might give me your hand *in marriage.*"

Tears were already blurring Chase's vision. "You want to marry me?" he asked, his voice thick.

Hunter nodded. "If you want to marry me?"

Chase snorted and had to stop himself from grabbing at the damn ring. "Don't ask silly questions. Yes, *yes!*"

There was a loud thump from under the table next to them with all the plates and bowls of salad on it. Lyla and Geena came scrambling out from under the tablecloth, a barking Trooper following right behind them.

"He said yes! He said yes!" Lyla screamed out to the entire backyard.

Apparently, every single person knew what she was talking about because they all burst into riotous applause. Kris and Gabriel came running up to Chase while Connor slapped Hunter on the back before turning to rescue the barbecue. In all the confusion, Hunter did manage to slip the ring on Chase's finger.

It fit perfectly.

Shelly was crying and laughing at the same time while her kids handed her napkins. Somebody produced bottles of fizz and there were cries and cheers as the corks began popping free.

"You told them?" Chase asked in disbelief, looking around as his grin grew wider and wider. "Y'all knew?"

"Well, we didn't know you'd say *yes,*" Kris admitted, pressing a cold flute of bubbly into Chase's hands. "But we hoped," he added with a wink.

Koby and Ginger Duvall leaned in to clap him on the shoulders. "Well done, man," Koby said. "I'm so proud of you."

Paul and Lucy both looked emotional as they offered their congratulations with Lyla bouncing around their feet. Chase had never appreciated them more. It was like he had real parents of his own for the first time in his life.

Chase looked around at all the people congratulating them. Dozens of faces were brimming with happiness for him. For them.

He threw his arms around Hunter and kissed him. "I love you," he said.

"I love you, too," Hunter told him.

Chase felt something collide with his legs. "I love y'all, too!" Lyla cried.

Chase and Hunter laughed as Chase picked her up to sit on his hip. Soon, she would be too big for him to do that. But for now, he'd do it every day he still could.

The three of them hugged together while Trooper circled their feet and the bubbles continued to flow around them. Someone had turned up the music and was playing the wedding march. Kris was already excitedly talking color schemes and flower girl dresses.

It was perfect. Everything was just as it should have been. And what made it better was that Chase realized this was only the beginning.

For now, they drank Champagne and celebrated with friends until the early hours of the morning.

This was the start of a new chapter in Chase's life.

He couldn't wait.

ABOUT THE AUTHOR

HJ Welch is a contemporary MM romance author living in London with her husband and two balls of fluff that occasionally pretend to be cats. She began writing at an early age, later honing her craft online in the world of fanfiction on sites like Wattpad. Fifteen years and over a million words later, she sought out original MM novels to read. She never thought she would be any good at romance, but once she turned her hand to it she discovered she in fact adored it. By the end of 2016 she had written her first book of her own, and in 2017 she fulfilled her lifelong dream of becoming a fulltime author.

She also writes contemporary British MM romance as Helen Juliet.

Newsletter: https://www.subscribepage.com/helenjuliet

facebook.com/HJWelchAuthor

twitter.com/helenjwrites

instagram.com/helenjwrites

www.ingramcontent.com/pod-product-compliance
Lightning Source LLC
Chambersburg PA
CBHW050836190726
48286CB00007B/2104